A Burden of Flowers

A Burden of Flowers

Natsuki Ikezawa

Translated by Alfred Birnbaum

KODANSHA INTERNATIONAL

Tokyo · New York · London

THE KAN YAMAGUCHI SERIES

Publication of this book was assisted by a generous grant provided by Ms. Kan Yamaguchi of Tsuchiura City, Japan. A select number of interesting works in English on Asia have been given such assistance.

The publisher gratefully acknowledges the support of Rengo Co., Ltd., and the Association for 100 Japanese Books for this translation.

The original work was published in 2000 by Bungei Shunju Ltd. under the title *Hana wo hakobu imoto.*

Distributed in the United States by Kodansha America, Inc., 575 Lexington Avenue, New York, NY 10022, and in the United Kingdom and continental Europe by Kodansha Europe Ltd., 95 Aldwych, London WC2B 4JF. Published by Kodansha International Ltd., 17–14 Otowa 1-chome, Bunkyo-ku, Tokyo 112–8652, and Kodansha America, Inc. Copyright © 2000 by Natsuki Ikezawa. English translation © 2001 by Kodansha International. Translation rights arranged with Natsuki Ikezawa through the Japan Foreign-Rights Centre.
First edition, 2001
ISBN 4-7700-2686-2

01 02 03 04   10 9 8 7 6 5 4 3 2 1

www.thejapanpage.com

1

KAORU

Bali isn't Paris, though both are islands—not that I ever really understood how the Greater Parisian Ile-de-France could claim to be an island in the middle of continental Europe. Or, for that matter, how so many Japanese, never having been abroad, could so easily confuse tropical *Bari* with gay *Pari* (*L*s and *R*s being all the same to us). As if Japan itself were the mainland and anywhere else just another blip on the map.

But then again, it never used to bother me that Japan saw itself as "not-Asia," a land apart. Maybe because at the time I, too, knew nothing about Asia. Meaning, I'd never been anywhere near places like Indonesia. Certainly the Paris-Tokyo-Bali connection was something I never expected.

In 1980, I lived in Paris, a foreign girl studying at the Sorbonne, staying in a Catholic dormitory on the Ile Saint-Louis, upstream from the Ile de la Cité. Strolling from the Quartier Latin along the riverside to the Pont Tournelle where I crossed, I often imagined how Little Louis must feel with his eternal tail-end view of his big brother Cité. One of these days they would sail down the Seine to the sea—to the Caribbean or up the Orinoco or even to Java. My little island was just waiting for the day, only big brother never seemed to make up his mind.

The early 80s weren't so bad. Not yet. America's war in Vietnam was five years history, even as the Soviet Union invaded Afghanistan. Thatcher became prime minister in England, though French President Giscard-Destaing still had a year to go in office. LPs and 45s and cassettes were the music media of choice. No merchandise in any store had barcodes. And one franc was worth fifty yen, so for an exchange student from Japan, Paris still bordered on the affordable.

France was a little more tolerant toward foreign students in those days. Certain stickling regulations aside, we were allowed to work up to twenty hours a week. This was even as refugees and immigrants and illegal over-stays were on the rise, not to mention a steadily spiraling unemployment rate. But apparently some sectors of society still had a degree of *largesse*. Anyway, most of us dorm students received no money from home, so we met day-to-day expenses by doing the odd job. I myself found part-time employment at a tiny *agence de voyage*—a travel agency, or more accurately a cheap ticket shop—tucked away at the St. Michel end of the Quartier Latin.

I was fifteen minutes on foot to the university and from there to work another five minutes. A pleasant walk, with plenty to see en route. After afternoon classes, I'd stroll across the Rue des Ecoles, cut through the "olive oil ghetto" of Greek and Turkish eateries on the Rue de la Hache, and a bit further along reach our *bureau*.

Volume was our selling point. Different cuts of customer came our way, but the majority were low-budget Euro youths, drifters bound for North Africa and the Middle East. Half of them moved north and south with the seasons like migratory birds. As spring turned to summer, the numbers heading for Scandinavia increased; when the weather turned cold again, they'd be off to the Mediterranean or to Cairo, Tunisia, and Morocco.

The other half were once-throughs: the eastbound crowd. They wanted out of Europe, preferably by land or sea, spending as little money and as much time as possible. The most dedicated of them never bought plane tickets; they only came to us for information about coaches, then bused out via Rome or Athens for the Asian continent. It wasn't unusual for last year's north-south vacationer to become this year's eastbound trekker. And once they walked out *that* door not many came back.

Japanese accounted for less than ten percent of our customers. While white people generally came in male-female couples, almost without exception the Japanese were same-sex pairs. One time, Yvonne who sat next to me behind the counter asked, "Are there really so many gays in Japan?" It was all I could do to keep a straight face.

The ultimate destination for eastbound whites was India. Most people on earth tend to move east, counter to the motion of the sun. Japanese travelers, however, invariably first headed west for Europe. Dozens of scruffy young Japanese backpackers told me they came straight across on the Trans-Siberian Railway. Strange kids, each holding that unique Japanese document, a single-issue passport in perpetuity, its pages to be filled with stamps from countless border crossings—as if the idea of staying away for years on end were their only source of pride. As if returning to Japan would sap their life away.

One day, an unusually well-dressed customer walked in. Tasteful gray suit and tie, neat horn-rimmed glasses, and slim black leather attaché case —unmistakably Japanese.

"I desperately need to be in Japan the day after tomorrow. The fare can be a little high," he said in impeccable French. Only later did he really look at me. "Japan? Vietnam? Not Korea or Taiwan. Certainly not as far south as Thailand . . . ?"

"*Nihon*," I answered in Japanese. This was maybe the second time I'd been mistaken for a *Vietnamienne*. Vietnamese friends never once said I looked like one of them.

"About the ticket, I know it won't be easy. It *is* almost Easter."

And Easter is peak season in Europe. "Yes, it *will* be difficult. But I'll see what I can do."

I made a few phone calls. There were no tickets to be had. "There don't seem to be any," I told him.

"I know, I went to the other travel agencies and . . . nothing."

Somehow his diffidence made me want to try just a little harder. Who knows why? But for the next hour, I called *everywhere*, sending feelers into the tiniest pipelines in the complex world of airline ticketing. Straddling agents, waiting, hanging on, flattering, interrupting. Until finally I had it— one single fare to Japan. Feeling rather impressed with myself, I immediately issued the ticket for the man. He beamed with gratitude, counted out a cash sum considerably higher than the going rate, then went on his way. The ordinary out-of-the-ordinary in the ticket trade, but it's still satisfying to know you can really be of service in a pinch.

The days came and went. I attended my language-and-culture *conférence* at the Sorbonne, did my hours at the *agence*, went to the cinema with friends, and wrote the occasional letter to Japan. Paris grew warmer with each passing day and the summer *vacances* were fast becoming the prime topic of conversation, when out of nowhere the man stopped in again. By then I'd all but forgotten his name: Monsieur Makino.

"You saved my life. I want to thank you. Let me take you out to dinner." This time he spoke Japanese straight off.

Poor student that I was, it would have been criminal to turn down such an open invitation. Lunch at the college cafeteria was quite a feast for five francs—starter and main course, even dessert or an *assiette de fromages*. All the same, sometimes I craved a fifty-franc dinner. And since the man was well-dressed . . . well, if he did have other intentions, I could deal with that when the time came. Anyway, the promise of one excellent *repas* dangled there before me. After two polite back-and-forths, I accepted for two evenings later.

The rendezvous was set for the Café Flore. Not entirely off-limits to studentkind, but too much of an intellectual snob's place for me ever to set foot in on my own. Paris is a city given to categorizing its inhabitants. Where one goes or doesn't go, what one wears or doesn't wear says everything about one's breeding and pocketbook and schooling and leanings. Thinking ahead to what restaurant might follow the Café Flore, I put on my only half-formal outfit, took pains with my makeup, and arrived exactly ten minutes late. He was sitting at a prominent table out front on the *terrasse*.

The tone of the place was a trifle *passé* perhaps, but any such reservations were more than dispelled by his pleasant conversation. At this sitting, I recall, he played listener for the most part while I talked about student life and the travel agency.

After thirty minutes or so, Makino suggested we leave. His car was parked nearby. A fairly posh, top-model Citroën. Sharklike to some eyes, a crushed slipper to others. A toy for a playboy. From his clothes and manner of speech, I had him pinned as a Japanese trading house rep, although trading houses typically had accounts with larger ticketing agencies. Even for personal travel, he'd never come to a discount shop like ours.

The Citroën ferried us to La Coupole. Why of course! A fitting and proper sequel to Café Flore. Although not an exclusive upper-class establishment —being a *brasserie*, not a restaurant—it *was* one of those places where only the right combination of clothes and conversation and wallet gained entry. An arena where successful freelance professionals went to be seen by one another. Trendy and snobbish and fickle, the sort of *milieu* where waiters and regulars alike passed impromptu judgment on every new face. Merely stepping through those doors was a dare.

It was becoming less and less clear just who this Makino was. What's more, he seemed to be a known presence there. The waiter addressed him familiarly, and he even greeted a number of other guests on the way to the table.

"So what do you suppose I do for a living?" Mr. Makino finally asked when it came time for coffee.

"I don't know. At first I thought you were with a trading firm, but you're not like that at all, are you? And you're not an academic either. And also not the artist-designer-composer-musician type." (At the word "artist," for one split second I saw my brother.) "A dramatist? No, let's not even mention journalism. I give up."

Makino smiled as he spoke those four inconceivable words: "I'm a Baptist minister."

Mr. Makino's—*Pastor* Makino's—story over our after-dinner *demi-crèmes* went like this:

"Both my parents were devout Christians, so naturally I was baptised as a baby, went to church and Sunday school every week. Public primary school, but then it was decided I should go to a Christian middle school. While I never doubted my own faith, I didn't especially think about the Faith. Never imagined a vocation.

"Middle school was no fun. I wasn't very studious, wasn't good at baseball or track, didn't make many friends. There had to be something else, something outside of school and church. As it was I couldn't apply myself, I was wasting my time.

"That's when I found bowling. I really had a knack for it, got good just like that. People made such a fuss of me, I couldn't get over it. My parents were easygoing; as long as my grades didn't suffer too much, they didn't say anything. I had a big allowance, and every day after school I'd head straight for the lanes. Weekends I practically lived there. Soon I was competing and winning money. The lanes even asked me to give lessons, which brought in more money. This was around the early 70s 'bowling boom' when they were building lanes all over Japan. Everyone was buying bowling shoes and bowling balls.

"Well, the time came for me to enter high school. There I was, bowling an outstanding average, but handing in less-than-average test papers. Why didn't I just forget about high school and go professional? I'd have more fun, make more money—wouldn't that be a better life all around? It seemed a fairly clear-cut decision to me.

"My parents panicked. However easygoing they might have been, this overstepped the limits. Whether or not I was thinking about college, at the very least they wanted to see me finish high school. Still I didn't budge. My argument rested on a very obvious skill—I invited my mother and father to tournaments, where they saw me take high-scoring trophies—and on just-as-obvious poor grades. My parents were in a quandary.

"In the end, we made a deal. That is, I would take the high school entrance exam and give it my full attention. If I passed, I'd go to high school; if I failed, I'd turn bowling pro. And the funny thing was, I passed the exam hands down. Which meant I had to go to high school. I promptly went back on my word and protested to my parents all over again.

"My poor parents. They went to their minister and told him everything. Let's just call him Pastor K. He was open and fair; he heard out both sides without comment or preaching.

"'Might I propose a third alternative?' he said. 'Say you don't go on to high school, or build your life around a game like bowling. The other day, a young man of my acquaintance formed a company. He asked me to look out for upstanding persons who might like to work with him. Maybe that would be best for you. You have the ability. Why not give it a try?'

"The company imported clothing from Europe and sold to Japanese department stores. Just out of middle school, I couldn't have been more out of place. Me, who couldn't tell a dress from a blouse, thrust into women's wear. But my parents put great faith in Pastor K, and in the end I turned around. I gave up bowling.

"My boss, Kei'ichi Goto, was twenty-five at the time. Thinking back on it now, he was awfully young for an entrepreneur. But to me, he was the image of know-how and ambition and resources and connections—I hero-worshiped him. Every day I ferried his samples around to the stores, talked to the buyers, took orders. At sixteen, I couldn't get a driver's license, so I had to dolly that huge display carton onto trains and buses. By evening I'd be dead tired, but it was a good kind of tired. I'd drag that fatigue to night school, and half-slept through French lessons. You see, Goto was already talking about me going along to Paris on buying trips. Not that my piddling French would help much in bargaining. But I had an ear, I guess. Because somehow I got the basics of the language. Day and night I worked at it. For several years, I picked up what I could. There are phases like that in one's life.

"The lines we imported sold. The start-up timing was good, Goto's eye for styles was good, our choice of outlets was good. Well-heeled women throughout Japan fought to buy our European fashions. The slightest edge over other importers translated into tenfold profits. Goto and I took turns on buying trips. My French had become proficient; I even started learning other European languages. I traveled the capitals of Europe seeking out the best *couturiers*. I'd snap up several dozen of each line, then head to the next city.

"The money poured in. I'd have to say we were one of the fastest-growing companies in the business. There I was, twenty-two and living in a condo overlooking the Imperial Palace, driving European imports. I had a steady stream of girlfriends. 'Growth' was a beautiful word to my ears. And all thanks to Pastor K!

"As the company got bigger, Goto thought, why keep bouncing back and forth to Europe, Goto-Makino-Goto? We decided to set up an office in Paris, with me as branch manager. I found a place, hired staff, and two months later our Paris *succursale* was on track.

"A year later, we decided to celebrate our first year in Paris, as well as the tenth anniversary of the company. Goto took a few days off from Tokyo and came over. We decided on La Coupole—that's right, this very restaurant. I came here on my first trip to France, and even after setting up in Paris I probably ate here twice a week.

"I invited Pastor K to the celebration, I wanted to express my gratitude. After all, it was on his advice that I'd made such a *grand succès* in the fashion industry. I wrote him, enclosing an airplane ticket, and he came. The celebration went wonderfully. Everyone was happy, we all believed in the company. My future was full-steam ahead, Pastor K was all smiles. Afterwards, I escorted him to his hotel and we sat in the lobby for a while. I told him again it was thanks to him I'd come this far; he'd pointed me in the right direction and I'd found my way.

"That's when the pastor spoke up. 'I'm very glad,' he said. 'But haven't you already done more than your share for Mr. Goto's company? You've made a great deal of money. Now might be a good time to resign from the business and become a priest. Seriously. From here on, that can be your work. Let me be the one to tell Mr. Goto.'

"Well, I was in shock. Here I'd spent the last ten years doing exactly as Pastor K said, acting the part he'd cast me in, so to speak. And now that was to change completely. I didn't know what to do. I don't even remember driving back to my apartment in Passy.

"Pastor K returned to Japan, and I did a lot of soul-searching. Of course, my instincts told me not to pull out of the company. And yet, recalling the lead he'd given me after middle school, I *was* tempted. What would happen if I listened to him again? The more I thought, the more confused I became. A week later, rather more exhausted than resolved, once again I threw in my lot with Pastor K. I resigned my job—Goto already knew—and entered divinity school . . . So now I'm back in Paris as a minister, satisfied I made the right choice."

I heard him out and could only sigh—I mean, what a life! What a gamble! Or was it just the daring of a strange character? And this Pastor K of his, reading others' futures—another character.

Mister-Pastor Makino called over the *garçon* and paid the bill. Then, turning to me, he said, "I'd like to show you something truly beautiful. Can you spare a little more time?"

The phrasing seemed just a little too smooth. It put me on guard. Another place after dinner? How was I to know if this story was true? Was he even a man of the cloth? If this was all just to lead me on this late, it was a cheap trick. Better beg off back to the dorm. Still, "truly beautiful" did sound interesting. In Paris, at this hour, what could that be? So in the end I accepted. (All right, maybe I was a little naïve about personal safety in my Sorbonne days.)

He nosed the slipper-shaped Citroën onto the *périphérique* and off we sped into the night. We were talked out, we hardly spoke a word in the car. I was a little drunk. Not having driven in Paris myself, I wasn't sure where we were headed. All I knew, it was out past the furthest *banlieu*. Too late now. I couldn't tell him to let me out in the middle of nowhere.

Through the car window I tracked the moon. When we first set out I was thinking "truly beautiful" might be moonlight filtering through stained glass windows in a tiny chapel somewhere. That'd be okay, I kept thinking —still thinking so thirty minutes later as we raced along. Ramping off the motorway onto surface roads, we swept past open fields, headlamps beaming down a dark tunnel of trees, until finally the car pulled to a stop.

"Here we are," said Makino.

Here we are *where?* Everything was pitch-black. There was nothing around, but I could hear flowing water. This is where he does me in, I thought.

The next thing I knew, he was saying he wanted to "baptise" me.

"To *what?*"

"Baptise you," he said, quite seriously. "Wash away your sins, make you pure again in the eyes of God. I *am* a minister, after all."

For crying out loud—*this* was his "truly beautiful" scheme?

"I don't think I want to be baptised just now, okay?"

"What *you* want isn't important."

"But I'm not even Christian!"

"That's why you should be baptised and become a believer," he insisted.

"Whatever you say here isn't going to change my mind."

"Listen. Your soul isn't subject to your whims. With baptism you begin a new life."

"I'm quite happy with my life up to now, thank you very much."

So by a dark river in the middle of the pitch-black woods, Makino and I sat arguing. Finally, I threw up my hands. If he wanted to baptise me so badly, well then let him. The soul part I could deal with later. What harm was there in him splashing a little river water on my head?

No sooner had I said yes than Makino got out of the car, opened the trunk, and pulled out a large, white, fluffy bundle. Robes or cassock or something.

"Take off what you're wearing and put this on. I'll wait outside." He walked around and opened the hood of the car. The trunk was still open, so there was no looking in from front or back. Next he brought out a black tarp and covered the roof, blocking the side windows.

Inside Makino's baptism-mobile my hands worked my clothes off piece by piece. Then I pulled his sheet—like a poncho or Greek toga or oversized smock—over my head. It took ages. I could hardly tell the neck from the hem in all that yardage. What was "truly beautiful" about any of this? I ducked under the black tarp and stepped outside.

It was June, but the riverbank was plenty cold. I was freezing under only a single layer of cotton. The forest huddled close around the car, the river flowing gently, twenty or thirty meters wide. But where was Makino? I couldn't see him anywhere.

"Over he-ere!"

I looked in the direction of the voice and there he was, all in white like me—in the middle of the river! Baptism midstream? Not for me, no way. I turned to go back to the car.

"Over he-ere!" called Makino.

All right, I'd already come this far, and I couldn't drive—even if I knew where we were. I swallowed what little common sense I had left and walked barefoot across the gravel toward the water. I eased myself in one step at a time. It was *so* cold, but soon I was up to my ankles, then my calves. The hem of the gown clung wet to my legs. The water passed my knees. It was still a long way over to Makino. I pushed myself forward another step.

"All the way over he-e-ere!"

One more step. The current was getting stronger. The wet fabric got in the way of walking, so I pulled it up slightly. My legs were numb, but I didn't want to lose my footing. The water was now over my waist. I really had to fight the next steps, the flow was so swift on the bottom.

I finally made it to Makino. And with not a moment's warning he reached out, grabbed my hair, and plunged my whole head under. Down I went, thrashing about for dear life.

I knew it! He's a homicidal maniac. Drags me way out in the middle of nowhere, miles outside Paris, hemispheres away from Japan, to kill me in some nameless river. Or only half-drown me before doing something worse!... He's hurting me... Why'd I ever accept his invitation to the Café Flore! Was La Coupole to be my last supper? Should never have listened to this pervert, this Baptist lunatic. Icy sharp fast scared angry pain—so many last thoughts in a single moment. Can't breathe. Can't breathe. Going to swallow water...

Just then, water gurgling in my ears, I heard Makino saying something up top—not to me, but to someone much higher up. And with that realization, the whole scene changed. My body eased up, I didn't fight what he was doing. Gone was the will to resist. Not that I accepted the Faith then and there—I'm still no Christian—I merely accepted his wanting to wash my soul clean, accepted the waters of the river, the dark stillness of the night. I accepted it all.

When I knew I wasn't dead, I felt happy. Happy to be alive. What seemed an eternity was over in an instant. Makino pulled me up from the water, his other hand—the one not holding my hair—held aloft. He spoke to the heavens, but only bits of it reached my ears.

I gasped for breath and, amazingly, there before my eyes *was* something "truly beautiful." The moon was reflected in the river, glistening off each ripple, framed between the muted silhouette of the trees in a high, vast sky. And the moon was beautiful; each and every moon-bathed riplet was beautiful; the shy, sweet stars were beautiful, too. Never had I seen anything like it. Maybe everything up to then was just to make me see this. If you're prepared to accept what's coming, the world *can* be this beautiful! Maybe that wasn't the baptism Makino intended, but that's what I experienced that night. And so, through no fault of my own, in a way I was cleansed.

Back on shore, Makino fetched a large, thick bath towel from the trunk of the car. Inside the confines of the car, trying not to get the seats wet, I dried off and squirmed back into my clothes in reverse order. Only then did I realize how much I was shivering. Chilled to the bone and couldn't stop shaking. My dress and coat were no insulation, even my arms wrapped around me did nothing for warmth. Then from outside I heard a distant "May I?"

I opened the car door and stuttered a barely intelligible, "Y-yes."

Makino had already changed back into his clothes. He stuffed the tarp and all our wet things into a big plastic bag in the trunk, then quickly lowered the hood and jumped into the driver's seat.

"Hallelujah," he announced, "—you've been baptised."

He turned on the ignition and the car started off—en route back to Paris, I hoped. The heater was on full blast, but my body temperature just wouldn't get back to normal. I sat there dazed and trembling, silently gazing at the dark road ahead. Makino must have been cold, too—tired or satisfied, I couldn't tell, but he just kept driving. Finally I suppose I dozed off.

"Where shall I drop you off?" I woke to Makino's words and pieced together where I was. The dashboard clock read 12:10. Too late for this Cinderella to make her midnight curfew.

"I can't get into my dormitory this late. Do you know any place I could stay?" I asked nervously.

"There's a little hotel I'm rather fond of," offered Makino, and fifteen minutes later we were there. He got out and arranged for a room, then came back to the car to show me up. When he handed over the key—everything paid—he never took one step inside the door. Then he was off without a word. I crawled into bed and fell into a deep, dreamless sleep.

That's pretty much my Paris story. I only saw Makino once again and I think I was too embarrassed to even thank him. The fact is, even after that singularly unforgettable night—my special personalized baptism—I don't even pray. Or maybe prayer is slowly silting the riverbed under my conscious thoughts, half-forgotten at the back of my mind.

The important thing is, when things get to a real pinch, just accept, don't resist. "Go with the flow," as the hippies used to say. If there is a God, He'll be there for you. If not, well—there'll still be something new ahead, maybe even something "truly beautiful."

Several days later, strolling along the Quai de Montebello looking at the Seine as usual, it occurred to me, supposing the Ile Saint-Louis weren't a baby brother but a kid *sister*? And what if the two islands headed off downstream each on its own? Where, oh where, might brother and sister meet up again—on the Caribbean or the Orinoco or someplace off Java?

2

TETSURO

Waking up.

Sluggish, weighed down, desperately immobile. Anything not to stir this slow, sweet sleep. But no, it just sheers away, floats off like smoke on a breeze, disappears.

Sleep is always shallow, inconclusive. Sleep marred by ominous intrusions, but still temporary shelter. No need to think, nothing to fear, just breathe nice and easy. Only that happy nowhere never lasts.

First blinking yanks a brutal ripcord—a landslide caves in from above, pressing down flat and suffocating. Body a catalogue of pains, pinioned up against the wall in some impossible posture, butting into the next body over. Sapped of strength to even move. Every joint hurts, eye sockets hurt. Better to sleep all day through, but the pain seems to have other ideas.

Morning. Another pointless morning. Still dark out. Some joker in the corner gets up, pads barefoot to the toilet stall, and pisses. Endlessly. There's no door and the sound alone's enough to remind everyone else to take a leak. Soon they'll be lining up and the stench will swamp the whole place. That's how mornings begin here.

Why'd you have to wake up? Why couldn't they pull the plug while you're still unconscious? The thought has occurred to you. Quietly switch off the works and let the body slowly rot—how much easier that would be. Let them come haul away the corpse and dispose of it somewhere. A dead object.

A heap of bones. Who could complain? Ugly thought, but right now, dying sounds positively irresistible. Wouldn't have the strength to resist anyway.

Starting to get light. A few people out walking, one or two cars go past. Birds chirping. Always the same birds at dawn here. Never knew how good it could be just to hear birds singing—*chippuy chippuy chippuy . . . tooop tooop tooop.* The chippuy bird. Others, too—*buru-ru-ru-ru-ru . . . pui pui.* One that simply goes *chi chi chi.* A regular chorus out there. The only music allowed these prisoners, and a live performance at that.

Foot traffic picks up a little later. This cage faces onto the busiest street in town, the whole front wall a floor-to-ceiling iron grating. Pedestrians can look in over that low wall and see *everything.* Passersby stop and gawk. It's a zoo. Families of the inmates come yell at each other. Mothers with kids. One babe in arms shouts so loud, everyone breaks up laughing. Probably said something like "Daddy, come home soon!"

Hide as far back as you can, you're still the foreigner. People point you out. You're the main attraction here. How can they allow such humiliating exposure? Outright disgusting, this rank-smelling hole. Dozens of men crammed in here together, itching to explode. The very sound of their language gets on your nerves. In spite of which, you occasionally get the odd whiff of solidarity. An insider's bead on the "outside world." Bitterness toward this island, the country. If you were in better health, you'd put such a curse on the place it'd slide into the sea. Or else, well—delude yourself that you'd break down the walls and escape. Bend the bars like King Kong, thunder out larger than life. Anger is power. Positively refreshing, didn't know you had it in you. Like it would do any good to rage at those jabbering monkeys. The real target is elsewhere.

So why not walk right up to the bars and get a better look outside? The blue of the sky, the green of the leaves, flowers maybe? Different colored buildings. People's faces. Sarongs. But more than anything, the color of the sky. If only you had brushes, paper, and paints, it might even put you in a halfway decent mood.

Hand on the floor to prop yourself up. Fingers feel sticky. All the dirt and dust and shit on the floor has sucked up sweat and mildew, forming a thin, greasy layer of grime. At first you used to wipe your hands off on your clothes, without thinking, until you saw how useless it was. You're already covered head-to-toe in filth from the tiles, the concrete, and other prisoners.

Yesterday was shower day. The guards take everyone out, a few at a time, into the courtyard, tell them to strip, then hose them down. They laugh their heads off at the pale, thin bodies, ribs showing painfully sharp. Jeering as they aim for the assholes straight and hard. The force of those hoses hurts a little, but feels good. Cold water can be nice, best thing you've felt lately. Afterwards, still wet, they make you get back into your dirty clothes and return you to the slimy prison floor.

For the moment, the pain is hunger. Hunger with no appetite. Your body isn't functioning—not digesting food or channeling nutrition to the tissues. Three times a day, those grim meals they dish out. Watery rice gruel. Stinking fried rice. Doughy noodles, not even cooked. No strength to spoon the crap into your mouth anyway. Putrid greens that float up in the bowl. Just leave it, somebody else will finish it. Once, out of sheer craving you forced some down, and threw up a minute later. And still someone "spoke" for it, gesturing from the sidelines—*If it's just puke-bad, I'll have it.*

At that point you could still eat. After those first couple of days of solid depression, for some reason you got your second wind. Breathing normally, more at ease. And with it, some hidden reserve of energy. A brief flare, purely psychological, then that too was snuffed out. Leaving only flat black despair and insensate fear. Deeper, harder to get at.

Fear is the worst. Thinking of what's to come. Even so, you can only explode at your own stupidity. The frustration boils right over, erupts like a bulldozer scraping into a water main. (Where'd that image come from? Don't remember drawing anything like it.) You were almost off the hook, you had it beat. So why'd you backslide? What was all the effort for? Slipped not once but twice, just couldn't make a clean break. You're such a fool. How many times have you thought this through? Chased round and round the same worn groove? And yet even now, you think, if only you had a fix all your problems would vaporize.

In Thailand you'd quit. Underwent "straightening by fire" at that temple. Returned to Japan, thinking you'd live out the rest of your life without heroin. For months on end, you forgot all about it. But your very next trip abroad, you met Nils. That was your downfall. Ever since Inge, your Sad Child Angel has been tagging after you.

So why did you do it again? Your body was clean, off the stuff. But your mind betrayed you, is that it? With that empty assurance—just a little now, you can stop any time. You think you're so strong, for no good reason. Been-there bravado that turns traitor on you, sells you out. Mind sides with any physical craving. Convinces and cajoles. Never pushing, only letting you slip. Over the edge, like falling deep down a well. First comes the physical shock, fracturing bones and whiplash, cuts and lesions. Next, the recognition—you've hit bottom and there's no way out. Then the near-miss backlash, the futile hindsight. Too late.

Here it's different from Thailand; here it's *dangerous*. Explains why Nils beat a fast retreat to Bangkok. You and your "one last shot." Pathetic. How could such a miserable patchwork of lies fool you into trusting that shady character? How could you buy from that shiftless bastard? Even before that, just taking Bando seriously was a mistake. No, can't blame anyone else. Anything could have started it off, really. Because you never really kicked your habit. Your Sad Child Angel was still hanging in there. There's no end to addiction, only intermissions. Prolong the last reel change before playing out the rest of your life—you'd have it beat. But no, you had to lose out *here*, in this place. Even if you get out alive, it'll always be the same. Win and you die, or lose and you die—game over.

You were so weak. Anyone could see clear through you. That's what Agus picked up on. Fucking police pawn. Sell to the foreigner, get him arrested, score points for the cops. That was his angle from the very beginning. He set it up right from the start. All scam and make-believe. A trap. And you just stumbled along, the unsuspecting fall guy

Right after the arrest came the questioning. As soon as you reach the police station, they sit you down facing the interrogating officer in a tiny room. Interpreter off to one side, stenographer behind. The interpreter speaks lousy Japanese, slurs syllables. Name, nationality, age, address in Japan, travel route since leaving Japan, local address, date of entry, reason for entry, cash on hand—so many questions.

All they had to do was look at your passport and immigration card. "It's all written down."

"Maybe. But we need hear from you."

Matter of formality, most likely.

"Occupation?"

"Artist."

And would you believe it?—the interpreter doesn't even know the word in Japanese. Rather than explain in English, you commandeer a pencil and a piece of paper from the steno, then proceed to draw the interrogating officer. No caricature, no flattery, just a normal drawing. In two minutes the sketch is done and laid in front of him.

"*That* is what I do." Spoken like a street-corner portraitist. And you return to your seat.

The officer is pleasantly surprised. He shows off the drawing to the interpreter and steno. He lightens up for one brief second, then turns hard, seasoned lawman again.

Now the real questioning begins.

"We found heroin in room at Pandra Cottages. Is yours?"

How to answer? You paid Agus for it and shot up once, so it can only be yours. They'll have their evidence, so no use denying it. Better play it honest. You've lived honest this far.

"Yes, it's mine."

It sounds like someone else's voice. Miniscule amount, first offense—they'll let you go with a reprimand. Or if it goes to court, they'll waive the sentence. Nothing bad's going to happen. You're a Japanese citizen. What's this country to you? These cops?

But you're still high. Was it the heroin in your system doing the talking? Made you so cocky, so careless? Oh yes, everything'll work out.

"How you get it?"

"Bought it from a pusher named Agus."

"Where?"

"In that room. When you police came barging in, Agus was still in the room. He was even doing heroin himself. Why wasn't he arrested along with me?"

"No such report. It will be investigate. Where you meet this Agus person?"

"On the street in Kuta. Practically hounded me to buy the stuff. I kept refusing . . ."

"But?"

". . . in the end I bought two grams."

The interrogating officer asks nothing more about Agus. Instead, the questioning turns to your "prior heroin habit." Yes, you'd used it before. But here in Bali only once, today, right before the arrest. No, you didn't bring the heroin in from Thailand, you bought from Agus, like you said. Why not just find Agus and haul him in? That'd set everything straight.

They take you to another room next door. There on the desk are various objects collected from Pandra Cottages. They point to each item in turn— "This belong you?" Backpack, clothes, passport, cash, traveler's checks, paintbox with brushes and watercolors, art paper and portfolio. Yes, yes, yes, they're yours.

"And these?"

A plastic pouch with a tiny dose of white powder. And a syringe, lighter, and spoon—what about these last items? Agus brought them, so where's the actual ownership? Does it transfer to you? Can't be bothered to think it through, just shake your head, yes.

"What about this?"

Beside the spoon is a half-crushed Marlboro pack.

"Agus brought the heroin in that. He took everything out and threw the pack away. It's empty, right?"

The interrogating officer pulls on white gloves, picks up the pack, and takes out five little plastic bags—every one of them filled with white powder. It has all the finesse of a magic trick.

"That's not mine!" you scream out the moment you see this sleight of hand. "Agus put it there, not me! I know absolutely nothing about this!" You lunge out, swinging, swiping things to the floor left and right before two policemen grab you in an armlock. "I never paid for any of that! All I bought was two grams!"

"So you say."

When you finally calm down, they take you back to the first interrogation room. Suddenly the tone is different.

"You are under arrest. Do you know what that mean? First time?"

"Y-yes."

"Unfortunately, possession against law in our country. We cannot simply let pass. We must detain you. Do you understand?"

Of course.

"Cooperate and we take into consideration. That quick way to freedom for you."

You say nothing. Your head is ringing, a big bell clanging in your ear— *freedom, freedom!*

"That all for today."

They tell you to stand. The two cops grab your arms from either side and march you out to the holding cage. They unlock the door and drop you in with all the others, then lock the door behind. Yet even then you still think you'll come through all right. Deportation or a waived sentence. At worst, you'll do maybe half a year. You're Japanese. They can't just lock you up forever in a place like this. You said what you had to say and they understood you. You'll be out of here in no time. Formalities are already being squared away on the outside. Just say you'll never do it again and that'll be that. Nothing to it.

The following day, they call for you again. Two cops take you by the arms and jerk you along, one slinky step at a time. Yesterday's strength is gone. You're a zombie, hand grazing the wall the length of the corridor. No, don't want to go to that interrogation room. Want to get out. *Freedom* is still clang-banging in your head. Okay, they've dragged you this far.

Today, however, it's not the interrogating officer, it's a Japanese man in a brown batik open-neck shirt. Compact build, graying pomaded hair, golfer's tan—what's he doing here? He sits there behind a professional expression, the lifeless bureaucrat. The type who—outside Japan or not—surrounds himself with other old boys duly cemented into the requisite Japanese postures. All his meager authority marshaled up front.

They deposit you in a chair across from him, one-on-one.

"Yoshizaburo Sato. Japanese consular officer here in Bali."

Okay, you nod silently, he's here for your case. The man looks down at his papers.

"And you are . . . Tetsuro Nishijima?"

You nod again. You're terribly groggy, a different person from yesterday. Slumped forward, you gaze vacantly at his chest and don't say a word.

"Yesterday, at your lodgings at Pandra Cottages in Kuta, you were arrested for illegal possession of drugs. Is that correct?"

The inside of your mouth is dry. Your voice is scratchy. "Can I, um, get out of here?"

The consul suddenly raises his voice. "Don't talk nonsense, young man! Getting out is out of the question. You have broken the law of this country. You have been arrested on suspicion of drug trafficking. A very serious offense. It's Japanese citizens like you doing things like this abroad who make our job so difficult. In any case, we will acknowledge the crime and ask for clemency. That is the best you can expect."

"What about a lawyer?"

"That's further down the road. I can't say this openly, but the legal system in this country is different from Japan's. It's not even the accepted practice to have a lawyer present at the time of interrogation. As a rule, foreign criminals like yourself are universally disliked here. And this is even when drug crimes do no direct harm to others. Which is to say, it's the country itself you've offended. So the country assumes complete impunity in dealing with foreign drug offenders. The law is, of course, on the side of the state, and almost always the ruling goes against the lawbreaker. You can only bow your head, admit to your crime, and hope for mercy. That's your line, young man."

The same thing the interrogating officer said the day before.

"But they didn't catch the guy who sold me the stuff. Are the police even looking for him?"

"I know nothing about any of that. Was he Japanese?"

Let's leave Bando out of this for now; strictly speaking, he didn't do anything. Agus is the one to blame. "No, *Java*nese."

The consul looks relieved. Javanese are outside his sphere of responsibility. "How does all this relate?"

"He hasn't been arrested. He got away."

"Who got away?"

"The guy who sold me the stuff. Hounded me to buy, then planted those drugs. But when the police came and fired their pistols and arrested me, this Agus, he just took off."

"This drug-seller is no concern of mine. You told them all that at the interrogation, did you not?"

"I did."

"Well then, fine. That's settled."

What's coming off here? No lawyer. Only this pompous Japanese official for a stand-in. The stiff doesn't even know which way he's facing. "If you say so. All the same, don't you think you could get me transferred somewhere a little nicer?"

"You still don't grasp the gravity of your situation. This country has its own laws and its own methods of enforcing them. If you expect me to put in a good word, you are very much mistaken. From what I heard, it was a sizable amount they confiscated."

"That's just not true! Only two grams were mine, the rest Agus left on purpose. I already denied it flat out, I told them that it wasn't mine."

"Let them take that into consideration later. That's what the trial is for. Just cooperate with the prosecution so as not to get death or life imprisonment, then ask the judge for leniency."

Death? Life imprisonment? The words drop on you like a bomb. Sparks fly behind your eyes. You want to scream. Who ever heard of anything so insane? How could they turn 2mg—barely more than for you alone—into a death sentence? Fear gurgles up from deep inside and overflows. Can't even ask the consul again to be sure. Did the police tell him? All the color drains from your face, blood siphons from your head. Tiny corpuscular crabs race over the sand, scamper into holes, and disappear—the serum tide's gone out.

You fall off your seat. The consul rises but, far from offering you a hand, opens the door and motions to the police outside. Two officers enter, jerk you to your feet, and drag you back to the holding cage. The iron door slides open and—push—in you go. Pressing your way through the other inmates, you find a wall and collapse. After that you remember nothing.

3

KAORU

It was just after New Year's when I returned to Tokyo. I'd missed the holidays, having gone to France at the end of November to work with a TV crew covering *Le Noël Français*—subtitled "Christmas in France" for the uninitiated —then taken off for Barcelona on my own.

"I'm back," I phoned in to Mom. "Spain was super cold."

"Oh," was her only reaction. Ordinarily I wouldn't have been able get a word in edgeways with her catching me up on everything that had happened in my absence.

"What's the matter?"

"Something rather serious has come up. We need to talk. Can you come over?"

It seemed pretty strange coming from her. Mom had never consulted me about anything, never confided in her own daughter tête-à-tête, but she wouldn't say anything specific.

I went the very next day. With my internal clock still out of kilter, I somehow dragged myself out of bed before noon and took the train to the suburbs.

"What's the matter?" I asked again as soon as I walked into the living room.

"It's Tetsuro, they've arrested him."

"*Arrested?*"

"The day before yesterday, there was a call from the Foreign Office.

Someone asking, was I the mother of Tetsuro Nishijima? I had a horrible feeling. And then he said . . . he said they'd been informed that Tetsuro's in custody in Bali, Indonesia, on a drug charge. And if the worst comes to the worst, he might get the death penalty . . ."

For five years after my strange baptism on the outskirts of Paris, I'd lived mostly in Europe, although in the end I never graduated from the Sorbonne either. Still, I got the language down and made a passable living. Part-timing at first, I eventually found a niche as a coordinator-interpreter, traveling back and forth from Japan for media productions about France. Jobs can come up at all times of the year, but autumn-to-early-winter is especially busy. April in Paris is also big, yet in recent years it seems the Japanese associate France particularly with harvest time and the arrival of Beaujolais Nouveau—and, for some reason, the Holiday Season.

That winter it was January 15 by the time I got back to Tokyo. I'm not in the habit of spending a traditional New Year's with the folks. Though not as extreme as my brother, I've never felt tied to the parental nest.

Mom sometimes grieved over this—the way the two of them, a father who went straight from university to the daily grind of automotive sales, paired with a mother who gave him moral support while raising the kids, could have produced such offbeat kids. I know that was Mom's take on the family, and I think it was the same with Dad. For better or worse, it was a solid partnership.

Ever since he was small, my brother was a self-absorbed child. Give him paper and crayons and he would play quietly for hours. From middle school on, he was winning illustration prizes left and right, getting commissions from magazines, right up until he finished high school and left home to start living on his own. His moving out came on the heels of a confrontation with his father. Dad, it seems, could never fathom Tez—that's my brother—or his lifestyle. A person was supposed to keep a proper distance from others, to implement his own powers within a cooperative framework, thereby contributing to the achievement of the whole. Dad was fairly adept at doing this himself. Never one to exert leadership, neither did he ever lag far behind.

An utter bore to talk to, though tell him that and it wouldn't bother him one bit. Likewise, Mom had no qualms at all about her own supporting role. Thinking back on it now, my brother must have seemed like the wrong baby, dumped on them from who-knows-where. And I probably came in a close second.

It's not quite correct to say my father and brother had a "confrontation." Their paths ran so totally oblique to one another there was never any possibility of a collision. To Dad it must have seemed that his son just walked out on him; he never understood why. While Tez's thinking was, I suppose, that he'd been provoked, that Dad was opposing him when all he wanted to do was develop his own abilities; so he had to exit Dad's sphere of authority. Of course knowing he could make a living was a big factor. Mom was all broken up. Meanwhile I stood by wide-eyed, watching everything just happen. Taking it all down in my indelible mental notebook: *Children must at some point leave the nest.*

Not long after my brother left home, I met him at a hamburger place in town and we talked. Eighteen and thirteen, strikingly similar faces, we must have made a funny sight. I mean, a teenage brother and sister who'd normally be living in their own little worlds, hardly exchanging two words around the house, yet here we were meeting outside and seriously discussing things.

Tez, affecting a self-conscious pose, said he was going to stay like this —away from home. He might just have well have been talking to *them*, the folks, not me. The two months on his own must have been encouraging, so probably all he wanted from me was to let on to the folks about this newfound confidence.

"Going to university, like, just isn't my way. Right now, each hour of mine's a whole lot more intense than anything the college crowd's got going. The idea, in this day and age, of attending art school and studying under some teacher—it's a joke."

I could only think, okay, why tell me this? The word "painting" didn't even figure in Dad's vocabulary. Try as he might to comprehend, you'd never hear him say "If that's your goal, then go to art school!" Did Tez really expect me to mediate between them? At thirteen, I stood equidistant from both my parents and my big brother. I was an interested observer, yes, but merely to see what would happen.

"You couldn't just up and leave without an argument?" I suggested. I was thinking back on the shouting matches between my father and brother. Dad's face a hot crimson, Tez in some kind of a huff. And Mom, of course, going to pieces.

"They'd never listen, not to what I'd have to say," he snapped, embarrassed that a little sister five years his junior should be questioning him. True, talk hadn't ever got through. Even I could see that. But I was still at home, under the same roof with parents who didn't necessarily hear out what *I* had to say. It wasn't fair, Tez, you making off on your own like that.

"This 'just finish college' crap—it's a joke. Painting's got nothing to do with university."

The next words out of my mouth came borrowed straight from Mom and Dad. "But, you know, you owe it to your parents who raised you."

"Parental love and obligation to support are two different things."

Score one for Tez. His adult logic floored my hand-me-down morality in seconds flat.

"Yeah, I was raised by them," he went on, "but so were Mom and Dad raised by their parents, who were raised by *their* parents before them. Just like me and you, Kaoru, sooner or later we're going to be raising our own kids, leading our own lives."

Me raise children? Would that day ever come? The very thought steamed up my head so fast I couldn't bring out a proper response. I mean, I was only thirteen. The big wide adult world still lay far ahead of me. But my brother was already there.

"Say, Tez . . . Bro?" (I always used to call him double.) "Why do we get along so badly as a family?"

"There are countries where it rains, and countries where it doesn't. Just like there's families who get along, and ones who don't. That's just how it is."

"Hmph."

"Anyway, I'm fine on my own. The money rolls in regularly, I do my own cooking. It's precisely what any high school graduate from a small town does when he goes off to university in Tokyo and starts living on his own. Just tell them that."

Entrusted with this message to the folks, from then on I became the one who knew what Tez was up to, or at least whatever he chose to tell his kid sister about. And several years later, when *I* halfheartedly went to university, I found I couldn't stand the scene either, and ran off to Paris, far away from the folks myself, pretty much following Tez's lead.

That winter, in France, going to church and visiting friends' families while writing up material on my first *Noël français*, I wasn't completely immune to memories of Christmas with my own family. Back when I was in fifth or sixth grade—which puts it around the time Tez entered high school—he was already having these run-ins with Dad, who told him to stop painting and do his studies, like any other parent talking to any "ordinary" child. Even so, those two or three Christmases were nice.

It's not like any of us were Christian, but still the Christmas spirit infused us all. Even Dad, who usually never spoke a word when he dragged himself home from the office, seemed a different person. Tez didn't hole up in his room either. For once we all sat down together around the dining table. Mom was a great cook and really went all-out for the occasion, spending hours over a hot stove roasting a big bird stuffed with who-knows-what, which Dad carved for everyone at the table. What a treat! Then we'd have tea—English tea—and Mom brought out a real plum pudding she'd baked and set aside months before. Dad sliced that for us, too. At Christmas and only at Christmas, neither Tez nor Dad started in with their bickering which always ruined dinner and left everyone miserable with cold food on their plates.

Later on, we brought out the gifts we'd chased up all over town for the last month. Even Tez gave things besides his own pictures. Usually all he ever thought about was art, but for once he actually went out and bought stuff. All told we exchanged twelve presents: four rounds of three boxes each, to unwrap while the others looked on, praising and appraising the goods, comparing them to last year's haul (not to mention the year before that—what long memories we had!). We'd try things on for show, plug in, switch on, happy just to hold our new *cadeaux*. For those few days I wished every day could be Christmas.

When Tez left home, there went Christmas. The remaining three of us didn't do anything the following year.

"Shall we send Tez presents?" I asked Mom.

"Why don't you send him something?" was all she would say.

So Tez and I continued to exchange presents as usual, but not Mom and Dad. That spelled out the situation to me; from that moment on I began to seriously consider my life as it would be without parents. Not being able to paint, I went on to university. Over their protests I found a place of my own, when I could easily have commuted from the suburban homestead. This made for a degree of financial difficulty, so that between part-time jobs and my studies, though nowhere near really poor, I had to wrangle up some scholarship money. At which point I dropped my college crash course on European language-and-culture and made for Paris, where I somehow managed to scrape by.

True to his word, Tez did quite well with his painting. At first, people in publishing he met when he won an illustration contest gave him the odd assignment: mostly little vignettes of everyday objects in watercolors and acrylics. Mom even discovered things he'd done in the pages of her favorite women's monthly. Then he began to get bigger work doing portraits, getting more and more covers. He even teamed up with a well-known writer to do a children's book. His drawings were unpretentious, painstakingly rendered, unsentimentally "dry" yet somehow lyrical. Sorry, I'm no good at putting my brother's art into words. All I can say is, his pictures, popular as they were, were obviously good. A single strawberry by his hand was instantly recognizable as a Tetsuro Nishijima. I'd like them even if they weren't my brother's pictures. Tez himself, however, was trying to break away from that staid pictorial style.

Occasionally I'd go visit him at his cluttered little studio apartment. In his case, a real-life studio. One time, saying how his life couldn't be better,

Tez showed me some samples of his work. Again he probably expected me to trot right home and tell the folks, which in fact is what I did; I told Mom everything I saw, as if it were my own little victory. Then two years later, my brother won a big prize for one of the children's books he'd illustrated. He was the youngest winner ever. Mom and I went to the awards ceremony, but Dad with his "life's not so easy, mark my words" attitude still couldn't accept or wouldn't trust his son's chosen lifestyle.

It was around that time that Tez started traveling. And not just, I believe, when he hit a "creative block." Commissions were coming in steadily. Every year I always had a calendar with his artwork to put up in my room. He was interviewed in magazines as the up-and-coming illustrator to watch. But somehow that still wasn't enough. He'd reached a ceiling doing pictures to order. He'd run out of things to paint. He was in a rut and he knew it. He did illustration work to get by, but eventually he wanted to be able to live off the proceeds of what he wanted to paint. To do that, he had to go "beyond," to the "other side" of his present self—I remember him saying things like that, though I didn't really understand at the time. Only later when I was thinking of dropping out to go to Paris did I finally appreciate Tez's reasons for wanting to see the world.

He was, for want of a better word, "molting" his old self. There's nothing wrong with wanting to widen your scope, but the human mind can be like a hard shell protecting you from unknown hazards. Inside those walls you can only grow so big. When you break out, you're all naked and tender, exposed to injury, until you can form a larger shell. A larger shell—that's why Tez started traveling, it kind of adds up now.

At first Tez took short trips. He joined tours to Europe, ones with a lot of unorganized free time, but soon realized he couldn't paint with others around. And anyway Europe just wasn't for him really. After that, I think it was somewhere in the South Pacific. I met him not long after he got back and remember him muttering something about the sun being too strong for him to paint there. He showed me his paintings, and even I could see the vast seascapes were too much for him. America was no good either. The next thing I knew he was off traveling in Asia. Which seemed to suit him better, because his absences grew longer and longer. Probably he found what he was looking for. He bragged about how expert he'd become at traveling well without spending money. It was Tez who gave me the bug to look outward myself. He'd get a steady magazine assignment that would force him to stay put and work for four months straight, then he'd head off for two months. Repeat that cycle twice and there was a whole year gone. Eventually he'd be away for four months at a stretch.

While traveling he painted exclusively watercolors. He showed me fresh, pristine landscapes from all over Asia. He never mentioned what he meant to do with those pictures, whether he was planning to exhibit or publish or simply stockpile images. Meanwhile the commissions kept coming in regular as clockwork. By then, half the time when I tried to get in touch he'd be gone. Just wouldn't be there.

"Tetsuro's in custody in Bali, Indonesia," Mom was saying, "on a drug charge. And if the worst comes to the worst, he might get the death penalty."

"*What* . . . ?"

"Well, that's what he said, this Foreign Office fellow. Where *is* Bali?"

"It's an island. A tourist resort, I think. In Indonesia, like you just said."

"Yes . . . right." She was completely out of it.

"Mom, please. Fill me in a bit."

"I don't know a thing. All I know is they want us to come. It seemed as if they couldn't discuss things over the telephone."

"And?"

"What do you think? I practically went into shock. It was all I could do just to take down the man's name."

"What about Dad?"

"Your father has his head in his hands. He wants *you* to go to the Foreign Office, Kaoru."

"All right. I'll give it a try."

So, the following day I went to the Ministry of Foreign Affairs.

"It's about the Nishijima case, I . . . uh . . ." I stammered the name of the official concerned at the first open door, before a junior clerk managed to locate a black-bound list amid the frightful clutter on his desk and told me where to go.

After wandering the dimly lit corridors devoid of any receptionist, I came to the entrance of an immense Administrative Department and tried to get someone's attention. Eventually I was directed to the man who'd telephoned. What I was able to get out of him was this: "A telegram came in dated the eighth of this month. Sent by Yoshizaburo Sato from the Denpasar mission of the Surabaya Japanese consulate. In which he writes, *Tetsuro Nishijima, age 29, arrested here on charge of illegal possession of drugs. Possibility of death sentence. Suspect holding Japanese passport, appears to have largely admitted to charge. Named his parents as contacts . . .*"

But surely there was some mistake, as Mom had suggested. No, not as far as the report received by the ministry was concerned. Of course there was still the possibility of mistaken identity. Say someone stole my brother's passport. Or maybe the police in Bali arrested the wrong person. Or a parcel he picked up as a favor had drugs in it.

"What do we do now?"

"For a start, you can go talk to the consul. There's nothing we can do for you at this end."

"Nothing . . . ?"

"We've been getting so many of these cases lately, and basically it's the legal institutions of the other country that decide things."

"And . . . ?"

"In any case, it's not the ministry's duty to extricate criminals."

Criminal? For one instant I flared red, then immediately controlled myself. These people! I'd run up against this same aggravating official attitude time and again as a foreigner in France. But getting angry here wouldn't do any good. This gray suit only wanted to send me merrily on my way. Okay, if that's how it was, I'd go to Indonesia. The man opened his Ministry Personnel Directory and showed me the address of the Bali outpost. *Outpost . . . sounds like the Foreign Legion*, I remember thinking as I jotted down his contacts.

"Please call the consulate first thing." That was all he said. Downhearted, I dragged myself down the dark corridors to the exit. Tez was behind bars in Indonesia. I walked along in a state, my mind a blank, my feet uprooted. As if on autopilot I took a train, then walked from the station to my Tokyo *pied-à-terre*. Indonesia? Where the hell was it?

Back home, I got hold of myself and called Mom to say I'd only succeeded in confirming what the Foreign Office already told her over the phone. It didn't seem to be any simple mistake. Tez was in jail. Someone had to go there.

"You go, then. It's overseas after all."

"I thought you'd say that. But you know, I've never traveled in Asia."

"France, Asia —what's the difference?"

One hell of a reckless generalization, though little good it would do me to protest. Neither Mom nor Dad seemed prepared to go along. Mom had never set foot abroad; she didn't even have a passport. It didn't matter what the country, nowhere in the world was worth the trouble of getting there. She was steadfast in her own little prejudices.

"What does Dad say?"

"He wants you to go."

"All right."

"But really . . . I mean, drugs?" Mom's voice swelled with distant irritation. "How could the child be so stupid!"

Only then did it hit home—*Tez was Mom's son*. Strange, I'd never really considered the possibility that she might still regard Tez (or myself, for that matter) as her "child." That time was long gone. We'd all graduated from each other by now, at least it seemed that way to me. It was as if she were trying to gather together strands I thought had long since unraveled, ignoring the way those ties had chafed on some of us.

I heard her out, but I'd stopped listening. Wasn't the death penalty a bit extreme, I wanted to argue, but the words caught in my throat. I couldn't bring myself to say "death penalty." My brother was going to be . . . *killed*. His body subjected to the ultimate violence. His life cut short. There had to be some mistake. It had to be a false accusation. Anyway, how could any country put you to death just for possession of drugs? Wouldn't it be enough just to deport the foreigner concerned?

On the plane to Jakarta I still felt optimistic, hopeful enough at least to take the positive step of going to Indonesia. Once I got there things would be straightened out. I'd tell them what's what and they'd understand. What exactly I would say I didn't know, but I'd untangle this huge knot they'd snarled up around my brother. I'd do my bit. Everything would be fine. I simply had to find the tail end of the knot and give it one good yank. That my own brother should be thrown into some Indonesian jail, let alone get the death penalty, well, it just couldn't happen. Words like "crime" or "trial" were so alien to me, they didn't even register. My first and only brush with the law was in Paris when my purse was stolen. Crime occurred in fiction; it was nice and unreal. Maybe that's why the in-flight meal on the way there tasted so good. It was my first trip to an Asian country, my first time eating spicy Asian food.

I changed planes in Jakarta for Bali. That's when my optimism began to wither. Only then did I recall the anxiety of not being able to communicate. Granted I didn't understand Indonesian—I didn't speak it and couldn't be expected to—but for them not to speak either English or French seemed, in the international scheme of things, a clear failing on their side. Particularly after all my efforts at learning languages! At that point I could still tell myself that.

Whatever happened to my brother had to be along the lines of miscommunication. I was no stranger to that helpless feeling when you can't understand what they're saying and they can't understand you, either. When I went to Paris for the first time I was resigned to the idea. Of course I wouldn't be able to get myself across. But then I was ambitious enough to think that all I needed was to study until I could.

Even after I'd already been at the Sorbonne for quite a while, I had problems. I took a one-off job with a Japanese trading company rep on a trip to Brittany to buy Calvados. I could get the locals to understand *me* just fine, but their country dialect was impenetrable. Here I'd gone along as an interpreter and I couldn't manage the simplest task. I was shocked. As it turned out, the first day involved very general discussions, so I faked my way through it. But come the second day, the numbers were flying thick and fast. I had them commit everything to paper on the pretext that it was safer businesswise. By the crucial third day, my ears were more used to their *patois* and I could actually make some sense of what they were saying.

What came back to me on the plane to Bali was my complete loss on that first day. Now I faced the same thing. I had to do something, but what? And the nightmare was, my brother's life was at stake. What if I couldn't get through . . . ?

The Bali-Denpasar Airport was chaos. The queues at Immigration were endless, people jostling back and forth not knowing which way to go or why. It should have been routine—land, pick up baggage, go outside— but here they delayed everyone for no apparent reason. Even out in the Arrivals lobby, the tiny place was swarming. And the smell! Granted all airports smell, but this was different. Nothing like the musty odor of Roissy-Charles de Gaulle or the ice-chill whiff of Moscow-Sheremetyevo. Take the smell of that Jakarta in-flight meal intensified a hundred times, liquefied in hot, sticky air, and pour it through the upper windows of the terminal building—that was the stink. Not three hours ago it had seemed delicious, but now the idea of breathing this day and night made me gasp and break out in a sweat.

No car came for me. Over the phone the consul had sounded none too young. He was curt and elusive, only barely cooperative, though I managed to tap him for the name of a hotel near the consulate. Then when I telephoned the hotel to book a room, whoever was at the desk distinctly said they'd send a car to meet my plane. I changed my money and was peering this way and that around the crowded lobby. There was no driver holding up any sign with my name on it. Which left me little choice but to drag my suitcase outside and take a taxi.

In a flash, a brace of men were all over me. "Taxi! Taxi! Chip wery chip!" All of them shouting at once. Just like Tunisia or Morocco. Try to negotiate a fare, they wouldn't even listen. "No problem! Wery chip!"

What could I do? I pointed to one of the drivers, a small man with a dark, sunburned face who went wild at winning out. He grabbed up my luggage and headed for his car parked a long way off. Only when I got in did I notice there was no meter in it. It was an unlicensed cab. *So that's how it goes here*, I thought, my uneasiness mounting. *At least I'm going to a regular hotel. There'll be a doorman. Nothing too terrible can happen.*

All I can say is, that driver really coaxed speed out of that noisy old hulk. I could tell the road was bad; every bump came pounding un-shockabsorbed through the seat. He went out of his way to pass trucks well ahead of us. French drivers are bad, but this guy was in a category to himself. He veered out into the middle lane into oncoming traffic, just barely cutting back in time after passing. I was at his mercy, clinging to the back of the front seat. Thin patches of forest dotted with the occasional building passed to the left, fields of scrubby grass to the right. Now and again, I could make out flat expanses of water beyond, probably the sea. A dirty mud-colored sea. Pretty desolate. Why would Tez want to come here? How could he, by whatever stretch, let himself get caught in a place like this?

Twenty minutes later—up a shady country lane, then a right turn—we were at the hotel. Grandeur befitting a consul's recommendation. Even in Europe I couldn't hope to stay anywhere in this class unless someone else were paying. This was a real resort hotel. We drove up to the portico, where the driver fetched my luggage out of the trunk. No doorman appeared. The driver looked at me and smiled: "Tenti taudan."

If only I'd memorized the exchange rate from the airport! I hadn't a clue how much "tenti taudan" was in yen, but as an opening bid I tried bargaining him down half-price. "Ten taudan," mimicking his accent. From my wallet I slowly counted out ten bills prominently printed with the denomination 1000 and handed them over.

"Tenti taudan," he pouted, not withdrawing his hand.

Oh all right, if I must I must. I counted out two more bills. Still no good. Another two bills. This time I looked the driver dead in the face, until he averted his eyes with a nod, "Okay," and got back in the car.

Still no doorman. Left wondering how much I'd been taken for, I grappled my luggage, pushing open the big door with my hip. The lobby was vast. Immense. Off in one corner, two bellboys stood chatting between themselves. I was furious. Never get upset first thing in a strange port of call, I know—but what a dump of a country!

The front desk was all the way over on the other side. I made it there unaided and gave the receptionist grief for not sending the hotel car. Which got me a brisk "So sorry." I insisted they deduct the amount from the room, but no could do, only when it coincided with a guest going to the airport, and unfortunately nobody was checking out today. Perhaps the explanation over the phone had been insufficient. So sorry they couldn't send anyone to meet me.

"So how much should the fare from the airport have been?"

"Depend."

What kind of answer was that? "How about 14,000?"

"Not so bad. If you bargain best price, you maybe get here for 6000, but official taxi chit sell at airport for 12,000 rupiah. But late at night, if many passenger waiting and raining monsoon, you pay 20,000."

In other words, I had to be prepared to haggle each time I took a taxi. Probably have to settle a price each time I wanted to do anything. But maybe that left room even for bargaining over my brother's sentence.

I went up to my room and called the consular office. A secretary answered in fluent English: the consul had already gone home for the day. I looked at my watch. Four o'clock. Well, in Paris too, embassies and consulates only receive visitors up to 3:00. And in some Arab countries, it's one hour, between 1:00 and 2:00 in the afternoon. In a tropical posting like this, dedication to duty is bound to run thin.

I checked the exchange receipt from the airport: nearly six rupiah to the yen. Which put the 12,000 rupiah taxi fare at roughly 2000 yen. *Hmm, that's all?*

I laid out my clothes. There in bottom of the suitcase, underneath my blouses, was the old middle school world map I always take with me traveling. I'd imagined Indonesia to be a tiny country, but here it covered a broad swath of Southeast Asian islands east to west. And it was south of the equator! For the first time in my life I'd ventured into the southern hemisphere. Bali was a speck just east of Java. The whole speckled mass formed an archipelago, which led to New Guinea if you kept heading east. Then there were even more islands up north. The map was crawling with them. But to the south was open sea, all the way down to Australia. So that's where I was.

The next day at 9:05, I signaled for a taxi out in front of the hotel. I now knew to fix the fare before getting in. We were supposed to be in the same general area of Sanur as the consular office, but when I showed the address, the driver didn't seem to know it and went over to ask a colleague before starting off. It was only a short hop.

Consul Sato seemed a colorless sort of person. He wore an open-collared light brown batik shirt and sat squarely behind a large desk. He gave me a who's-this-girl look when I first entered, but immediately erased his slate face and addressed me: "Kaoru Nishijima, wasn't it?" He then launched into a mechanical explanation of how a Tetsuro Nishijima had been arrested for illegal possession of heroin, taken into police custody in the state capital of Denpasar, undergone interrogation, and currently awaited due process.

"Is my brother well?"

"He's obviously quite distraught. Mind you, they all are. It's always a shock being arrested in a foreign country. Added to which, police treatment here is none too good. The other day when I went to visit him, he didn't look all that well."

"You talked to him then?"

"That's my job. He said he wanted to get out soon, but—what can I say? The fact remains, he is being held suspect."

Suspect—it grated on my unaccustomed ears. A nasty word. "Can't the consulate take any steps?" I wanted some token assurance, something to shift the grim balance just now impressed on me.

"No, it can't," said the consul on the spot. Not "We will do what we can." Not "We will try every possible . . ." Not even "It's very difficult"—this was "No." "It's not the Ministry of Foreign Affair's business." Said in a voice designed to nip my little hopes in the bud. "Your brother was apprehended in this country and is to be tried by the legal institutions of this country. Diplomacy begins first and foremost with respect for the sovereignty of the reciprocal country. We have no place interfering in their internal affairs."

It was the same official communiqué I'd heard only a few days before at the ministry itself.

"But in our passport it says, 'The Ministry of Foreign Affairs of Japan requests all those whom it may concern to allow the bearer, a Japanese national, to pass freely and without hindrance and, in case of need, to afford him or her every possible aid and protection . . .'" I'd committed the wording to memory in my spare office hours at the Paris travel agency.

Consul Sato's expression soured. He wasn't used to such rebuttals. In Europe, a young woman who expresses herself in a clear, logical manner can generally expect to get her way, but here it obviously wouldn't wash.

"Indeed, it does say that. However, criminals don't fall within those bounds. Nowhere does it say that if a person killed someone from this country we should ask them to let him 'pass freely and without hindrance' right out their jurisdiction."

"Killed someone?"

"Drugs are, in a sense, an even more serious offense."

"So you'd just abandon him?" Even as I blurted this out, I knew I'd gone too far.

"Say what you will," allowed the consul, turning away. "We appreciate that our salaries are paid from citizens' taxes, but that doesn't oblige us to come to the aid of each and every Japanese who comes to Bali. We are simply unequal to the task."

"Can't you send a letter of protest to the local court?"

"Out of the question. No country does that."

"And that's the bottom line?"

"You have to realize that your brother represents something of an embarrassment to our country. What I *can* do perhaps is introduce you to an attorney, who can acquaint you with the judicial system in this country and how drug cases are handled on the whole."

"Okay—please." Under the circumstances, just avoiding an argument was an achievement. What constitutes debate in Europe, in Japan is mere bickering. Time I got that through my head.

"Nevertheless, when it comes to the trial, the decision whether or not to go with this attorney is entirely your own. Contractual arrangements are up to the private individual."

"Understood."

"That and" (here the consul relaxed his bearing slightly) "just a friendly piece of advice. Running around everywhere by taxi and *bemo* can become a real bore. I expect you'll be making regular trips back and forth between your lodgings and the police and the courthouse. Hiring a driver is easier and, above all, cheaper. I suggest you use one of our regulars, Wayang. I guarantee he's one-hundred-percent trustworthy."

I accepted the offer gracefully. If introducing a driver was the best the consul could do, then I should know enough to be grateful. What good would it do Tez for me to bitch? It was sure to be a long haul ahead. "One last question. Am I allowed to see my brother?"

"A visit should be no problem. Would you like to go right now?"

And so I found myself riding into the state capital Denpasar in a big, lumbering sedan, the newly acquainted Wayang at the wheel.

Wayang was a short, middle-aged man, dark-skinned, with a twinkle in his eyes and a minimal command of roadside English. He and I came to an agreement: I engaged his services for 6000 rupiah an hour, running or waiting regardless. The consul's word was good enough for me. The world is full of dishonest drivers, so if the man had proven himself to the consul over the years, surely he wouldn't cheat me.

Not long after leaving the consular office, we were in town. The car slowed to a traffic-jam crawl. Shop-houses hemmed us in on both sides of the road, cars increased in number, people walked the streets in even greater numbers. Children darted out in front of cars without a thought for their lives. I pressed my face to the glass to take it all in. It was my first time in this corner of the world and everything was new. I had to know what I was up against.

On the footpath along the storefronts, I saw bouquets of flowers in shallow boxes or maybe folded paper. Or no, folded leaves. Each shop had one, the way restaurants in Japan put out little saucers of salt by the door before opening time. It was only then I noticed Wayang had a similar box of flowers on his dashboard: no bigger than a paperback book, with something under the flowers.

"Wayang, what is that?" I asked.

"*Chanan.*"

"What is it for?"

"For god."

God? Which god? Flower offerings. Like for *bulsudan*, the family altars back home? But now was no time to be asking about gods, not in a car. Religious explanations always get long and involved. I made a mental note to ask him about it some other time.

The car window was open a crack. The air was damp and thick and pungent. Those same smells from yesterday at the airport, only much more powerful. Blended to a sickly potency, a wall of smells that blocked the way. Suffocating. I'd never get to like it.

There was plenty of greenery in town. Rows of very large trees lined the streets, and more trees sprang up between the buildings, all spreading dense growths of branches and leaves and vines; dusty red soil feeding them from below; the moisture in the air, even the sounds of the city lending support. Sewer water ran in open ditches, brown half-naked children scampered here and there. It was all too much for me, as if my whole body were wrapped in an invisible, clinging net. A stinking net.

As the buildings along the road got bigger, I knew we'd reached the city center. We passed a large, market-like structure, then what seemed to be a park, then some kind of stadium. We turned the corner and there was the police station. Wayang parked in back and helped me out of the car. *What a kind face this man has.*

I followed him out into the street, then stopped in my tracks. I'd been working out in my head things I was going to say when I got to see Tez in whatever visiting room arrangement, thinking I had to make sure to get it right, when suddenly I caught sight of the iron bars. There behind a chest-high concrete barrier and across a courtyard was the lockup, an entire wall of metal grating. In it were prisoners. There in plain view. Just like at the zoo.

Wayang, you can't mean my brother is really in there? Not among all those men, crouching, sprawled flat, pacing around that cage? I just stood there, dumbfounded, scared. My eyes had strayed where they didn't belong, caught in the iron crosshairs. I couldn't look away.

Little by little I could feel the men fixing their eyes on me. What I wore distinguished me. My face set me apart. My eyes and nose, my build marked me. Somebody among them had spotted the young foreign woman and the news spread, not so much by word of mouth as sheer tension. A clotting of curiosity. Nudging each other, whispering, pointing with their chins, they all focused on me. And I just stood there in the rub of their combined gaze.

From deep in the shadows a pair of eyes found me. He was dirty and sunburned, more disheveled and sunken-cheeked than anything I remembered. Practically a stranger, but still nothing like the local faces. Tottering to his feet—it was my brother, no mistake. Our stares locked . . . until finally I summoned the strength to break away. I wanted to collapse right there. I placed a steadying hand on the concrete barrier wall and looked down. Wayang was next to me, quietly reassuring—"All right, Miss?"

"I'll be okay. It's just seeing my brother in there like that . . ."

"Yes. So sorry."

"Uh, do we have to meet in there? Isn't there someplace without all the others?"

"Can do."

Entering the police station, Wayang presented a formal visitation request from the consul, along with a letter verifying my identity. I showed my passport to the duty officer and was conducted to a small room with a crude wooden table and two chairs, plus another chair over by the wall. Everything inside the building smelled of cheap paint over heaven-knows-what else. Compared to this, the rotten-vegetable air outside was a whole lot fresher. For fifteen minutes they kept me waiting while Wayang stood out in the corridor.

Then the door opened and in came Tez. Slowly, as if he were blind, he sat down at the table. He looked terrible, sickly and wasting away. His hair was a scraggly mess. He was looking right at me, yet didn't see me. The guard who led him in took the seat by the wall.

"Tez?" Easy now, easy.

There was no answer. Tez was sealed off inside.

"Tez, I came to help you." Not the words I intended, but what was I to say? "Everything'll be fine," I began again, then burst into tears. *No, I can't be crying like this.* "It's okay . . ."

My brother just sat there dazed, afraid to open his mouth. As if the whole world would go to pieces the minute he uttered even a single word. Arrested, locked up, then I waltz in from out of the blue—where now could he hide? Is that what he was thinking? The more I thought about it, the more I cried. Uncontrollably, uselessly. I planted both elbows on the table and looked at Tez swimming through tears. Everything was a blur, my cheeks were all wet.

I kept repeating, choking: "It's okay . . . we'll get you out of here."

That day my brother spoke not one word the entire fifteen-minute visit. His blank expression stayed glued in place. I cried myself hoarse and out of breath. It was all I could do to offer a weak "I'll be back" before standing to leave.

The following day, after a troubled night, I went with the consul to meet his attorney. This was in Denpasar again. A small office more like a rural records bureau, where a smiling, solid-girthed Attorney Darsana took a seat next to Consul Sato.

"Did you meet with him?" asked Darsana straight off in English.

"Mm, I went there yesterday. Horrid place."

"Well, it's just until they file his report. Once papers have been sent to the Investigations Division, he'll be transferred to solitary confinement somewhere else."

"And then what?"

"As soon as the trial begins, he'll be moved again."

"What about bail?"

"Not much chance."

"And the prospects for the trial?"

"Yes, well, the prospects . . . ," said Darsana, glancing over at the consul.

"Let's not be too *o-pu-ti-mi-su-to*," pronounced Sato, vowel-by-vowel in Japanese schoolbook English.

"And just *what* is too optimistic!" I snapped back. These two were speculating about Tez as if he were an exchange rate. "When things can't be any worse and we're searching for possibilities, what exactly is optimism?"

"Don't worry," said Darsana. "No judge likes to pronounce a death sentence."

I couldn't speak. Words like that don't just trip off the tongue. Could this man really be so tactless? Or was the situation really that bad? Tez—Tez and me—had been thrown into alien territory. Common sense told me that a trial was a "due process" and that lawyers were trained to "reason logically," but now all that evaporated. My whole being went limp.

The consul nodded gravely before my disbelieving eyes.

"Just leave it to me. I can guarantee less than life imprisonment," Darsana was saying. "Less, but well, still life. We'd be doing well to get the sentence reduced by twenty years."

"Did my brother actually have drugs on him?"

"They arrested him and they're conducting an investigation, so very likely, yes," said Darsana, smiling as always.

"What you're saying, isn't that looking at things backwards?"

"Backwards?"

"Doesn't the trial begin with trying to establish whether or not he really was in possession? At least from the defense's side, shouldn't that be the tactic?"

"But drugs *were* in fact discovered at the time of arrest, so that line of argument is out."

"What if it were false evidence? The whole case might be a set-up."

"Family members always look for conspiracies," the consul interjected, "but no police in any country in the world would go to such trouble. What would be in it for them?"

48

"Well then, what about the amount? Is possession of one milligram a capital offense here?"

"From what I heard, it was quite a large amount," said the attorney. "Much more than for individual consumption. Hence the trafficking charge and the possible death penalty."

Could it be true? That Tez was not only a user but a dealer too? No way. Why would he need to? He was too well off. Where in Asia would he have picked up his habit? I hoped beyond hope it wasn't true; it had to be a lie. But just supposing it were true, what was I to do? What if Tez really had been running heroin? I still couldn't just write him off. Whatever Tez had done, he was still my brother. Whatever it took, I had to get him out of that hole.

"If I decided to engage your services, what sort of defense could you foresee?"

"As I said before, we could appeal to the judge's better nature to abrogate a death sentence. Any more than that is unrealistic."

"Is that how all your trials go here in this country?"

"You would do well to lose that tone and look at the facts," the consul cautioned. They were a fine pair, him and this attorney. "Your brother *is* imprisoned in this country, after all."

"As to my services: I would personally argue the case. I would prepare all the necessary papers and take care of procedures. Assuming three sessions up to the ruling, the total would come to two million rupiahs or thereabouts."

I wasn't even asking, thank you. *Just see if I let you put a price on Tez's life —on Tez's freedom!*

Even more depressed than yesterday when I saw Tez, I returned to the hotel in a foul mood.

4

TETSURO

Two days after the consul's visit, you're back in the interrogation room, a sheaf of typed pages in front of you. A transcript, they say. The investigating officer slowly reads the whole thing, paragraph by paragraph in Indonesian. It takes forever. And his dumb interpreter takes even longer to translate it all into something like Japanese. You listen in silence. It seems close enough to what you said; still, better play it safe. You haven't lost all your wits.

"Everything you say. You sign."

A self-respecting thought finally forms on your lips. "I'll have a lawyer read it, then I'll sign."

"That not allow. You sign, you get out quick."

What to do? "Get out quick." Remember what the consul said: "Just cooperate." About the only thing you've understood since incarceration. Can barely manage to sit up, but somehow you comply. Your hand moves by itself toward the pen, reaching out to the promise of life. Besides, the interpreter really did sound like he was translating.

"One more copy. Duplicate."

Again you sign.

Remember those two Americans they brought in a couple of days ago? Happy-go-lucky bastards, impossibly optimistic. They saw you weren't a local and struck up a conversation. You talked in your workaday English. Or rather, they did the talking, a hundred words for every one of yours. To them it was one big joke—"You got caught with only that much smack? What a laugh!" You stared in disbelief. They were in for heroin, too.

"Hey, you're a foreigner, same as us. So relax, something'll work out."

"Work out how?"

"Just you wait and see. Uncle Sam to the rescue, from our big bad motherfucking Land of the Free. Old Man Suharto's real good buddies with America, right?"

What if it were true? What if your own country *did* pull weight and intercede? That consul talked a hard line, but behind the scenes he was probably making some sort of arrangements. Any day now maybe you'll walk free. You cooperated, you even signed their damn papers. No, that doesn't make any sense. Desperate dreaming is all it is. Yet the next minute you're all worked up again over your imminent release, jerking yourself this way and that.

But then what happens? Those two really *do* get let out. A guard comes for them and they never return. They couldn't have been executed, they must have been released. Never got the details, how much they were holding, how they got arrested. Whatever, they're gone.

No such luck for you. Seems Old Man Suharto wasn't so tight with Japan. No call came saying you could leave this shit-plastered zoo of a jail. Still, they can't kill you, can they? You haven't committed any real crime—it's just unthinkable. Who'd play a trick like that? No, you're not going anywhere; you don't even know what the wait now is for. Waiting for trains and planes, waiting for visas to be processed—waiting is something you got used to when traveling. But never just waiting indefinitely, never so totally at someone else's mercy.

The empty hours are torture, but the idea of what lies at the end of the wait is even worse. *Death*—the word flares up in your head. A blaze too intense for the eyes, it sears right through you, impossible to look at straight on. Every cloud floating in your head catches the light and reflects it back at you. Death is the sun, with no place to hide, no way to slip past. Picture yourself dead. A pathetic corpse. Inert matter, airplane debris, a sack filled with muck. That thing lying on the ground—that's you. *Don't want to die. Please.*

Lying there in detention, you notice everyone is peering out of the cage. They've all seen something. Out on the footpath beyond the courtyard wall, a face you swear you know. So very familiar, but confused and worried, and she's looking this way. Peering in with wide, grave eyes. The instant you recognize your sister, your self-defense mechanisms spring into action, shutting down with an audible *slam*. Just seeing Kaoru there jams all conscious thought, overrides the will.

From the arrest until now there hasn't been a soul around you knew. You came here alone, stumbled into a trap by your own stupidity, suffered solitarily through arrest and withdrawal, met with that nonentity the Japanese consul. Hallucinations all. The heroin was bliss while it lasted, bliss that was just as unreal. Ever since you met up with Inge, it's all been like a bad dream. But your sister *does* exist. She's part of your real life, not a figment of your imagination. From earliest childhood she was there. And now she's *here*, breaking through the trance, a link from the distant past to your real self. No illusion, from any perspective. But it only signals how bad the situation is: her arrival is a death sentence in itself.

Later, you'll see Kaoru up close in the visiting room, her face drifting in and out of focus. You'll hear her voice but won't respond, hear without listening. Her voice flowing by, a river you can't wade into. There's nothing to say, nothing to ask. You're a condemned man.

Twenty days ago you came to the island. Why Bali? Why here and not somewhere else? Even more to the point, why didn't you return to Japan? In Bangkok you met Nils and got yourself hooked again. You vowed to quit, didn't you? Even after that "one last shot" you could have made straight for Japan. Like the time before, when you kicked the habit at that temple. A living skeleton, feeling like shit, not remotely "normal"—but no temptations to shoot up. Where's there to score in Japan? The Sad Child Angel gave chase, but couldn't lure you back to heroinland. So after half a year, you were your old healthy self again. You showed that angel. If you'd kept straight, you would've been clean. What stopped you?

Took heroin a little too lightly, that's what. One time addicted real bad, one time clean. Slip again, you can always pull through. Just grit your teeth through the worst of it. You and your cold turkey achievement badge. An addict's twisted pride—he who quits and survives is stronger than he who never gets hooked in the first place. Was that it? Sure Nils provided the excuse, but who was the one who fell for it? So cocksure you could stop cold right there in the pit of fear. Addicted to the cycle of addiction and detox.

Still humming in the afterglow of that last shot, you arrived on Bali. You negotiated the long queue at Immigration and were waiting for your luggage when the withdrawal symptoms hit. Okay, it was in the cards, only much sooner than expected. Once through Customs, you head outside and grab a taxi. Say the name of the cheap digs Nils told you about, Pandra Cottages in Kuta. Don't bother to look at the scenery. *All these tourist areas look alike anyway*—or so you tell yourself through the mounting discomfort. The same hostels and guesthouses, signs and façades. Nothing real until you make for the countryside. No strength to take in these new bearings, you surrender to any idle thought that comes along.

The taxi, however, can't pull up to the guesthouse entrance. Pointed down a narrow path, you hoist up your backpack and walk. Groaning step by step, you eye the passing faces—hardly any Japanese, just Australians and Northern Europeans.

By the time you reach the lobby and check in, you really feel like shit. As soon as you show your passport and sign a traveler's check to pay in advance, you collapse on the floor, retching. The next thing you know you're crawling across the floor gasping, nothing in your stomach to even throw up. No appetite or much of anything to eat for days, yet you're sick to your gut, insides writhing. A storm rages in your nerves. Someone comes to help. *Sorry for being such a nuisance*, you want to say, but no words come. Face and scalp are slick with cold sweat. A chill spreads through your entire body, your limbs. Fingers are stiff, ten stalks of throbbing pain.

The guesthouse staff are kind enough; they don't turn you away for being sick. A young man from the front desk lends a shoulder and walks you to your bungalow; another carries your backpack. They seem used to this, even when you tumble onto the floor of the room. Ah, peace at last. The young man fetches a bucket and sets it down beside you, just in case. There's no private bath, and in your state you'll never find the shared toilet.

The next day, you're laid flat, having vomited through an anguished night. Nausea in exchange for those two months of euphoria. Bartered karma. A small price to pay, but what are these pains all over you? No, not the knife stunt again, please. The blade's buried deep in your pack, you wouldn't have the strength to dig it out. That's some relief.

The following day you still can't move. The young man comes to check up on you, then enlists another guy to help drag you to a car and take you to a clinic. Probably cause problems for the guesthouse if they let you get any worse. The doctor who examines you asks them about your symptoms, then comes out with the diagnosis.

"Is heroin, no?"

"Y-yes," you snivel, barely audible. Does the law here require a doctor to inform the police? Haven't done any on Bali, they can't arrest you for anything. Questioning at most.

"Look bad. You not have heroin now?"

"N-no, quit in Thailand . . . before coming here."

"Everybody say like that. But okay. You want we treat methadone?"

"Please."

You've heard of the surrogate drug, the relief it's supposed to bring. How it also makes your body recall the high, makes you want the real thing. But as long as there isn't any around, you're safe. You won't slip up. You can't.

"Can't give much. Just two tablet. You still bad shape tomorrow, you come back. Give out drug one day one day. Bring down slowly."

"Fine."

The methadone is expensive, but it works. The nausea subsides so you can actually sleep. But you're still not strong enough to walk, so they take you to the doctor again next morning.

For three days you go to him for methadone. Other than that, you sleep. By the third day you're able to hold down a little food. The fourth day, the doctor doesn't give you methadone but some other, weaker drug, and a laxative. Thanks to which, after an hour on the john, brow greased with sweat, the strain in your bowels eases slightly.

The following day you manage to walk to the doctor on your own. Pick up your substitute drug and laxative, then drop by a big hotel on the way back to use the restroom in the lobby. Don't want to monopolize either of the Pandra Cottages' two communal toilets.

Soon you're beginning to eat and regain your strength. You're through the worst of it, you tell yourself, as if it were a major achievement. Even the surroundings start to shine.

It's after that you decide to poke around Kuta a bit. It looks similar to a Thai town, if a dash more colorful. Streets scarcely wide enough for cars to pass are flanked by precarious footpaths. Here they arrange brilliant flowers in folded banana-leaf trays. New flowers each day, set out early in the morning and discarded by nightfall, apparently. Curious, but a nice custom. While making a few purchases in a shop, you ask about the flowers.

"That *chanan*. God flower," comes the reply. "Bali have so much god and spirit, offer much flower, make much much festival. Wery busy."

So many gods and spirits? Sounds promising. As soon as you get a little stronger, maybe those *chanan* would be a good point to start sketching from again. Nice subject.

Partly because it's a tourist area, the town is solid commerce—rows of little shops down tiny back alleys catering to fast turnover. The hawkers' street food, once your stomach is back in form, proves quite palatable. Not so chilipepper hot as Thai food; no sugar in everything either. Nor so overboard with the *masala* spices like in India. The *bami* egg noodles are good, as are the *nasi goreng* fried rice and *nasi champur* vegetables on rice. And that chicken soup *soto ayam* is the best of all, truly delicious. Aside from that there's the ubiquitous tourist-trade Italian eatery, a little pricy but decent. Also a Japanese restaurant, which doesn't even merit consideration. Throughout Southeast Asia, these Japanese haunts are so expensive and offer such mediocre fare, they don't even make you homesick. Anyway, you didn't come all the way overseas just to hang out with other Japanese.

Lots of peddlers out on the streets, too. Watch-sellers trying to flog their big, flat boxes to every tourist in sight. Bright gold Omegas and Longines and Seikos for only 30,000 rupiahs. That's 5000 yen—no way they'd be real;

stop on you the next day. Or no, everything's quartz nowadays, so at least they'd run. Fakes you can flaunt anywhere. Who makes the things? Who channels them here? Now, that's an intriguing question. Not that they'd ever tell you. Probably wouldn't even know at this end of the chain.

Ten minutes' walk from the guesthouse is the sea. The beach stretches off to the north, broad white sand as far as the eye can see. Plant yourself down on the sand and relax. The sun feels great. Maybe it's time to bring out the art supplies. Long overdue, actually. Sunset ought to be beautiful. Nice tones for watercolors, especially with the sea. Come to think of it, haven't done a seascape in ages. Sea and sunset—all color and no form, good practice after all this time. The open sea, should be simple.

At these low latitudes, when the sun sinks into the sea, they say sometimes you'll see a "green flash." One last spark of light, green on the horizon after the sun's gone down. Supposed to be fantastic. Later maybe you'll come to the beach and try to catch it.

"Hey you, Pandra Cottage!" A voice out of nowhere, speaking crappy Japanese.

You look up to see a short, dark man standing there, grinning like an idiot. Shifty character, open-neck batik shirt over baggy pants and beach thongs. Doesn't seem too together; his eyes wander in and out of focus.

"Me, Agus. You name . . . ?" More pidgin Japanese.

Just ignore him, look away.

"Other day, I see you," he says, slipping into English.

"See me what?"

"You know, you go doctor."

So he knows.

"Smack, right? You need, any time, just tell me. Get fast."

A damn pusher, this jerk. Which means there's heroin on Bali. Well, makes sense. It is a tourist area after all. So why'd Nils have to go all the way to Bangkok to score? Didn't he say Bali was dry? Though the folks at the guesthouse seemed unfazed, and the doctor *did* have methadone. All these different thoughts arise, but in the end the only one that sticks is the realization that they have it here too.

"No thanks."

"Yeah, ha ha, soon change mind. You tell Agus, okay? Price chip, good stuff, safe safe."

"I said no."

"*Daijobu*, no problem. I wait."

"Get lost."

"Okay, later sure thing." And off he goes. You fling a handful of sand at his retreating backside, but of course it misses, mixing indistinguishably with all the other sand.

Little more than five months ago you went to that temple on the outskirts of Bangkok. A refuge of Buddhist compassion known for helping addicts to recover. Thailand produces heroin, up north in the Golden Triangle. It gets shipped overseas via Bangkok, so of course it makes the rounds inside the country, too. Mobsters and prostitution rings push it onto countless new addicts every year. At the point when it became a social menace, the Buddhist Sangha got involved in relief efforts, with "chill temples" where you could go if you couldn't pull through on your own.

Back then, you were running scared. Your fix was escalating nonstop. A breathtaking ride while you were high, but grinding agony when it bottomed out. And the roller coaster kept getting more extreme all the time, not a spare moment for your art.

You didn't plan it that way. You were in control, you could quit any time you liked, it shouldn't have been too hard. Do as Inge taught you—work up gradually over two weeks from a small pinch to a heroin binge. Shoot up once a day and lie around doing nothing. Then for another week gradually cut back, until you're able to return to normal life with hardly any withdrawal symptoms. Beyond that, just commit to doing it only in that one village, and you can go completely without the white powder until your next visit.

The fact is, you *did* follow this formula of hers. Reducing the amount was no trouble. You were coming off clean, ready to get back into the swing of artwork and travel. But with only three days left, there was that fateful accident. And now ever since, the Sad Child Angel has hounded you, sent you spiraling toward a sky-high fix. You can't live in the outside world any more. The only reality is in the shelter of the drug, a shelter that's real as long as you're in it. Perfectly fulfilled just sitting and breathing. You can gaze at your shoes for hours on end. There's no such thing as boredom.

Why paint pictures? Everything's designed to lead you to heroin—why leave the embrace? Quitting is bullshit. The angel won't hear of it. You, a known artist again? Let the vicissitudes of easy pleasure go on forever.

But it gets scary. A fair dose for first-time users might be 5mg; less-than-4mg thresholders aren't uncommon. If you're careful, you can play out the balancing act a long time, quitting and starting again all in good stride. After the fateful tumble, though, your intake skyrocketed. 100mg can kill; 500mg is dead certain—and you're shooting twice that. One whole gram each time. Even in Chiang Mai where the scoring is easy, it gets expensive. Back in Japan you still have savings, so you get your bank to wire you funds, while they last at least. If that runs out . . . no, don't even think about it. Every bone in your body creaks with alarm.

When withdrawal hit, the pain was impossible. Memory cut out. You felt surrounded by enemies. Everyone, everywhere. By the time you blur back toward sanity, punctures all over your left arm are trickling with blood. Did you really grab a knife to cut out the pain when the screaming in your bones became unbearable? Lucky you didn't sever an artery.

It's a wonder you were still alive. Nutrition, antibodies, cell replenishment —all of that went. And yet the absolute minimum maintenance-level functions hung in there.

You tried to quit, but lacked the confidence to go where no drugs were to be had. You merely put off the next fix. The stuff runs out and the anxieties begin. Half a day later, the pains. So shoot up—the raging floodwaters will subside. Those insects crisscrossing your insides with straight razors will scurry off. The world's in your pocket.

All you could ever think about was scoring the next round, then the next. Heroin was the cause of your suffering and this same heroin brought the end of suffering. All it took to wipe *samsara* clean away. No cares, no hangups, just floating in a void. Buoyed in a warm bath of pleasure, adrift on gentle ripples washing in and out over those vast open shoals between sleeping and waking. Such perfect bliss, doing nothing at all. Existence itself is a blessing, an Oriental paradise manifest in a living death. Hell veiled in a vast, blissful vision of heaven. Divine deception, exquisitely wrought. To die alive, to vegetate and turn to stone, to abide a hundred thousand years —this is Inge's miracle ideal.

After half a year you've reached your limit, a voice tells you—a faint murmur from the shadows of what's left of your rational mind. So you flushed the last of the white powder down the toilet, ground the syringe under your heels, and caught a flight to Bangkok before the terrible withdrawal hit. Whatever it took to drag yourself to the temple.

Wasted to nothing, barely able to stand—the only person who'd have anything to do with you was an English-speaking monk. Radiating intelligence in his brilliant saffron robes.

"You come this far mean you have will to quit drug. We help you, but you must use will to carry you through. No drug in bag?"

You shake your head. A young acolyte leads you to a large, breezy scripture hall. You see men lying about here and there on the floor, small enamel pots stationed beside each of them. No one moves. Weird scene, like a well-lit opium den. You sit down and another monk brings you a pot and a bowl of liquid, prompting, "Drink all." It's some kind of infusion, horribly bitter, with a strange smell. Almost time for your fix, but nothing to shoot up. This time you're quitting. You steel yourself—it's going to be torture.

For the next three days you drink quantities of the brackish herbal potion, vomiting constantly into the pot beside you. You do nothing else. Your stomach lining is a gravel-strewn wasteland. Somehow you've held on, physical strength being the only thing that let your addiction get this far. Otherwise you'd be dead by now, or been scared off long ago.

Three days you lie immobilized on that temple floor. The monks come around to bring you medicine, rinse out your slop pot, bring you water— never saying a word. Not even an encouraging pat on the back. Some addicts can't take it and disappear; new addicts come in. Most are Thai, but none has the energy to speak to anyone else.

The fourth day, they show you to a different building and give you some thin rice gruel. How many days has it been since you ate anything? Miraculously, the stuff stays in your stomach. A week later you're eating and walking like normal, filled with gratitude. You offer your heartfelt thanks, donate as much as you can, and leave the temple behind you.

Then a plane lands you back in Japan. It was good to be off heroin, but you're still weak. So emaciated that gallery acquaintances shudder just to look at you. Their eyes condemn—*Has he got some disease?* You're not up to the art crowd, they make you feel ashamed. Tokyo's threshold is too high. So, okay, take it slow. Roam rural Japan until you recover.

You stay in cheap inns, walk and eat a lot, sleep even more, recouping. Ease back into art from simple sketches, just to warm up your technique again. An interesting exercise, refreshing in its way. Before long, when you think it's all coming back, you take up the watercolor sketchbooks you had couriered from Vietnam. Makes you nostalgic. An and Tanh's faces. The villagers. What times those were.

You try doing oils from the watercolors, but nothing really clicks. Something's missing. Or too much. Maybe the models were better suited to watercolors. You retrace An's back and it becomes something else. After a few more attempts, you give up. Better just leave it all as is. Until you can work it into some other composition, whenever that might be.

But you aren't alone, you're being followed. Over your shoulder the angel is always there, you can tell. No longer glowering in your face, but watching all the same. Silently observing, seeing whether by some outside chance the taint of guilt no longer reads. No pressure, only vigilance. Nobody forced it on you; you brought it on yourself. You who lived so lightly as a child, with one false move you brought down such a heavy freight of blame. And now it's your lot to carry it around for the rest of your days.

At a small inn somewhere in the remote hills of Shikoku you make the angel a proposition: shall we give this weight a shape?

"Dark night tonight. It's a new moon."

So it is.

"Only the light of the stars. No one going out till morning."

Seems not.

"Gives me the shakes, just looking out at the shadows on the village path."

I know.

"Three nights I've been scanning the night sky—no new moon yet? I even checked the newspaper."

And?

"I've decided to fast."

The angel says nothing. Silence by way of benign neglect—*As you wish.* Or else a warning—*Don't even try to lighten your load.*

For twenty-four hours after that you abstain from eating. A minor physical inconvenience, but it makes you live in constant tidal awareness of the lunar moment. You sit on a riverbank watching the heavens, and as the moon narrows to a sliver, you sense the time drawing near. Like it or not, you're being led back. You await the dawn on an empty stomach. It's all you can do, you tell yourself, telling the Sad Child Angel who still haunts you at a distance the same thing, but the angel says nothing.

You continue to circle through back-country Japan a little longer. From Shikoku to Kyushu, then hopping the Goto Islands out to Tsushima by boat, calling at Iki and Oki on the return. Following the Japan Sea coast north by local trains, staying a night at every stop, until at long last you're back in Tokyo. Full of vigor again, you can get down to work. Take on a shitload of jobs, whip off illustrations left and right just to recoup all the money you spent on heroin. And after a good long stint at the grindstone, when you think you're back on course, you set off again in search of *real* images

Like picking up the frayed end of a string, first you head to Bangkok. You don't even consider Chiang Mai. Your appetite hits full stride and you really stuff yourself. Stepping out every three hours to wolf down a bowl of hawker noodles or fried rice. Portions in Thailand come small, but then everyone's eating at all hours. Right in front of this hippie hostel on Khaosan Road it's a day-and-night food bazaar. Altogether, a convenient jumping-off point. So where to next? How easy is it to get a visa to Burma? You're lazing there considering your options, when a knock comes on the door. You undo the latch and it's the concierge.

"You okay share room?" Must be peak season overflow.

He turns around with a "Come on" flick of the head, and in stoops a tall European youth. Mouth buried in a shaggy brown beard, he flashes his teeth in a grin. "*Ja.*"

"Ya," you respond in kind.

"Nils. From Holland."

"Tez, Japan. Only one bed, so if you don't mind, it's mine. You take the floor. You over there, me over here." You draw an imaginary line the length of the room.

"Okay." Nils unhitches his pack and begins to lay out his sleeping bag and kit on the floor.

"Where'd you come from? Not straight from Europe?" you ask as you fall back onto the bed, languid from the afternoon heat.

"Nah, I was in Bali. About two months. Nice place. Small island, lots of people and rice fields. Green and beautiful. Nice buildings, too. Stone temples and gates. Real nice vibes."

"Maybe I'll go." A glimmer of incentive.

"And the people, they're so funny. I mean, each village's got its own thing: festivals or music or handicrafts. And they're all so high just doing it, there isn't an alcoholic on the island. Except maybe in Kuta—which is a real tourist trap. You really oughta go, out to the villages. Everyone's real friendly. Food's great. Wanna see a guidebook?"

Nils hands over an English tourist guide to Bali, then steps out, saying he's got some shopping to do. The book proves thorough and informative, if written with a European slant. You start leafing through it, then settle down to read in detail. Bali seems to be a crossroads, both urban and rural. "A rich culture that defies classification." Certainly, the traditional architecture in the photos looks distinctive. And their *gamelan* music sounds interesting as well, the variety of dances. It's a resort, but the locals seem above it all, more together than the tourists at least, living at a higher intensity. "According to Balinese cosmology, a mystic energy emanates from the mountains and fills the human world, then flows out to sea." Fascinating. Makes you want to see their mountains, their coastline. Stone buildings and intricately carved gates. Especially this *candi bentar*—a "split gate" the English text calls it. "Picture a gigantic sculpted tower cut in half, symmetrically down the middle." Now that would be something to paint!

That night, not long after your fifteenth snack of the day, Nils shows up.

"I'm thinking about going to Bali," you tell him.

"Way to go. First thing, maybe you should stay in Kuta, at Pandra Cottages. Just long enough to pick up information. Then I'd recommend you head as far out as you can. If you wanna see art and crafts and shit, it's Ubud, but there's lots of other places besides."

You never said a thing about being an artist; it's Nils who brings it up, though the guidebook did say there were many painters there. You start to fantasize about the place, imagine the stimulus its hillscapes might give you. You can just see the pictures you'll paint.

Nils pulls a small plastic bag from his pocket. "Just scored this. Wanna try?" Heroin.

You react calmly, but shudder inside. After all you went through to kick the habit—here before your very eyes. But you're okay, it's been half a year. "No thanks. I quit a while back."

"Oh? Sorry, man. Don't mind me doing a pop?"

"Fine by me." So polite, just minding your own business. You couldn't tell him to stop. "I'll just go outside for a while."

"Didn't mean to bring you down or anything . . ."

Can't say you weren't tempted. But no, a nightmare is a nightmare. So what if Nils gets nice and high, you don't want to know about it.

You go out and wander the late-night streets of Bangkok. It's an ungodly hour, but kids are running around shrieking. This city really never sleeps. There's plenty to look at, but you're thinking about the heroin. You're off the stuff, right? Safe and sound. But what if you go back and find Nils blissing out half-asleep, wouldn't you think twice? No way. Keep walking. Three prostitutes come on to you and three times you wave them away. You don't buy sex.

When you get back to the room in the wee hours, Nils is sprawled atop his sleeping bag, gazing up at the ceiling. Spaced out. He has a small box by his head. Contents—a syringe and cigarette lighter, a spoon, a mini-bottle of mineral water. It's all there.

You snap. Your little voice has already defected—*Just this once won't hurt.* The Sad Child Angel smiles, beckoning. The daylight clarity after shooting up comes back to you. *Just a tiny bit, one time won't get you hooked*—even as your hand reaches out. Or does the thought race to catch up with your hand?

"Can I score just one time off you? Only a pinch. Repay you the stuff tomorrow."

"Go ahead. Use as much as you want," Nils slurs a slow response.

There's nothing more to think. The prospect of "one time" has your head in somersaults. You unpack the Coleman stove from your things to boil water. An interminable wait. You drop Nils's syringe into the scalding cookpot to sterilize it, retrieve it with your trusty traveler's chopsticks, adjust the needle and plunger. No scales, so you have to eyeball it. You crease a scrap of paper with the white powder in the fold, tap out 15mg—more or less—into the spoon. Mix with a little water, heat to a boil with the lighter. Then you draw up the liquid heroin into the syringe, give it a squirt, take a deep breath, and inject it into your left arm.

That's all it took for you to slip back into your former state. A classic "one time" turnaround. For the next week, you and Nils shoot up constantly. Nils sticking to a constant fix, you soon hitting 100mg. You stop eating completely. You vomit sporadically.

On the eighth day, the heroin runs out. Paranoid with pain, you resurrect an image of yourself streaming with blood that time before. You've got to get out of here, leave this country. Vow to make a clean break this time. Paint pictures like you should. But where to go? It's almost comic, the way you cast about for a sign. Yes, the guidebook—Bali it is.

You tell Nils and somehow pack up your things, then take that last "one-for-the-road" to boost your spirits and a cab to the airport. There's no heroin in your bags, you're sure of that. Crossing borders with the stuff is dangerous and stupid—and besides you're quitting, remember? Just wait, you can get yourself cured on Bali. Withdrawal symptoms are bound to coincide with your arrival, but it'll only be a three-day ordeal. You've already quit once. You'll be all right now, because now you're cutting all ties with heroin forever.

You'd done with the doctor and started walking around to get a feel for Bali. Got your strength back, sure to go clean this time. Taking care to eat well, filling in the gaps. A healthy person is a strong person. Still hadn't done any artwork, but that could wait until you made for rural Bali. Meanwhile you explored the network of narrow lanes, browsed the shops examining the unfamiliar goods, never intending to buy. Just a little longer and you'd be drawing again. How about a sketchpad? They had to sell paper here somewhere. One day you traipsed up the beach —not easy going on loose sand—all the way from Kuta to beyond Legian. At a luxury beachfront hotel restaurant you had some Australian beef, then felt so tired you took a taxi on the way back. The sunburned face in the hotel lobby mirror was a stranger to the pallid invalid of only a few days back.

The taxi drops you off near Pandra Cottages. As you get out, who should be standing there at the top of the path but that same creep from a few days before—the pusher. The last person you want to talk to. He sees you and ambles over. You look away.

"Hi, having good time on Bali?"

Thanks for the concern. You wave him away and start walking. He follows, keeping pace a few steps behind.

"Better shoot soon, no?"

Ignore him.

"Good stuff. No mix with lactose. Hunded percent."

Who cares.

"You try some go straight to heaven."

Persistent bastard.

"Well later then."

Oh, lay off.

"Anytime you want I always have." And with that, he slinks away.

Scum. Want nothing to do with the likes of you. Ever! you snarl under your breath as you walk on. Then ten steps on you happen to think—*What did he say his name was again? Agus?* Now why'd you have to remember that? Better to just forget.

Shunmei Bando makes his appearance the very next day. More than once you'd brushed by a Japanese man in the lobby. Big build, heavyset, round face. Dressed like a surfer, though the aloha look did absolutely nothing for him. Each time you passed he twinkled at you, an unwanted familiarity just as soon disregarded. But that morning, as you crossed the lobby to head out to the café a few doors down for breakfast, someone called after you.

"Excuse me, but aren't you Mr. Nishijima, the artist?"

You turn around and it's that Japanese guy. Have you met somewhere before?

"The name is Bando. Shunmei Bando. With Taiseido Books. Editorial Department? Two years ago I commissioned you to do the cover and illustrations for Oscar Wilde's poem *The Fisherman and His Soul*?"

Ah yes, slowly it shifts into focus. Nice book, as you recall. A young fisherman parts with his shadow in order to win the love of a mermaid; but the shadow is really his soul, and the soul tries desperately to return to its master, the fisher lad. So it travels the world, telling all it has seen. You did the cover and the title-page art, as well as a number of quarter-page cuts. It was a children's book, but you put a spin on it with decidedly adult illustrations. Whether or not as a result, the edition did well critically. And he was the editor.

"No, it couldn't be, I told myself—he looks so different from when I last had the honor in Japan. What a coincidence! This *is* a nice surprise!"

Smarmy character. You acknowledge with a vague nod of the head.

"I heard you were on the road half the year, and sure enough—it's true."

Heard from whom? "So what brings you here?"

"I'm almost ashamed to say. I'm a weekend surfer. But one gets tired of the beaches at home, the waves are so small; and, well, I heard it was good here, so I came down. Just the day before yesterday in fact."

"And how are they? The waves, I mean."

"Exhilarating. Barely got my board wet yesterday, though. I don't suppose . . . that is, do you surf?"

"Not me." Try not to sneer.

"Ah, what a shame. Great surf here. Yesterday I went to a place called Nusa Dua on the eastern shore. The breaking point is rather far out, so they have to row you out in one of those long outrigger-canoes. *Jukung* I believe they call them. Actually, it's not the best season for surf. They say one should really come in summer and do the western points. But I was up to my neck with work right up till the end of the year. Just impossible to take off a block of days until now, so one really can't afford to be choosy about which waves on which side. In any case, yesterday's surf was fine by me. I plan to go again today. You know, I almost had second thoughts about coming here alone, but the people in the surf shops seem friendly enough. At least so far so good."

What a ninny! At least he didn't try to drag you into going with him.

"Off to breakfast? Mind if I join you?"

Spoke too soon. Wonderboy has invited himself along. You order a hot "juffle" sandwich and café au lait; he has the same—only two of each. Now what's there to talk about? Good thing he didn't arrive a few days earlier. Wouldn't have wanted him telling the Tokyo gossip-mill about the wretched state you were in.

"You know, when I said I'd heard you spend half the year traveling . . . well, I mean, do you?"

"I suppose."

"For the discipline of it, as praxis for your art?"

Those fawning eyes, looking up at you like a dog. Is that supposed to be a sign of respect? "Nothing so deliberate, I'm afraid. Just for enjoyment. I'm just a gypsy."

"A gypsy! Brilliant! And with your talent, you must be positively swimming in commissions."

Makes a big deal out of every little thing, this guy, as he shovels in his double breakfast.

"Well, I'm heading for the waves," he announces eventually. "But what do you say —shall we have dinner together?"

"Fine." You'd like to tell him to get stuffed, but for some reason it's the only thing to answer. A need to reconfirm your return to health in others' eyes? Since when have you wanted to share meals with anyone? Let alone another Japanese—a Japanese who knows you professionally, what's more. Dangerous ground.

That night the two of you go to a middle-of-the-road tourist restaurant. Bando talks a streak as he consumes platefuls of *saté* and *gado gado* and *achar* and *ikan asam manis* and *nasi goreng*, all washed down with Bintang beer. You're bored stiff. How can he talk so much? You'd think he hadn't spoken Japanese in three years, not three days.

"No beer for you?" asks Bando, surprised by your iced tea.

"No thanks."

"No stronger alcohol, either?"

"Never touch the stuff. It doesn't agree with me."

"And you don't smoke, either. What *do* you like?"

"Just travel does it for me." There you've gone and said it. Now he's going to bubble over—*Fabulous!*

"What about, you know . . . drugs and all that? Ever take any on your travels?"

"I wouldn't know." You cringe inside. Not because you lied to this chump; it's the topic itself that triggers a reaction.

"I'm fascinated, myself. As a surfer I've smoked my share of grass. But no real fireworks, no cocaine or heroin or LSD. Just once I'd like to have the experience."

"It's not to be taken lightly." Your heart skips a beat. As if unwittingly he'd spoken the one name dearest to your innermost thoughts. A secret from everyone, the love-of-your-life through thick and thin and painfully thinner, who only just left you after beating your head against a wall. What was this ignoramus doing speaking that name?

"Oh, then you have . . . ?" His eyes are twinkling.

Too late, you've implicated yourself, you can't change the subject. "It wrecks you physically. Makes you turn your back on society, on everyone and everything—apparently."

"But just once wouldn't hurt."

"That's what everyone thinks."

"What about you? Did you ever get hooked?"

"No." You're getting more and more irritated. Fatuous fool. If it's "just once" he wants, why not give him his fucking first go? Let him see for himself how deep he has to go to reach the heights. A full three times it took you to finally ascend. So high you never wanted to come down. But that first long, hard climb up a trail of thorns, the first time is always hell. You'll score a hit and teach him a lesson. After that it'll be his own responsibility.

Not that you ever intended to procure only for Bando. Anyway, whose "own responsibility" means anything when it comes to heroin? You know only too painfully well: one time and any notion of responsibility fades clean away, cautious words evaporate. The only thing that matters is the next shot. Can't say you haven't been there.

Thinking back on it, the whole gambit was aimed at yourself—it's so obvious. Telling such transparent lies, conniving by any means to score again. Ever since returning to the land of the living, a neon sign—*One Last Shot*— has kept flashing in your skull. Can't turn it off. Can't disconnect it And that big oaf stumbled onto the forbidden button.

You can see it all. how you'll score just a little to give him his "experience," how you'll lay the real stuff on him, prepare a test whiff, set down a syringe alongside, and invite him to shoot up. You'll explain everything—the initial reaction, the high once the body builds a tolerance, the inferno thereafter. "Not for a nice boy like you, Bando." And when he doesn't go for it, you'll flush the stuff down the toilet right before his eyes, crush the syringe . . .

That evening, however, you contain yourself and say nothing. Let Bando prattle on, silly drunk, you're screening *One Last Shot* full-frame the whole while. Like caressing a bare shoulder, you stroke the phrase over and over again.

A trap always has two parts: first the bait, then the closing door. Lure and snare, that's how it works. Which explains why you run into Agns the pusher on the way back from the beach at noon the next day. Like he's been waiting for you to show (as in fact he probably has).

This time you approach him. In your own mind, you're buying the goods to show Bando. But the scenario you've scripted is really just a trick, a sick ploy to dupe your cured self.

"I need a bit."

Agus's eyes shine. "Heh-heh-heh, way to go."

"Two grams, that's all."

"Got more if you want."

"No, two grams is plenty." It's two grams or nothing.

"Later, I bring you room."

"Can't we do it outside?"

"No no. *Damé damé*. People see."

Oh well. "Okay, I'm in 2-A. And a syringe?"

"Sure thing, boss. In two hour."

"Oh, one thing. If I'm not in my room at that time, consider the deal off. Canceled." A little voice tells you to leave yourself an out, just in case. The rational self still has its say in the addict's world, only in most cases the voice isn't very vocal.

You spend the next couple of hours arguing with yourself. There's still time to turn back. So you placed an order with Agus. Just don't return to your room. Stay away for the next five hours. Then check out and move to another place. If you stay in Kuta you're bound to run into Agus again, so head for the other side of the island. Or leave Bali altogether. Go somewhere they've never even heard of heroin. There's always that route.

But you've already kicked the habit once, you have the strength to quit if you make up your mind to. That's what the *basso profundo* claims, underscoring the entire opera. The tenor voice of reason counters that it's just the sort of excuse one-time addicts always fall back on. And back and forth it goes, an hour-long command performance on the beach. You sit and think, and reach a conclusion: you'll return to your room, pack up, and be out again in thirty minutes.

Once back in the bungalow, however, the whole idea of nixing the deal just vanishes. Who are you kidding? The anticipation is immense. Slowly your body begins to float, rising silently through the gray choked air, far above the noisy streets below, all your troubles wafting away, lighter and lighter up through the cloud layer, finally reaching the ethereal clarity of the stratosphere. How can the sky be so blue? Body sublimating into emptiness, ballooning out to envelop the whole sky. You're one with the sky—and does the sky worry? Pleasure so immediate, all you have to do is wait for it.

A knock comes on the door, a beggar's timid tap. Once, twice, then silence. You get up, both rehearsing to say you still haven't made up your mind and knowing full well you can't resist. Split personalities, each recognizing they've only got a few more steps to go.

Agus stands there looking at you with doped eyes. Half-glancing behind, he steps into the room, practically pushes you out of the way, and lands himself on the floor. From the pocket of his dirty shirt he produces three disposable syringes still in their sterile packaging. Followed by a teaspoon, a cheap plastic lighter, and a small bottle of water. Last of all, a pack of Marlboros. He cuts the seal on the Marlboros, extracts two tiny cellophane-wrapped cocoons, and tosses the cigarette pack across the room, then looks up at you and grins. "Two gram, two hunded dollar. Chip."

You can't say take it back, not now. Two bills swim out of your pocket automatically. Everything's in order for shooting up, but for one brief flash you entertain the Bando idea again. What a righteous coup, to flush it all away as he looks on! Two whole grams! Of course he'd never need that much, dozens of times more than the usual amount for a beginner. Even for someone who's been off for so long, twice a veteran or not. Maybe you only have to dispose of a little in front of Bando. No, you can always get more. Thinking about shooting up and dosages takes on a weird life of its own.

"You try, this real thing. No want you complain no good later."

Yes, that's the correct protocol for these transactions, isn't it? And with the stuff just sitting there, who can resist? The familiar ritual begins. You snap open a syringe, then unwrap the cellophane and tap out about a third of your usual dose into the spoon. Carefully set the spoon on the floor, open the water bottle, pour in just a trickle. Now hold it over the lighter and wait for it to boil. Ever so deftly, switch hands, pick up the syringe, draw in the liquid. A little squirt to force out air bubbles. There, just like a pro.

The thought occurs that you can still stop, but it's thunder rumbling in the distant hills, nowhere near. You roll up your shirt sleeve to the shoulder, hunt for a vein between your scars, slide the needle in. That familiar pinprick of sweet pain. Almost there, just a little bit more. Slowly depress the plunger and your body glows with pleasure. Now here, now there, like lights coming on room by room in a dark house. You're weightless, floating. Yet solid stone, Inge's petrified ecstasy. Yes, *this*. Should have done this so much sooner.

"G-good stuff."

"Like I say. Now some for Agus, okay?" His voice sings from some far-off heaven.

You hand Agus the morsel of cellophane. He goes to the window, plants himself down, puts a scant pinch of the white powder onto a piece of paper from his pocket, then rolls another scrap of paper into a little tube. Snorts into one nostril, then the other. You mean he's just a sniffer? Not much of an addict. Okay, but why is he sitting over by the window? They'll see him from outside like that.

Just then comes a barrage of footsteps, the door is flung open, and in rush five uniformed cops. Before you can even comprehend what's going on, one of them draws a pistol and fires three shots in the air—*bang! bang! bang!* Sulfur smoke fills the room. You shrink to a quivering fetus on the floor. Make no sudden move, that much common sense you still possess. Two cops bear down on top of you, wrest your arms behind your back, and handcuff you. Then with a good sharp tug they make you sit up. Even so, the drug in your veins suffuses a soothing calm. You're positively tranquil, self-possessed. Despite your desperate straits. You hear a voice saying, *This is nothing, nothing at all.*

The two of them hold you in an armlock, elbows and shoulders, from behind. Another cop pulls on gloves and proceeds to gather up the syringes, the cellophane rolls, the lighter and spoon, depositing each in a separate zip-lock plastic bag. You idly watch the circus. The remaining pair of policemen take up positions along the walls. Meanwhile, the evidence collector goes after the Marlboro pack in the far corner of the room, carefully picks it up, and places it in a bag. But that's just Agus's camouflage container, you remember thinking, it's empty. All sealed pieces of evidence go into a sturdy wooden case, your clothes and dufflebag into a cardboard box—a box with a Hong Kong noodle company trademark, you notice, as they set your half-filled artist's daypack alongside.

An important captive, you're trotted out at the head of the squad. The guesthouse staff and others in the lobby see you off without a word. Agus, however, is gone. Back in the room the cops didn't handcuff him or even try to detain him. By the time you're marched into the lobby he's nowhere to be seen. Through the rosy heroin haze it finally dawns on you—why Agus moved over to the window. Why he was snorting so anyone could see him from outside. And why the police burst in with such immaculate timing.

You've been set up.

5

KAORU

What a loser of an attorney! I'd never met anyone in the legal profession before, but I could tell he was useless. Left to that man's devices, Tez would get the death penalty for sure. Or spend the rest of his life in that monkey cage. That self-serving Darsana just wasn't up to trying.

The consul wasn't any good either. All he cared about was riding out his posting. He'd do nothing out of line, then retire happily ever after, or serve on some board of intercultural deadweights. I could beg and plead, he'd never come up with anything. Probably only had dealings with his ministry and didn't even know anyone locally. No help whatsoever to Tez.

I had to locate someone on my own. Someone who would take the case seriously and really hustle. But for that I had to be in Tokyo. Why waste my time here? Back in Tokyo, I knew people. Connect the dots and I was sure to hit on the right person.

Okay, I'd book a flight tomorrow, but first I had to see Tez one more time, to tell him I had to backpedal a bit but I'd return soon, then we'd talk. I still needed to hear his story. Give him a good shake, snap him out of that spaced-out death mask—did I say *death*? Never, ever. I must be positive. Mustn't break down in front of Tez again.

I telephoned Wayang. A woman answered. Thinking she might not understand, I asked pidgin-politely for "Mis-tah Wa-yang," only to be answered in fluent English: "Please hold on a second. I'll go get him."

At last Wayang came on the line, and I told him I wanted to go to the police station tomorrow morning.

"The woman just now, Wayang. Was that your wife?"

"Yes. Wife."

"Her English is so good."

"Wife, work in hotel."

Oh, Wayang! Why couldn't you take lessons from her? It would make this so much easier.

The following morning, Wayang met me at the hotel with a well-practiced "Good morning." Then he handed me a newspaper. "Today paper, news you brother."

There beneath a front-page headline in Indonesian was a photo of a policeman sitting at a desk with a carton of American cigarettes placed front-and-center. What was it all about?

"Police chief call reporter. He say he catch Japanese drug man."

I wanted to know more, but it would overtax his English. I packed the paper away. I could probably get a translation at the consulate, but there wasn't time. Nor was I inclined to ask the consul for anything.

When we got to the police station, I rushed right in. This time I didn't even look at the cage. I didn't want to see my poor brother in there. But then the duty officer said something that made Wayang smile. "Brother now change him only one room," he tried to explain.

Good, so he wasn't in that cage any more. Something of an improvement. Had the consulate pulled strings?

I was shown to the visitors' room, another tiny, stinking place with an old wooden table but no policeman standing by. I took a seat and waited. They brought Tez in. He slouched in through the door, eyes downcast to avoid mine, and sat down across from me. Would this be another silent session?

"I hear you're out of that, uh . . . group cell." I hesitated to say "cage." As if the police here could understand Japanese.

He looked up. Oh, Tez. You really looked a fright. Last time I seemed to sense you were holding back. Out of contrariness or who-knows-what.

But today it was clear you just didn't have the strength. I was devastated. "You've got a cell to yourself now?" I tried again.

A minute later he actually spoke.

"Yeah. They sent my papers on. That got me in solitary. Some rule here." His voice sounded hoarse. Distant and out of sync, like a bad telephone connection.

My eyes swam with joy. I started to reach for my handkerchief, then checked myself. I didn't want another sob session. I was glad about the new cell, but we had more important things to discuss. "I'll be popping back to Tokyo, either today or tomorrow."

My brother gave me a look. For the first time, really looked at me. There was a mysterious something in his eyes I couldn't place.

"There's the trial to think of, you know."

Tez nodded.

"Yesterday I met with an attorney introduced by the consul here, but he was no good. No initiative at all. But I don't know how it works here, so I've got no way of finding anyone else. Back in Tokyo there are people I can ask. That's why I have to head back for a while."

"Why bother? Just leave me here."

"How can you even think that? If I just leave you to it, you'll get the death penalty for sure!" There I'd gone and said it again. *Death penalty.*

"Fine by me," said my brother with no expression.

"Get a hold of yourself. Why do you think I hauled myself all this way in such a hurry?"

"Didn't ask you to. Not on my account."

"I'm not hearing this." I was furious. There was no getting through to him in his present state. He'd lost the will to do anything, along with any prospect of ever getting out of there. Okay, so maybe it was up to me to bring him back to his senses.

"Say what you will, I'm going to do what I can. If the death penalty agrees with you, fine. I personally don't fancy people saying I saw my own brother to his grave. Self-centered of me, isn't it?" Not bad for twisted logic. Tez said nothing; he obviously didn't want to argue.

"Just tell me one thing. Did you in fact have any heroin?"

A moment's silence. "Yeah. I bought two grams after I got here, from a pusher. Some guy named Agus I met on the beach in Kuta. He must've been in with them."

"A pusher? Why would he inform?"

"Probably made a deal. Set me up and—*bang*—the cops move in. They get points for drug control, he gets protection, and the fall guy's a foreigner so the locals are happy."

"If you're so smart, why did you fall for it?"

"Because I'm a sucker," he taunted himself.

"So what you're saying is, you *are* an addict?"

"Yeah."

"But how could you?"

Silence again.

"Just something I got caught up in on my travels. That's all."

"But heroin, is that an automatic death penalty?"

"I don't know," said Tez, almost as if talking about someone else. "In Japan, of course, I had nothing to do with the stuff. But I read somewhere, first offense gets off with probation. If they actually jail you, six months at most. Foreigners I guess they deport. For possession, that is. If you bring stuff in and sell it, then it gets serious."

"But we're only talking possession here, right?"

"Right. Just possession. All this death penalty talk, I don't get where it's coming from."

"Well, then there must be some mistake," I said.

"Yeah." My brother sank back into his fog. Why get him worked up on cheap hopes anyway?

"In any case, you're going to need top-gun legal help, so I'm returning to Tokyo for now."

"It's okay."

"It's okay *what*? Don't you want help?"

"What's the point? A lawyer from here's fine."

"Come on, don't be so down."

"I'm *not*," he protested, but I knew he hadn't any fight left in him.

"Look, I'll take care of everything. I'll find a good attorney and I'll get you out of here, Tez. I can't just leave you in a place like this."

"Why not?"

I thought it over for a minute: why *was* I helping him? "Because I'm your sister."

Tez couldn't say anything to that. "Because I'm your sister" was just too straight, too obvious. Embarrassed, we could hardly look at each other.

"Is there anything you need?"

"Well, clothes maybe," he said after a while. "Jeans and a T-shirt and underwear. Could do with a pair of shorts, too. Better ask first, though, before you go ahead and bring it in."

"All right. Before I leave today, I'll do some shopping. I should have the things to you before noon. If they only allow one visit a day, I'll have them delivered."

Tez nodded.

"So, I'm off. I'll be in touch. You write when you can. I'll be sure to include paper and pens in the package. How about paints?"

"Don't bother."

With that I left him in the room. But just as I was getting into Wayang's car, it struck me. Tez admitted he had heroin, but death for two grams? The laws might be different in Japan and Indonesia, but where did this death penalty talk come from? If they failed to mention it at either the time of the arrest or the interrogation, Tez must have heard it from the consul. It was the consul and that miserable attorney who put it to me. But where did *they* get their information? From the police? Who was telling what to whom? Tez had every reason to be paranoid. "Set up" or not, there was something else funny going on here.

I couldn't leave like this. Unless I had some idea of what the police were up to, I couldn't plan my next step. And well, there I was, standing right outside the police station.

"Wayang, could I . . . Is there a way I could meet the police chief here?"

This caught Wayang off guard, but my stern expression forced his hand. And so back we went inside. Wayang approached the duty officer, who said he'd go ask, then showed us to a small waiting room. An hour later we were still waiting. I remembered how I once spent a whole week waiting for a visa at the Tunisian consulate in Marseilles. I went every day, waited from morning to afternoon, and every day the visa would be ready tomorrow. Officials in these countries keep people waiting forever. Seems that's their job.

Eventually the duty officer reappeared and led us to the Denpasar police chief. A big man in a short-sleeved uniform, seated behind a monstrous desk. He stared at me silently as I entered, as if sizing up merchandise.

"May I speak English?" I asked.

He nodded, but still said nothing. Unnerving.

"I'm the sister of Tetsuro Nishijima. Did you arrest my brother?"

"I conduct his arrest."

"And the charge?"

"Illegal possession large quantity of drug."

"When you say large quantity, my brother says he only had two grams."

"That we make clear at trial."

"Then what did you say at the press conference?"

"You can read in newspaper."

He'd agreed to see me, but apparently not to have anything to do with me. I could tell Wayang was on edge beside me. Was this police chief so very scary?

"The Japanese consul said my brother might be sentenced to death. Is that a possibility?"

"Judge decide that. My job only arrest suspect, secure evidence, and prepare report."

"*Is* there that possibility?"

"Our fair and just court system decide that."

Was he just playing with me? I decided to change my tack. "My brother says his arrest was a set-up. Is it true?"

"Set-up? Why we need to do?"

"Then what about this Agus character?"

"Who? Maybe you not know, Miss, million person named Agus in our country."

Stupid me. The police chief was getting impatient.

"Honest citizen inform on suspect. When we search he have drug, so we arrest."

"Who was this honest private citizen?"

"I see no need to tell you. I see no need me to meet you now. Only person I need to meet is suspect. You not belong in this." With that the police chief finally grinned.

"And what does that mean?"

"Mean be careful not commit crime here in our country, not make everything confuse."

"Is that a threat?" I stared straight at him.

"No, just warning. Not do thing police mistaking for crime, not do thing tempting our good citizen make crime. Foreigner very much causing trouble here. Particularly women."

Come to think of it, he *was* eyeing me with a little more than circumstantial interest. Sizing up my face and figure. He could have me detained on any pretext. Or just plain have me.

The more worked up I became, the more I realized how powerless I was. Nothing I said would get me anywhere. This cop had absolute authority, and he'd play whatever hand he wanted. Argue rationally or act the "sassy female"—none of that would alter the situation. It wouldn't make a dent in him.

Wayang cowered in his chair.

"Okay, then. I look forward to this 'fair and just' Indonesian trial," said I, and stood to go.

I'll show him. We'll win that trial. We'll wipe that smirk off his face. My thoughts took a spiteful swipe at the police station as we left.

When I landed back in Narita, I already had someone in mind, the one person in Tokyo with the right contacts. My biggest fear, though, was that he'd be overseas on a story, but by some miracle he was in Japan.

Kei'ichiro Takami was a freelance TV director with his own production company. A news-breaking locations man, he covered international affairs —Arab countries and Latin America mainly—and occasionally came up with the most amazing scoops. I knew how good he was to work with; I'd been his interpreter on three trips to francophone Africa. I'd seen him press his luck to the limit and ride it into some great footage. After a while it dawned on me that the secret of his success was that he was on the level with everyone. Never took sides or played up to anyone; he just said the right thing at the right time, at all times. He came across as a real person, no-nonsense but very likable. Disarmingly so Which let people be themselves and forget the camera. One interview would lead to a second and a third. A brilliant memory for faces and places, he kept up hundreds of contacts over the years. Since the better part of reportage work is dealing with people, being a "people person" makes all the difference.

I rang up Takami, saying I needed to see him urgently, then went straight to his office. I knew he'd listen and bounce back with a plan. Here was no typical Japanese, weighing only what others in his small island circle might think. He was more expansive, more "continental." Sometimes a bit too broad-minded, if anything. I only hoped he wouldn't have me chasing halfway around the world. I told him what I knew; I could see the wheels turning.

"Well, there's that fellow . . . Yuzo Inagaki," Takami said, summoning up a name.

"Who's that?"

"Old Indonesia hand. Got real pull where it matters."

"Pull?"

"Do you have any idea how strong economic ties are between Japan and Indonesia? The sheer amount of money and business and people moving back and forth?"

"No, not really. To be honest, until this all happened, I didn't know a thing about the place."

"Very well, shall we have ourselves a little briefing?" Takami leaned forward. "Before the war, Indonesia was a Dutch colony, then the Japanese army went and occupied it. At first, the Indonesians welcomed the Japanese for having liberated them from Holland. In general, up until the war, Japan was quite popular throughout Southeast Asia. Today's so-called developing countries were all colonies of Europe; the only ones in the whole of Asia never colonized by Western powers were Thailand and Japan. We were industrialized. We even beat Russia militarily. Japan was a shining star to a lot of Asians, a valiant big brother, maybe even a liberating knight on a white horse."

I must have slept through this in school. I shut up and listened.

"But the truth of the matter is, while freeing Indonesia from the Dutch, the Japanese military merely ushered in their own brand of colonial control. Their aim—to secure wartime resources and expand their power base. Our troops were an arrogant, abusive lot. They forced the Japanese language and Shintoism on the Indonesians. Even today, Japanese words like *romusha* and *bakayaro*—'coolie' and 'idiot'—are still part of the vocabulary, so you can imagine how tempers flew. And in no time, the Japanese became an anathema.

"That much said, two groups of people living next to each other for any length of time makes for familiarity. Besides the soldiers, more than fifty thousand civilian Japanese were transplanted there, too. Not all were over-bearing, and of course there's also this thing that happens between men and women everywhere. More interestingly, though, Japan's Greater East Asian Co-Prosperity Sphere made a pretext of turning Indonesia into an independent nation, with preparations moving ahead for a constitution. Anyway, two days before the war's end, dovetailing onto these preparations, Sukarno declared independence. And after the war, several thousand Japanese officers and infantrymen opted to stay on in Indonesia. Those who put down roots were called *Japindo*—'Japanese Indonesians.'

"The minute the war ended, the Dutch came back and tried to pick up where they left off. Sukarno waged a four-year War of Independence, and finally succeeded in throwing them out. In that War of Independence, many *Japindo* took an active role. I once did a story on them, although their numbers have really dwindled, as you might expect."

Takami was recalling faces, I could tell. Probably he'd met a sympathetic soul or two in the course of that story. And probably they'd passed on since then.

"But where was I? The most important element in Japanese-Indonesian relations belongs to postwar economics. Japan paid reparations, which primed Indonesia's recovery and growth. Naturally, politicians in both Indonesia and Japan flocked to this money. Japan did the funding and Indonesia did the projects. Building dams and power plants was beyond Indonesia's technical expertise, so of course Japanese contractors went over, too. Eventually there were rebates paid, the same general mechanism as ODA today: money paid out ultimately found its way back to Japan via corporate channels. And some portion always wound up in politicians' pockets.

"So the ironic thing is, thanks to losing militarily, Japan forged much closer relations with Indonesia. Professor Inagaki was among those working there during all of this. I don't exactly know what he did, but his reputation is clean."

"Meaning he wasn't in it for the money?"

"Apparently not. He seems to be one of those rare individuals who believes in what he does. Seriously believes he personally has a hand to play in improving Japan-Indonesia relations. At least I don't hear any bad rumors about him and kickbacks."

"But will a man of his stature listen to the likes of me?"

"Never know until you try. You're the desperate one, right?"

Which is how I found myself paying a call at the offices of Yuzo Inagaki. It was a disaster right from the start. I had Takami write a letter of introduction and even call ahead for me. I showed up right on time. It was a tiny place in downtown Nihonbashi. I presented my letter to the receptionist and took a seat on a folding chair out in the corridor. Fifteen minutes later the receptionist led me to a makeshift visitors' area where I waited another fifteen minutes before Professor Inagaki showed. I rose and bowed.

"Take a seat. Please," said the professor, a plumpish figure with a round egg of a face and a bald pate, big round eyes, and thick lips. Complexion on the well-seasoned side. He was maybe seventy, but full of life. "I read Takami's letter. Do you have a card?"

"I, uh . . . no."

"Come asking for favors and you don't even take the trouble to print up a calling card? Only common courtesy, I'd've thought."

I didn't expect to be lectured out of the blue. I'd come to beg help for Tez, yet here I was tongue-tied.

"I swear, young people these days. So your name is . . ." Professor Inagaki glanced at the letter in his hands. ". . . Kaoru Nishijima. Says here you're an excellent co . . . co-or-di-na-tor. All these fancy new foreign job titles. Just what is it a coordinator does?"

"I help with footwork for television shoots. I gather advance information, track down prospective interviewees, arrange for appearances, take care of any official clearances. I reserve local transportation and go along with the crew to handle on-site negotiations. Translate, too, when needed. That's pretty much the work I do."

"In which country?"

"France is where I'm most at home. But I've been to West Africa with Takami."

"I get the drift. When Takami did that *Japindo* program, he had someone along of that stripe. So what's this all about? All it says here is that you have an important request."

"My brother's been arrested in Bali. They've said that he might get the death penalty . . ."

"For what?"

"Possession of heroin."

"And did he? Have heroin, that is."

"Yes, I'm afraid so. These past few days, I was over there trying to verify things. My brother says he'd bought two grams when they arrested him. So actually it was only that one particular time."

"And the seller?"

"He disappeared. My brother says it was a trap."

"Accusations like that won't get you anywhere. He had it in his possession, however briefly. Sorry to be blunt, but—is your brother a, um, a doper?"

"Excuse me?"

"I mean, is he addicted?"

"Yes. By his own admission."

"And when was the arrest?"

"The beginning of January."

Professor Inagaki cast an eye at the calendar on the wall. "Why, that's all of a month. What on earth've you been doing with yourself? Time's already been and gone. They've got the jump on the case."

"I was away in Europe for work. When I came back I went immediately to the Foreign Ministry, then straight to Bali. I met with the Japanese consul and my brother and the police chief, then came straight back to talk with Takami and—"

And now, I heard myself saying . . . (Had so many days really passed? Could the timing be so impossible?) . . . *And now Tez was going to die for it!* The thought was too much for me. No, come on, be strong, be cool. I can't let him see a weepy woman trying to buy sympathy.

"Stop that. Please. I don't like being cried at."

"Me either . . . crying's . . . not my forte." I covered my face with my hands and reached for the handkerchief in my bag, when I remembered Wayang's newspaper article. "Here . . . please have a look at this. It's about my brother."

While the professor concentrated on the newspaper, I managed to pull myself together. I knew I must look a sight.

"This here's a mighty different story," said Inagaki, looking up from the article.

"Excuse me?"

"The Denpasar chief of police held a press conference—that's what the article's about. Says they caught a runner for the Japanese drug mafia, a Japanese student named Tetsuron Nishijima. Police arrested him entering from Thailand with heroin. Says a major seizure of two hundred grams is rare for Indonesia."

"It's all lies. There's no mafia involved at all. And my brother's name is Tetsuro. And he's not a student, he's a painter. And the heroin, it was only two grams, bought on Bali. It's true he arrived from Thailand, but they didn't arrest him then and he didn't smuggle in anything."

Professor Inagaki went silent. A secretary leaned in to announce that our time was up and the next appointment was waiting.

"Have them wait," huffed the professor in a voice that broadcast everywhere. Had he decided to help Tez? "This thing's blown all out of proportion. Too big for a backwater like Bali. Let's see—we might get the case mandated to Jakarta . . ."

"Y-you mean you'll find an attorney for us? Someone on the ball, someone we can trust. That's what I came here today for."

"I know, I know. Just hold your horses." Inagaki rushed out of the room and returned with his agenda. Flipping pages, he picked up a telephone and dialed a long string of digits, carefully checking each number one by one. He said something in Indonesian. First to one person—pause—then to another—pause—then to yet another. Then finally with this last person he talked for fifteen minutes. I had no idea what about, all I knew was his Indonesian sounded as fluent as his Japanese.

"In a couple of days, I'm going with you to Jakarta," he announced after hanging up. "We still might be in time."

"Thank you so, so much."

"I can't say why, but I've taken an interest. It's a tricky one. Better not to get your hopes too high. I've been working with that country ever since the war, pretty much as a co-"—he looked at my letter of introduction—"a coordinator like yourself. So I have some cards to play. I'll look into things, pull what strings I can, and if it seems in line, I'll find you a decent attorney. I'll try, but it'll be well nigh impossible to iron out the whole mess. I've been making it my business to see what *profits* both countries for so long, it'd do me good to get behind what's *right* for a change. Guess this is what they call getting emotionally involved."

On the plane to Jakarta, the professor hardly said a word. He sat looking straight ahead, eating the meal when served, then sinking back into silence. Until thirty minutes before landing when, in one brief concession to logistics, he finally leaned over and said: "When we arrive, there's a man I must see. A good, good friend of thirty years' standing, and the person I trust most in the country. You'd better wait in the hotel. We'll be talking *Bahasa*—in Indonesian—and anyway I already told him most everything over the phone. He's very well placed to gather information, and he'll have a take on the situation."

Still with no game-plan, I bowed to this man who held the lifeline to Tez. Glad as I was, though, I couldn't figure him out. What had moved him to get involved when he could have said "No can do" like the consul? Who knows what really motivates people? Back in Tokyo, Inagaki said he'd always worked for profit so it was time he did something on principle—but he couldn't be so profit-oriented as all that, just look at his tiny office. Maybe, like Takami said, he really did value good relations between the two countries more than money.

Outside the airport, Jakarta was a sprawling metropolis. My first Asian capital. Our taxi route seemed to meander between two parallel cities. The main avenues were broad, well kept—and empty. But once we slipped behind that façade, the narrow backstreets roiled with pedestrians and motorbikes, people pulling foodcarts and strange half-breed bicycle-rickshaws. The whole place in an uproar—frantic, standstill traffic boxed in by rickety houses, and all those smells! This must be the real thing, how the people actually lived. Compared to which the big modern office buildings were movie sets thrown up for show. Neither was any place I wanted to venture into on my own.

Professor Inagaki dropped me off and I checked into the hotel by myself. It was no five-star Intercontinental, though clean and adequate. My room on the eleventh floor faced onto the pristine modernized side of the city, where the scale of this unknown Asia seemed somehow less intimidating from high up. By evening I started to think about dinner, but, deciding I'd better stay put for when the phone call came, I ordered room service. *Nasi goreng* ("Indonesian pilaf")—which turned out to be ordinary fried rice with an egg on top and shrimp crisps on the side—and a Bintang beer. I finished about half.

I felt uneasy not being near Tez. Was he still running himself down? I'd gone all the way to Bali and couldn't do a damn thing for him. The most I'd managed to do was buy him a few provisions. Saving my brother meant coming here to the capital and brainstorming. Me, an outsider with no bargaining chips of my own. All I could do was sit still, anxieties on hold.

Tez's burden of proof—to demonstrate how a tiny amount of heroin bought on Bali from a vanished police pusher had become "smuggled in from Thailand," the quantity multiplied a hundredfold—it all added up to bad news. Overturn *all* the inconsistencies and would it be enough to free him? Deportation, even two or three years' time would be a blessing. But realistic? How long would I have to hang around for the verdict? The same thoughts kept churning over and over in my head, with nothing to break the loop. The more I tried, the deeper I spiraled down. The police chief's gloating face loomed up with a vengeance.

I could feel my bile rising. Who ever heard of such a country? Selling drugs to foreigners just to string them up on trumped-up charges! They could make their capital look fine and decent and modern, big hotels serving their phony fried rice on bone china, but behind it all they were still primitive. I could just tell what sort of trial it was going to be in this tribal swamp. No way I'd ever take a liking to this place. When this was all over, I'd never ever come back here. Let them drown in disasters, I wouldn't even read the newspaper reports.

I began to feel ridiculous and mean. Okay, no more letting my temper get the better of me. I closed my eyes with my knees tucked up in a ball. Not asleep, not awake. It was 11:00 at night when the professor's phone call came.

"Tomorrow, from 9:00, we're meeting with an attorney. Have your breakfast and be ready in the lobby." That's all he said, then hung up.

So he'd gone for legal help. We wouldn't be breezing Tez out of the country without a trial. That night I tossed and turned through a sequence of oppressive dreams.

Our appointment the next morning was at a grand office in a grand thirty-story glass tower. A thousand times more impressive than the professor's little cubicle in Tokyo.

Two men were waiting for us: an older gentleman, portly like Inagaki, who introduced a somewhat younger man to the professor. They shook hands. Then Inagaki presented me to the first man in Indonesian. I bowed slightly, then also gave a bow to the younger guy for good measure. The professor neglected to tell me their names.

We faced off in pairs on two grand sofas, the professor chattering away animatedly with the older man. Probably recapping a drinking anecdote from the night before. Then, as if he'd only just noticed me sitting there, he paused to clear his throat and finally introduced his friend in a language I could understand. "This is Pirungati. We go back a long way."

"*Konnichiwa*," said the older man in tenuous Japanese. Then, switching to perfect English, "That's all the Japanese I know. May I continue in English?"

Almost immediately the professor interjected in Indonesian, and Pirungati smiled.

"Our friend Mr. Inagaki says he doesn't speak English, so we'll have to keep shuffling between three languages. You and me in English, me and Inagaki in *Bahasa*, you and Inagaki in Japanese. Oh, and yes, this is Mr. Gatir, attorney-at-law. He's all right with English."

The younger man nodded. By younger, I mean he was probably fifty. But much skinnier, with big, sharp eyes and batlike ears. In order of skin color dark-to-light, it was this attorney Gatir, Pirungati, and Professor Inagaki. And Inagaki, to my eyes, was already quite dark.

"Mr. Gatir was formerly a police investigator," said Pirungati. "And now he's a top attorney. Please tell him everything you found out in Bali up to now."

I proceeded to relate what I heard from Tez, what I saw at the Denpasar police station, then asked him what he thought. Would he be willing to take on the job? Gatir's English was more than just "all right."

"I get the overall gist of the case. As I see it, there's considerable leeway as to how this might develop. Probably the most desirable outcome would be a no-trial annulment, which in actual terms would mean deportation. They'd release him and send him away, saying don't come back. Let's first try for that."

"Please. Anything you can do."

"And if that proves out of the question, then he'll be subpoenaed to stand trial."

"And the death penalty?"

"Legally, it could go that way."

"My brother did buy and use heroin. But he did *not* bring it in, and *not* two hundred grams."

"Certainly, going by what you've told me, there does exist the possibility of a police frame-up. I also saw the newspaper article, and my reading is, for the police chief to hold such a press conference while everything is still under investigation suggests ambitions to make a name for himself in a 'big case.' Very likely the man is not from Bali, but was posted there from Jakarta and hopes to return to the capital by scoring points. Also, whoever sold your brother the drugs, if he was indeed a front for this police chief, he'll never show in court. Or if he did, say as a witness for the prosecution, he'd probably say *he* was buying heroin *from* your brother. Which would be a major setback for our side."

"Is there nothing we can do?" I leaned forward to ask.

"Let's not rush to conclusions. There's no point entertaining unnecessary fears *or* groundless hopes. Nothing is decided until the final ruling. A trial is an open forum and it's up to the defense attorney to use whatever means to channel that ruling to our benefit."

"Understood."

"Let's pursue this further. Say he had brought heroin in from overseas, it would cease to be mere possession. It would be interpreted as transporting with intention to sell."

"Is there no lenience for the fact that he's a foreigner?"

"On the contrary. Forgive me for putting it so dramatically, but your brother is accused of committing a monstrous crime against the nation of Indonesia. I don't want you to view this in an unduly pretty light."

And the uglier the case, the bigger your take? The better for you all to extract what you can from my brother and me—there's also that angle. Still, at least ransom offered an out.

"Bringing in drugs is tantamount to pressing Indonesian citizens into drug addiction. And drug addiction is regarded as a tragic end, more miserable than slavery. And rightly so, I would have to say. Your brother would be seen as selling our people into slavery. In which case, why shouldn't the country be angry? At least that's the spirit of the law dealing with drugs. You probably have similar laws in your own country."

"Yes, but . . ."

". . . *But*, whether this law actually applies to this case is to be decided only after due examination in court. However, let me warn you—young as you are, and this being the first time someone in your family is to be tried in court—do not for a moment think that the court exists to elicit the truth. The onus of the court is settlement, *not* revelation. No matter what actually happened, the facts as recognized by the court are the facts. And the task of the attorney is to press for a favorable recognition of those facts."

"So even if it's a lie, if the court says it's so, it becomes true?"

"Yes, you could say that—but I would put it another way. In cases where there is a divide between what's right for the individual and what's right for society, the court must decide where to draw the line of effective and acceptable justice."

"Which means, it could go either way . . ."

"The individual and society are at odds, so no matter how the court metes out justice, both sides will be dissatisfied. Though conversely the court has sufficient authority to absorb all such dissatisfactions. That being so, judgments once rendered are not open to question."

"So, my brother, he really could get death?"

"Unfortunately, at this point, we can't wholly rule out the possibility. With drug offenses, the pendulum can swing very wide. A deterrent show of punishment is strongly indicated, especially with foreigners. This holds true not only with Indonesia, but represents the general trend throughout Southeast Asia."

"Are there any similar precedents?"

"Certainly. Just recently, two Australians were caught in Malaysia and sentenced to death. Australia applied diplomatic pressure to forestall execution, but this seemed to produce the reverse effect. Malaysia took offense and renewed its stance. The execution could take place at any time. Those two lives are candles in the wind."

Here we go again, he's trying to scare up his price. What was with the police and lawyers in this country? Whatever Tez did or didn't do, this place was calculating and evil. So this is Asia? If only Tez hadn't been casting about on this side of the globe, if only he'd gone to Europe like me. And yet this piece of information about Australian diplomatic pressure was good news. The Japanese consul in Bali is a dud, but maybe the embassy here in Jakarta could do something? An ambassador's got more clout than a consul anyway.

"So now, what's for me to do? And if I ask you to defend my brother, what will *you* do?"

"First, we want to try the no-trial route, as I said. If you allowed me to act on your behalf, I'd go to Bali and meet with the prosecutor."

". . . And I'd go to the International Police and Bureau of Investigation," piped up Pirungati.

". . . But," continued Gatir, "if we see it coming to trial, at that time there would be any number of ways to fight it."

"Okay, then I'm asking you."

I made up my mind there on the spot, without even consulting Professor Inagaki. At least his explanation was logical. Unlike that deadbeat in Bali. Even if they did things differently from Japan or Europe, I didn't want to be bullied, I wanted someone I could talk to.

"Nonetheless, if for any reason this does come to trial, I would need to draw up a contract with your brother—not you. What does he have to say about all this, incidentally?"

"With the shock of arrest and imprisonment, not much of anything, I'm afraid. But if there were a trial, I'd convince him to put up a fight. I think he'd listen to me."

"I'll go with you to Bali," the professor reassured me. "I've got an acquaintance or two who could prove helpful. Let's just leave it at that for now. When you need to come back to Jakarta for anything, tell Pirungati. He's got clout and he's a straight shooter—a good man to have on your side."

6

TETSURO

"Because I'm your sister." It floored you to hear that—or rather to see Kaoru looking so disconcerted, so at a loss. That pained expression of hers nudged some secret place inside you. Okay, maybe it was time you listened to her and dropped your just-leave-me-here attitude. Maybe her energy would prove contagious, pull you out of this hopeless slump. In any case, there was no stopping her. Not Kaoru. Something like gratitude stirred inside you.

But your *little sister*? How did it come to this dumb kinship thing? Because at times like this, all you can finally depend on is family. Unconditionally, no double-dealing, no games. Mind, your folks wouldn't do it; they were too old, worlds apart in their thinking. They'd never understand. So that left Kaoru. Dumb, corny, but in the nick of time, your secret trump card.

It's your fault for not having friends or lovers to stand by you. Obvious, isn't it, the reason why you never had anyone who stayed around?—you're too damn selfish. You chose art over life, especially a life in Tokyo. The famous illustrator. Yes, there were women from time to time, but none for long. One of them lasted three years, then it became demanding, too stifling, and you broke it off. What a painfully pointless end to the affair. That was five years ago. After that only flings, always just short of "serious." In the end, you always chose travel over women. And no matter how close you'd been before leaving, by your return they'd have found another man. Which made things easier, actually. Funny you never met anyone who made you want to suggest traveling together.

An—now *her* you miss. If you had one fairy-tale wish, those'd be the days to relive. Since Vietnam, you wrote her three letters. Faithfully addressed to Ngyuen Ti An—beautiful Vietnamese name—enclosing sketches from your travels. After Inge, though, you never wrote again. When you get out of here—*if* you get out of here—promise you'll go visit the village. Go see An and Tanh again. But what if An's not alone any more? Everyone's got a life to live. Everyone who's not made of stone.

So that leaves your sister, with god-knows-what expectations. "Because I'm your sister" was probably the most honest thing she could have said. Because I'm your sister, stupid! Because I'm your sister, what choice did you give me?

Of course she's no longer the little Kaoru you knew; she's a woman now. A woman who's lived abroad and charted her own experiences. Kaoru has changed these past five years, probably more than you've changed. She's not the tomboy running out to play after school, nor the girl posing for you with a pot of flowers. No puzzled teenager standing between you and your parents. You'd better believe she's your salvation.

Where did you hear that hokey story about siblings helping each other out? In Goa, that's right. At the guesthouse café by the river. From that headstrong Finn who tagged along with you for a while—what was his name? You remember the country, but not the person. Draw a person once and you never forget the face, but the name won't come.

Some Goan boy was trying to sell you both something with the usual "Hello brother!" and the guy came down on him—"I'm not your brother!"

"Oh, but brothers, they are helping each other out. And I am just wanting some help is all. So you buy my ganja, I am grateful for the money and you are happy for the dreams. Both sides happy, isn't it?" Him standing, the two foreigners sitting—always the stronger bargaining position.

"Your sales pitch is wrong. Brothers do *not* help each other out. Now you listen. A brother is the very first competitor you meet in life. Ever hear of sibling rivalry? Anyone who can't beat his brother won't get far in the world."

"But my elder brother, he helps me if something happens."

"That's because times are good. Life has never been as easy as now . . .

Look at the birds: they lay two or three eggs." The Finnish debating champion placed three matchsticks on the table—that's right, he smoked a pipe. "They need to raise one egg, but they lay two or three as spares. If anything happens to the first one, there's the second, and if anything happens to the second, there's the third. The first one hatches, the parents quickly bring it food. The second one hatches, more feeding. The third one hatches, but by then there's little food to go around. If two chicks grow, no need for a spare any more. The first to hatch wins the race to survive." One matchstick forward and one matchstick back by way of illustration.

"But people . . ."

"People are no different. Only these days no one starves, so we don't have to compete for the same food. But if things get desperate, believe me, brothers will fight. No good calling everyone 'Brother, brother.' That's a mistake from the start—and we won't buy your ganja."

The boy withdrew, looking really pissed off. Probably thought we were making fun of him, but we weren't in the market for marijuana anyway.

"Your sibling survivalism is kind of skewed," you begged to differ.

"How so?"

"When brothers do compete during the early stages, it's because at that point they need to grow and develop. So, a shortage of food means fights, for sure. But once they get past that stage and learn how to fend for themselves, learning to cooperate becomes the smart thing to do. Since the parents have shared out only so much DNA, by cooperating they ought to be able to combine more potential. Get more food, defeat more enemies, produce more kids than just brothers who're always fighting."

"Well, that makes sense I guess," he admitted, just a heartbeat too late. "What do I know? I'm an only child. I had the advantage of my parents' undivided attention. Which I suppose now, you'll say, puts me at a disadvantage."

"Brothers are your first 'others,' but they also share a bond of kinship. No guarantee you'll get along, but when you do, trust runs deep. Stronger than with strangers. Seems to me that corporations come out of that family all-for-one-ism. Uha and Brothers Co., Ltd." Uha—you remembered his name.

"Point taken. You got brothers?"

"Just a younger sister."

"Ever compete?"

"Nah, we had enough to eat." Very funny. "Never helped each other much either, see her maybe only two or three times a year. But I guess I'd rally to her cause if she needed me."

"Or maybe vice-versa?" Touché. How could he have known?

"Come to think of it, in Japan there was an ancient belief that sisters could . . . well, sort of watch over their brothers. They were said to have special powers, almost like family witch doctors. When a fisherman went out to sea, he took a strand of his sister's hair as a lucky charm. And if there was a shipwreck, the sister's spirit turned into a white bird that flew out to guide him to safety. Island seafaring superstition. Long before there was anything even called Japan, a male may have ruled—the kingship idea, from the Asian continent—but it was his sister who guided and protected the country spiritually."

"But weren't the samurai on top? Weren't women way down the social ladder?"

"That was way later, during Japan's feudal Middle Ages. This was back in prehistory. Originally it was the women who had the clout."

What did you talk about next? The standing of women in the West? The whole chivalry thing. How men put women on a pedestal while they ran around on their "quests." That male artists painted female nudes, but female artists never painted male nudes—what few female artists there were. What else? Not a bad little comp-culture survey for a college dodger. Inconclusive, but seems we talked a long, long time.

Kaoru didn't just arrange to send clothes, she gave her hired driver money for your food. And he paid a shop near the jail for several meals in advance. That very day at noon a boy came right to your solitary cell to deliver hot *nasi goreng* in a scruffy plastic bowl, along with a flimsy aluminum spoon and a cup of water. Either you were hungry—a sign your health was improving—or maybe the rice really *was* good. Compared to the regular jail slop, this was heaven. Even the shrimp cracker was tasty. *Kerupuk udang*, think he called it, the other shop boy who came to collect the bowl and spoon two hours later.

He leaves and you're still thinking about family witch doctors. Kaoru's no white bird of hope, but maybe if you'd carried a strand of her hair, you could have avoided this whole ordeal? No Inge, no angel chasing after you. But if it's anything like Shinto, divine protection is pretty black and white. Half-faith gets you nowhere. And you never could believe. A hair is easy enough to carry around, but you can't just start believing retroactively. Black hair, white hair. Was pubic hair also a lucky charm?

You've never seen Kaoru naked. You've drawn her face, painted her in that flower picture. But no pubic hair. Seen her in a school bathing suit when you took her to swim class for your mother. That would've been when she was in second grade. From the time of puberty on, you never even thought about Kaoru having pubic hair. Never knew about her first menstruation. What older brother would think about his own sister *that* way? Was it all so unconsciously taboo? Internally censored, excluded. Naturally you know nothing about her first man, either. Never asked. Your imagination stopped long short of that line. Even when you did that painting, you never viewed your sister as a young woman-to-be.

No, redirect your thinking. Sexual talismans for a spiritual quest. To tempt fate. Without fate no one ever finds what they seek. Fate is always there, they say, if only you've got the power to coax it out. No one ever meets what has no connection. Spiritual readiness precedes actuality, a latent necessity before the phenomenon. Unseen, invisible. Hit the magic combination and who isn't a fatalist? Yes, but to really believe?

When you met Inge, you met with heroin. An unforseeably inevitable, prearranged accident. She had your number. And you without your strand of Kaoru's hair. Nothing to protect a brother in his travels, not one lousy sketch of her face. Your defenses were too damn thin. So now, to make up for not having spiritually inoculated you, Kaoru has to do all this running around.

Inge must have used some kind of psychic hocus-pocus to find you out. It was too easy, too many hidden workings behind that fateful encounter. You were ripe for temptation, ready for that beautiful paralysis: concentrated essence of sleep while still awake, death seeping into every nerve ending. Blessed vegetative happiness, mineral contentment. Brain stimulated and body dozing—you lovely Sleeping Beauty!

Inge came selling pure pleasure. Eros on ice. Pirouetting across death's divide, a graceful dance devoid of heat. No body temperature, physical being rarified to a dancing shadow. A person's got to die sometime, so why resist? Why indeed, when it's so much simpler, lighter, to slip over to the other side. Once there, you never need die again.

Death, so irresistibly seductive, because you have none of your sister's life-force, her eros suffused with energy—and no image of her pubic hair. And that sketch of An is over a year old now, probably lost its potency. Oh, to see An again!

You were in a train station in rural Thailand. In a waiting room along with dozens of others. All afternoon you've been painting water buffalo wading through the paddies nearby. The green of the surrounding trees, the blue of the sky reflected in the shallow water, the beautiful curves of the buffalo horns and body lines. You're pleased with the picture.

When you reach the station the sky is still light, the color of jade. Not so very hot, a nice breezy afternoon. Everyone's lulled into quiet lethargy. The train will come . . . oh, maybe not on time, but what does anyone here care about schedules? They come and they wait, that's all there is to do. Once in a while someone new turns up and greetings go around, gossip is bandied about to gentle laughter here and there.

You notice there's a disturbed guy in the crowd, muttering to himself. His voice has a different tone from the others. You can see he's still young. He sidles up to people and babbles in dead earnest, but everyone conspires to ignore him. He wanders over to a young mother and child. Wild-eyed and mouth skewed, sputtering as he speaks. The mother pulls back, drawing her baby in close. Everyone looks out of the corner of their eye, but the situation doesn't seem to warrant intervention—not for the moment.

The youth leaves the mother and immediately goes looking for someone else. This time it's a large middle-aged woman. Rather well-to-do among the present company, to judge from her body weight. The youth walks up to her, spits out a stream of verbiage, hands flapping, then throws himself down on the floor in some kind of plea. The woman says something. Happy that someone's finally spoken to him, the boy's antics become even more exaggerated. You steal glances from afar, a mixture of curiosity, apprehension, and sympathy. The large woman pulls a cloth bag from the bosom of her dress, a purse with a long string tied around her neck. When she takes out a single coin and puts it in his hand, he lets out a yell and throws himself flat on the floor, bowing over and over again. But the next moment, he's stretched out a hand and thrust the coin back at her. His voice gets louder and louder. Everyone tenses a notch. The middle-aged woman snatches back the coin and puts it in her purse, then turns stiffly to one side with feigned indifference. Too late for the youth to object.

The odd boy is apparently a familiar fixture of town life. He may act a bit funny, but show him a minimum of attention and there's no harm done. Treading a fine line between what he can and can't do, he's in control and not so crazy as he appears. It's all theatrics to him.

Next he goes over to a monk. A poised eminence of maybe sixty, who nods not-really-listening, occasionally tossing in a reply as the young man blathers away. It seems to be a little homily, which gets a token of attention. But each time the monk finishes, the ranting starts again. Only the first few words pretend to be addressed to someone—anyone he can find to launch him into his own monologue—the rest doesn't even come close to conversation. The monk plays along, telling him to please settle down and not bother the others. You watch the goings-on, but it's the monk's beautiful orange robes—not saffron at all—that interest you. You're okay, you blend right in. No one's looking, you reassure yourself.

Only the next thing, the young man comes over to you. He crosses his legs on the cement floor and begins remonstrating with great determination. Glaring at you dead serious, rapid-firing his verbal slingshot, showering you with word-spittle. You don't know what to do, but you can't take your eyes off him. He lifts his hand and slaps it palm flat down on the floor right beside your shoe. Almost of itself, your leg flinches back a half-step.

"I-can-not-un-der-stand-a-word-you-are-say-ing," you tell him quietly and slowly in Japanese.

As if provoked by this, he lets out a scream at the top of his lungs. Oh-oh, answering him was a big mistake. What can you do now but look away? The boy keeps raving, inching forward on his knees. Too late now. He huddles over your shoe and gently, lovingly, begins to stroke it. His words become more and more excited—*I've always wanted shoes like this, you can wear nice shoes like this but I go barefoot, I'm human too yet have no shoes* . . . Now he's wiping his hands on his lap as if you and your shoes were filthy. You almost want to kick him on impulse, but restrain yourself. Finally he plucks up courage and makes to climb into your lap.

At that, several men rush over and grab him. He clings to your legs, but they drag him away and slap him hard, *whap-whap-whap* on the head, shouting him down—*Don't bother the foreigner!* He sobs operatically, flailing his arms and stuttering apologies. A few more slaps and shows of repentance, and gradually the commotion dies down. An awkward silence ensues, then everyone starts chatting with their neighbor like before. Only a lot more subdued, a conscious effort to forget what just happened.

You didn't lay a hand on the kid, though it was you who made him overstep the line. But even more depressing—you obviously don't blend in. You, the foreigner in the corner, the one with the backpack. You wear your nationality, body and clothes. A rich person in sneakers. Here, maybe a tenth of the people have shoes, another half rubber thongs, and the rest are barefoot. They know your kind, but choose to ignore you. Only the disturbed youth bucked the general disregard. No, a painter isn't all eye-to-hand, seeing-but-unseen. Whatever you do, you're a traveler; wherever you go, you stand out. You're a target.

Thailand is also where you met Inge. Land of hot, steamy light. Land of rain-fresh, limpid colors. Where Buddhist monks stroll by in persimmon robes. Where voices lilt in high singsong. Where they douse the most exquisite flavors and fabulous ingredients with heaps of chili and MSG and sugar.

It was a village two hours on horseback from Chiang Mai. You'd vowed to walk it, but a horseman overtook you from behind, pointing to his extra horse, miming money with his fingers. Primitive pressure-capitalism. You dropped off your things at a cheap guesthouse, then spent the next four days walking around with your camper's canvas pail of water and set of paints and an empty can you picked up somewhere for washing brushes. Didn't bring much paper this trip, so you make do with a school drawing pad bought at a stationery store in Chiang Mai. Shitty Chinese-made pulp, not enough sizing so the paints bled, but manageable once you get the hang of it.

You were painting a temple up on a hill at the edge of the village. The day before, you climbed the long stairway and went inside, tried to paint the Buddha seated on the altar, but for some reason just couldn't get it right. The enigmatic smile kept turning cynical, as if sneering at human weakness. Not a Buddha of salvation. Again and again you put pencil to paper, but each attempt went wrong. So you gave up line-drawing and switched to color washes. Still nothing worked. The shape of the lips was there on paper, but it didn't convey anything. Okay, so what?—except that it was the most profound expression in all the world and you couldn't get it. This was one golden Buddha you'd have to pass on.

So the next day you forego the temple interior and climb further up the hill behind the *wat*, scouting for the best angle from which to paint the roof through the trees. Your aluminum-frame backpack folds out into a little camp chair. You anchor the drawing board on your lap, tack down a sheet of paper, and block out the rough forms in soft No. 4 pencil. Then work in more details in ultrafine .02mm black ink. Take out your palette, begin filling in color areas on the monochrome ground. A whole vista looms up. It never fails to fascinate, no matter how many times you've done it. Line can render, but color *is* the world. You think you're painting a temple a hundred meters away, but the real subject is the space between the temple and yourself. The dampness in the air gives a faint glow. That's so important. Light doesn't travel in a straight line here; it soaks into the air. Europe never said "landscape" to you; the air was too dry, the outlines too sharp. This luminous humidity is everything.

Inevitably, the angle of the sun shifts as you paint. You pack up quickly and move to another spot. By the time you've nearly finished three pictures, someone's standing there behind you. Probably a villager. You're used to it. Or maybe a monk from the temple. Too quiet to be children. Don't turn around, just go on painting. Some famous painter—who was it?—went to Paris with his young wife and had her set up an easel twenty meters away as a decoy for onlookers so he could work in peace, knowing that most people will flock to a pretty woman even if her painting's crap. But here you're on your own. A monk in your own way. You finish the picture and wait for the surface to dry. Little by little the paper starts to buckle.

"Very nice," comes a woman's voice. A shade low-pitched, in English.

"Thank you," you answer, your eyes still fixed on the watercolor, not looking around.

"From how you've painted it, you can almost tell there's a gold Buddha inside."

Give me a break. You crane your neck around to see . . . a white woman. Tall, at least from below she looks tall. Late thirties maybe? Hard to guess *gaijin* ages. Then she crouches down and you see she's older than you thought. A mature, defined face. Clear blue eyes, the color of a distant lake. But tired, not altogether there.

"Come on—I'd still paint the same picture even if I never saw inside the temple."

"Well, *I* can see the Buddha."

You swing around to examine her face. You habitually "sketch" people in your head, but this one resists. She doesn't look anything like the people you've met these past few months. She reminds you of a bad likeness of a movie star. A breeze brings a whiff of the woman's perfume from twenty meters away.

"Yesterday I went inside the place and saw it too. Had real problems with it. I couldn't get the smile, couldn't draw it."

"You're Asian and you couldn't get it? You from Taiwan? Japan? Korea?"

"Japan. Asia's a big place, and it's not all the same Buddhism. And I'm not really Buddhist anyway. Japanese don't go to temples any more than Americans go to church."

"Oh, but I'm not American, I'm German," she says, "and Europe is a big place, too. But not so big. Anyone does not fit in, we send them to the New World. Ha!" Strange laugh.

As a traveler, you end up talking more to other travelers than to locals. The same thin membrane that separates travelers from the soil of the place seems to connect the strange community of outsiders. So you talk to this German woman about Asia, and she proves reasonably knowledgeable. To hear her, she's been coming here regularly, visiting this very village for ten years now. And she never really understood that Buddha either.

"One time, I thought I understood. But that was because I used special means."

"Special means?"

"My little secret. Worked wonders all around. Almost got to know the Buddha personally. But anyway, I like the picture. The air's so wet."

She has eyes! Most of the time people feed you casual comments. Rare to find someone who actually *sees*.

"Southeast Asia is nothing if not humid."

"Are you a professional artist?"

"A professional *illustrator*. What would it mean to be a 'professional' artist anyway?"

"Because being an artist is a matter of self-awareness?"

How long you'd waited for such a conversation! This faded flower is sharp. And even better, she speaks clear English. You can't begin to follow young Americans, but her English is simple and direct, compressed and slow. You've traveled Asia, looking at the scenery, people's faces, their lives, painting what you see. You love it here, but you never found anyone to talk about these things. Local people will watch from the side, praise you as you paint their landscape, but to them there's no mystery: it's just what's there.

But then, since when was it particularly Asian to spout theory? That's something only urban intellectuals versed in European thought do. Ordinary people just take their surroundings as is. But for foreigners, that's never enough. It's not as if you longed for cutting-edge discourse, merely a chance to discuss what you see, the wonder of seeing. Talking to hippie types never goes anywhere, but this German woman seems to have a little more depth.

Later, then. There's still a little more sunlight to do a few more pictures, and she has places to go. You find out she's staying in the same guesthouse (there's only one), so there'll be time. You stand to see her off and size up her silhouette—*very* tall.

The next day it rains hard and heavy from the morning. A deluge to drown the whole world. Crossing the road for breakfast you and several others from the guesthouse get soaked, then soaked again on the way back. The rest of the day everyone just sits by their windows gazing out at the rain. Everything is a washed-out gray. Nothing worth painting. An hour later, bored with your vigil, you step out into the corridor and bump into the German woman.

"Rain," you pout.

"Rain," she echoes.

The narrow corridor adds pressure to the encounter. Was she attractive when she was young? Prettiest *mädchen* in her class, then prettiest girl in the school, then not-quite-prettiest girl in town. Germany is not America, so they probably don't hold those stupid contests. How did white people measure out their standards of beauty? She's got a decent face, slim body with long arms and legs to spare—so why does she look so tired, so listless?

"Care to talk?"

"Why not? It's raining after all."

This is no fancy city hotel. There's no proper lobby. The rain is coming down even harder than before, so there goes any idea of going out for tea. This is a don't-anyone-come-outside downpour. Only one place to suggest. "Well, there's always my room."

"Thanks for the invitation." She flashes an impressive set of teeth. "My name is Inge."

"I'm Tez. Pleased to meet you. Again." Pleased that her name is at least pronounceable.

You enter the room and Inge's mere presence fills half the space. You sit cross-legged on the bed, she camps diagonally opposite on the floor, bottle of mineral water in hand.

"Your painting yesterday, very nice and quiet."

"Thank you." What was that supposed to mean—"quiet"—unassuming? Weak? Non-assertive? Meaning "Asian." Something in you wants to lash out at that European attitude of theirs.

"Any other pictures?"

You show her what you've painted on this trip, traveling all over Thailand by train and bus. No need to verbalize what you were trying to do in each image; she has eyes, she really sees. Like laying out your latest portfolio before an art dealer. Or an auction. Just having a European look at your work is a boost. And why not? This woman knows her stuff.

Slowly, one by one, Inge picks up each watercolor from the floor, thinking aloud as she goes—"Hmm, color over form." Yes, you *are* more of a colorist. If only you could tamp a piece of paper over *everything* out there and take an impression while it's wet. Color pure and direct. "But there's also monochrome. Doing away with color right from the start."

"That's not 'doing away' with it. Black is the sum of all color. Not exclusion, total inclusion."

"*Ach so.*" Germanic Zen.

"And do you paint?" A counteroffensive.

"No. I just enjoy looking."

"As part of your work?"

"No, my job has nothing to do with art. I'm an accountant." Every year around this time, she tells you, once she's done balancing the books, she takes off and comes to Thailand. She used to paint when she was small, but no, she's not an artist. More of a critic by her own admission, she likes looking at other people's pictures. Rigorous, but not academic—a collector? Only Europe produces such people. Brainy heirs to gray light and cold stone architecture. The air in the room is still, yet you catch the same scent from yesterday.

"I did have one interesting experience painting not long ago," you offer. "In the southern part of Laos. A typical farming village scene—rice fields, palm trees, raised mud paths. Very picturesque, the palm trees especially. So I began to unpack my watercolors. The sky was a bit overcast, but the light was good. Saturated colors. So I went at it with a broad no. 16 sable flat.

Fifteen minutes and I was done and thinking about doing another picture, when all of a sudden the sky turns black and it starts to rain. Two minutes later I was in the middle of a tropical storm. I didn't even have time to put away my painting—no point anyway while it was still half-dry—so I wrote it off. My clothes were soaking wet and there was no shelter anywhere around. I just sat there in the rain."

Yes, it was a good twenty minutes' walk to the farmhouse where you were staying. Your first day, a bus had let you off in the middle of the village, where you started sketching one of the houses. People gathered to watch. You singled out one man, a little better fed than the rest, and drew his portrait to get on his good side. He put you up for the night. You didn't have to speak a common language; the picture translated. That's another "art" of yours—spongeing.

"So there I was, the painting I'd just finished dissolving before my eyes. The paper soaked through, the outlines blurring, fields and palm trees and sky all running together. As if seen though a fog. Or a rainstorm. My hair was all wet, my clothes were all wet, raindrops dripping from my eyelashes. I just sat there in the rain watching the picture change."

"Mm," came her guarded response.

"And you know, it looked more natural. As if my second-rate effort had been baptised by the rain and returned to nature. Amazing process . . . I saw a good painting make itself before my eyes. Or should I say 'unmake' itself?"

"Interesting."

"Yes, interesting. Though I couldn't claim to have painted it. Nature lent me a hand, rain's a much better painter. I could never intentionally get the same results. If I tried 'natural effects' they'd come out unnatural. Paradoxically, that's the trade-off. It wouldn't be art."

"You really think so?"

"If you're asking good pictures of nature, then you might as well not paint anything to begin with. Just gaze at the scenery and go home. But if there's a person, if it's me who's doing the painting, then there has to be some technique, some *doing* to it."

"The scenery is beautiful enough without you, my young painter friend.

But you're not painting for the scenery, you're painting for people."

"Exactly. The scenery is beautiful even without my being there. It was beautiful a thousand years ago, it'll be beautiful a thousand years from now. Assuming there are eyes around to see it. No need for pictures, just go and show it. Goodbye painter—I seem to be talking myself out of a job. So where to find a niche in the paradox? Some gap in the equation?"

"No, what sees the beauty is the soul of everyone who ever lived and died there. Seen from the other side, from the stillness of death, it must look even more beautiful. Think about it. Nothing left to intrude, all the dead can do is look." Inge spoke in low tones, darkly in tune with this rainy Southeast Asian afternoon. What was she saying? The dead, witness to the ages? "The world never dies. People who live in it, look at it, die. But by dying, people can finally see the world as it is. Only then does the scenery become a perfect canvas. If ghosts could paint, their art would be nature itself. Beauty with not a nuance lost."

What is she going on about? You can't think of anything to say. After an uneasy pause, you pick up the loose end of your Laos story. "Eventually the rain stopped. Just like that—gone. The sun came out and everywhere was shimmering in waves of mist. I peeled the wet watercolor off my drawing board and held it out in the breeze. Steaming like everything else. And after a while the paper began to dry. I sandwiched it into my paper block and walked my soggy way back to the house. Then I put the picture out in the sun."

"And?"

"When it dried, there was no picture at all. Just a piece of paper with a faint smear. I threw it away."

"Your picture was short-lived."

"Yes. Beautiful while wet."

"Because there was no real death in your painting."

What was that supposed to mean? Paint death into a picture? Dissolve death-pigments in water? No, you can't paint the perfect landscape. Nor can the dead, of course. But to have the eyes of the dead while still alive . . . What did Inge know that she wasn't telling? What was this bedraggled blonde doing here in backroads Asia anyway? In this rainstorm, talking about death?

7

KAORU

Next day Professor Inagaki, Attorney Gatir, and I caught the morning Garuda flight to Bali. As soon as we landed, the whole plane filled with that sickly sweet flower-and-fruit-and-soil smell again. Cloying, fetid, hostile. And this was only my second time here. How many times after this would I be in and out of Bali? When would I finally be free of here?

I'd called ahead and Wayang was there at the airport to meet us. Count one positive thing for Bali. He smiled when he saw me and waved. Naturally, I was happy to see him, and glad to be able to offer the others a lift. We all piled into the car, while Inagaki gave Wayang directions. On the road to Denpasar I looked out at all the colors. Garish reds and yellows and purples radiating out of the thick greenery. Intense sun and midnight shadows. Layer on layer of unbearably strong contrasts, even the soil burned with color. Back on this island, am I? This time Inagaki and Gatir might make a difference for Tez. I'd done part of what I set out to do.

I'd thought we were en route to the police station, when instead we pulled up in front of a small two-story building just outside of town.

"There's someone I want you to meet," said the Professor, getting out of the car.

I got out and looked up at the sign. It was a Japanese language school.

Inagaki introduced me to the principal. "This is Mr. Kondra, another good friend of mine," he said. "You're going to need an interpreter for the trial, if it comes to that. I hope you'll take him on."

Sole proprietor-instructor of the school, Kondra was in his mid-fifties. He seemed calm and composed, and spoke excellent Japanese. "I owe so much to Professor Inagaki. He put me through my studies in Japan. I only hope I can be of service." Very polite, too.

"Yes, we all owe him a lot." I bowed slightly to cover my confusion. So this was one of his Bali acquaintances. Yes, the trial probably would require language skills, and the man did seem to know his stuff. But hiring another stringer? Why hadn't he told me? What else had he already decided but neglected to mention? Was this his wartime experience taking command? Okay, what choice did I have at this point? I guess I should count myself lucky.

Introductions done, we all crammed back into Wayang's car and were off. The four of us, like Momotaro the Peach Boy in the Japanese children's story, with his entourage—Pheasant and Monkey and Dog. Or maybe more like Dorothy with the Tin Man and Cowardly Lion and Scarecrow from *The Wizard of Oz*—me being a girl and all.

At the lockup, Tez looked a lot better, if not quite back to normal. Still awfully pale, but maybe that was just by comparision. Everyone else here was so dark-skinned.

"Tetsuro," I said in my formal go-visiting voice, "I'd like you to meet Professor Inagaki, a famous Indonesia expert. And this is Attorney Gatir. And this is Mr. Kondra, who has consented to translate for us."

My brother bowed. Gatir came forward and began speaking in Indonesian, pausing every now and then for Kondra to translate into Japanese. Professor Inagaki looked on silently.

"As an initial step, I'll meet with the prosecutor this afternoon and see what I can find out. Our immediate aim is for a no-trial. Whether that's possible or not is hard to say just now, but let's not rule it out. At any rate, if I am to act on your behalf, you have to decide to engage my services." Whereupon he explained his fees for research and negotiating a no-trial.

Tez looked up with a start, as if he'd only just then remembered there was something called money in the world. "That's twenty percent of my annual income. I can afford that."

Kondra wondered whether to translate this back to the attorney, then stopped himself.

"You're on," said Tez in a clear voice. And for the first time so far, I felt Tez had some fight in him. I was so happy. I didn't know what I would have done if he'd bowed out now, saying "Please don't bother" or something.

"Then I accept," said Gatir (via Kondra's translation), maybe a touch overdramatically. Tez began to recap the events from the time he arrived in Bali up to the present, with the attorney taking notes and asking questions as he went. It was the most detail I'd heard, but it only confirmed that, while that Agus character may have hounded him, he had bought heroin, of his own volition. Guilty as charged of purchase and possession. He hadn't, however, smuggled any in, nor of course sold to anyone. Suddenly it seemed quite reasonable that we might get a no-trial on condition of deportation, swearing never to come back. Or was that wishful thinking?

Maybe so, because when Gatir heard that Tez had signed two testimonies, he raised his eyebrows. "Odd. Ordinarily there's only one transcript. Did you make sure both copies were identical?"

"No. They told me it was a duplicate."

"They might have got you there. It's a trick they sometimes use, especially with foreigners who don't know Indonesian. It could easily have been a completely different document."

"Oh, great," said Tez, with me wincing inside.

"Let's assume coercion. We can argue that you signed both papers because otherwise they'd deny you permission to see a lawyer. They, on the other hand, will insist you only signed one document. Still, I think we might get the testimony dismissed as evidence."

"Would we need to get it dismissed?" I asked.

"Probably," said Gatir gravely. "The police seem to be stacking the odds. In any case, I'll meet with the prosecutor."

At that the three of them left and headed for the hotel. Not a word out of Inagaki from beginning to end. I stayed on and talked to Tez, after arranging for Wayang to come back and pick me up.

"I brought you some paper and crayons. I'll pass them to the policeman later."

"Thanks. But I don't feel like drawing."

"Why not?"

"All I can see out the window is a small patch of sky and one branch. Seven damn leaves and no flowers. The sky's always blue, not even a cloud."

"We'll get you moved somewhere with a bigger window, you'll see. Professor Inagaki's got connections. Knows all the ins and outs here in Indonesia. He's our ticket."

"Oh."

I'd hoped he would have praised my efforts in locating such a luminary at short notice, or at least thanked me, but Tez seemed plain uninterested.

"How about the attorney?"

"What about him? He's the first lawyer I ever met in my life."

"Well, same here. But if we do get a no-trial, that'll solve everything, won't it?"

"Let's save the rejoicing for when it happens."

"I'm so glad you're in for the fight."

"Guess the heroin's out of my system," he said. "I want to get out and paint."

"You'll get out of here, I promise." Maybe it was irresponsible of me, but it seemed to reassure him. A bit too much, maybe—he didn't have a lot to say after that. I told him I'd be back tomorrow, and left him in the visitors' room. Outside, Wayang was waiting with the car.

That evening, our team got together, the four of us, at the hotel restaurant. Gatir reported on his meeting that afternoon with the prosecutor—in Indonesian for Professor Inagaki, with Kondra translating into Japanese for me.

"In a word, the no-trial line is going to be very difficult," he began. "The police chief is an academy man from the capital, smooth and eager to build up a quick track record and climb the ladder. Which means he's on top of this case. If he lines up his evidence and files a full report, there's no way they can avoid calling it to trial."

I held back my disappointment and focused on his lips. "Is that the end of it?"

"One option that leaves us is to try to get the Japanese embassy in Jakarta involved. Even the prosecutor himself said so. He has ties to the capital but seems committed to holding on to his post here in the provinces, an honest official by the look of him."

"What's going to be in the police chief's report?"

"Well, it being key evidence for the prosecution, he wouldn't say much, of course, but he did have me understand the content has been 'adjusted' substantially. It's very likely to say that your brother brought in a large amount of heroin with the intention of selling it. Hence we may assume that he was in fact tricked. Not a good situation, I fear."

A moment of silence passed between those present. I felt outraged all over again, but kept my feelings to myself. I guess that meant we were going to trial.

The professor spoke up first. "I'm heading back to Tokyo tomorrow via Jakarta. I'll touch base with the embassy, but it's up to you, Kaoru, to meet with the ambassador or liaison officer as soon as possible. I've seen my share of ambassadors rotate through, but that doesn't give me any special lever-age. You have to be the one doing the asking. I'll just give 'em the general picture."

"Thank you." I didn't know what else to say. I guess I was kind of worked up.

Meanwhile Inagaki and Gatir adjourned to another room. No, I wouldn't ask what they couldn't talk about in front of me. I'm sure I just looked worried, and they didn't want to upset me. Fake reports, crooked trials—what more was in store?

The next thing I knew, Mr. Kondra was there in front of me. I hadn't noticed how big his eyes were. Large lips, broad nose, very black hair—a trustworthy sort of face. Still I felt uneasy. Maybe I really was all alone here, isolated and without support; maybe everyone was just leading me on. Kondra looked at me patiently. "*Daijobu*," he said, trying to comfort me. "It's all right. Things will work out, they generally do."

"Yes, I guess they do," I said, though inside I was fuming—*What did he know!* Even so, soothed by his fluent Japanese, I decided to wear a happy face for another five seconds. I had to remind myself how ineffectual I'd be on my own. I needed to do something about my attitude. "Can we talk here for a moment?"

"Yes, of course. I must say, I admire you, a young person holding up under the strain of something as big as this."

"He's my brother." Some explanation. Who wouldn't help their own brother? But Tez wasn't just any brother, he was the only one I had. "Tetsuro is a great artist. Paints wonderful pictures. Sees things no else one can. His pictures are that good. He's painted me, too."

"Painting is a valuable gift. Artists are highly respected on this island."

"Tell me more about Bali." I wanted to change the subject; all this talk about Tez was getting to me.

"Ah well, Bali . . . It's special," said Kondra. Like "He's my brother," a flat declaration, very emotional, explaining nothing. "Indonesia's a big country. Not that big is necessarily good, but the country *is* bigger than most Japanese people realize. It covers forty-one degrees longitude east to west, with five times the surface area of Japan and one and a half times the population."

"Really?"

"Sorry, I slipped into my schoolteacher's voice."

"Don't apologize. It's easy to follow."

"But, well, Indonesia was originally so many different little island-states, each with its own individual culture. It came together as a kind of federation. Probably no one short of a dictatorial leader could run it."

"You mean Suharto?"

"Now, yes. Before that, Sukarno. That much said, the island of Bali is something of an anomaly. Indonesia is predominantly Muslim. Only here is Hindu. Islam never gained a foothold. There were too many gods here, too many demons."

"Which is why you offer them so many flowers?"

"Definitely. Every day we offer them *chanan*. We placate them with music and plays. We have grand festivals. It's endless. I can't even begin to tell you, not at a time like this. But you should see Bali for yourself; it's not the evil place you think caught your brother in a trap."

"What do *you* reckon? Was it a trap?"

"In a way. No doubt you'll think me prejudiced if I say it was all the doing of the Javanese police chief posted here. But you see, to us Balinese, the Javanese are a different race. The Javanese are sharper, better at business, quicker to succeed. We're more passive, always thinking about gods and demons and fun and games. Which is good *and* bad."

"Fun and games?"

"All sorts. Really, just about anything: dancing, music, theater, festivals, funerals, crafts, cockfighting, painting—we enjoy it all. Whatever's going on, the whole village gets into the act and that's all they think about. Then they get tired of that and something else begins. If you feel up to it, you really should take a look around Bali, there's so much to see. It would do you good. After all the misfortunes you and your brother have met with on this island."

"Yes, I guess so," I answered. This was no time to be sightseeing. But in order to fight for Tez, it helped to believe that his enemies—our enemies —weren't Balinese. I wanted it to be true. Talking to this man was, I don't know, relaxing. More than with Gatir, for sure. More than even Inagaki. Kondra's musical Japanese gave me a living color image of the place, the people in the street. Those enticing words of his made my hardened feelings waver.

"Do you think my brother was a fool?" I asked him on a sudden impulse.

"How do you mean?"

"I mean, his getting addicted in the first place. Because even the trap— if it was a trap—depended on his addiction." That horrible word.

Kondra thought it over. "Let me tell you about King Nara," he began, then paused as if trying to remember how the story went. "It's from the ancient Indian epic, the *Mahabharata*."

"I've heard of it at least. Never read it, though."

"Well, you see, this being Hindu territory, the *Mahabharata* is part of life here. The whole of Balinese culture is literary as well as theatrical and mythological." Did I detect a hint of pride in Kondra's voice? Could I, an interpreter like him, talk about Japan with such pride? When French people made their farfetched comments about Japanese culture, I generally argued right back. That was more anger than pride (then and only then, my French poured out in torrents.) It just made me so mad to be lectured about my own culture by ignoramuses. But would Kondra, proud as he was of Bali, take similar offense? Somehow I just couldn't imagine him ever getting mad.

"King Nara cut a dashing figure," said Kondra, assuming the tone of a storyteller. "And this magnificent king fell in love with a beauty, sight unseen, in another kingdom: Princess Damayanti by name—and very voluptuous she was, as Indian princesses tend to be. Well, she likewise fell in love with King Nara, sight unseen. But as Damayanti was the royal princess of the land, the selection of her consort was a matter of state. Many suitors came forth, men of superior standing and even four gods as well. She was that beautiful, you see.

"Of course, Damayanti chose to be wedded to King Nara. Whereupon the four gods turned themselves into the very image of the king, which played havoc with everything. Except that gods cast no shadow and gods don't sweat, so you could tell them apart if you looked carefully. Thus the two were happily wed, and in due course a daughter and son were born.

"The evil goddess Kali, however, was jealous of the couple. She incited the king's younger brother to challenge him at gambling, while Kali transformed herself into a pair of dice, so there was no way that King Nara could win."

"Very sneaky."

"Exactly. The king gambled away all the gold and silver statues in the palace, then forfeited his many chariots and jewels and other adornments. Each time he lost, he flew into a rage, but always found something to wager next. He always lost, but he couldn't stop gambling. He kept thinking next time he might win, just one more roll of the dice and he'd get back all he'd lost. So the competition went on forever, and he was reduced to dire poverty. Any bystander could see it, but he himself was blind to what was happening. Plead as Damayanti might, he had no ears. Such is the nature of gambling." Kondra paused and looked at me.

"After many months of this, the king had lost his kingdom and all his possessions. Finally, when there was nothing more to bet with, his brother asked, 'Care to wager your wife?' That was the final blow. The king stormed off, as did Damayanti, each their separate ways, each to great hardships. But in the end they came back together and lived happily ever after."

"And . . . ?"

". . . And so, there are traps in this world not even the smartest people can escape. Gambling is one of them. And drugs are surely another."

"And maybe drinking too."

"Ah, not in Bali. People are already drunk on the air here—no need for alcohol. It's true, there are literally no alcoholics here in Bali."

The following day, I returned to Jakarta with Professor Inagaki. And the next morning, after he headed on back to Japan, I went to the Japanese embassy as arranged and met with the liaison officer. With the result that —conclusions first—I learned the embassy would not become involved. Exactly what the consul in Bali told me. Their official duty was to the Japanese people as a whole, not necessarily to each and every citizen. Intervening in another country's due process was, as a rule, not something they liked to do.

"It's most unfortunate," said the liaison officer, "but we cannot press the Indonesian side for a no-trial. While diplomacy has its bargaining aspect not unlike trading, were we to ask the national government here in Jakarta to have the regional prosecutor in Bali bury the case, we would be racking up a very big debit. Giving them a wild card to play, as it were, which would be counter to our own national interests. We diplomats must be able to cost out these things, you know. Even Professor Inagaki himself admitted as much."

"Which is to say my brother isn't worth the trouble to you."

"We're not in a position to judge the worth of each individual in need."

"Though in the Customs officer bribery case last spring, didn't the embassy take action?"

"Professor Inagaki told you about that, did he?" said the official, looking rather displeased. "Those were special circumstances. Up until then it was the accepted practice to pay certain under-the-table gratuities in order to speed up Customs clearance. Then one day, out of nowhere, government policy changed and it was suddenly regarded as bribery. Moreover, they neglected to inform foreign trading companies. So all at once there were multiple arrests. Now, cleaning up 'hidden fees' and payoffs is all very commendable, but where is the necessity in arresting twenty foreign import-export traders to enforce this policy, I ask you? Nor were we the only ones: Australia, Luxembourg, India, many countries issued strong protests to the Indonesian government on this account."

"I'll take your word for it," I conceded.

"A country has its pride, just as a person has his. No country likes others interfering in its internal affairs. Especially in the case of a crime committed by a foreigner."

The word "crime" rubbed me the wrong way. I wanted out of there. Call me a quitter, but when I see an entrenched position, I run out of things to say. Beg, plead, what's the use?

"However, it may interest you to know that we have looked into the matter, and it seems that, at this particular moment, the Indonesian government is cracking down on drug crimes. There is talk of pressure from America. Or perhaps the American First Lady Mrs. Reagan's War on Drugs campaign of a few years back still strikes a receptive note with Mrs. Suharto. Nancy Reagan's nephew died from drugs, as you will recall."

"And in such cases, a nation swallows its pride?"

"America—that is, the American government—is a special player. Treated specially by every country in the world. That's just the way things are."

"Oh, is that so?"

"If the outcome of the trial is very bad, we might be able to take steps to have the punishment reduced or commuted. This is not without precedent."

"You mean, if they hand down a death sentence."

"Well, in situations of that sort."

"Thank you very much. I'll try my best not to let it come to that." That was the most I could bring myself to say under the circumstances. So a trial was unavoidable. With maybe a noose waiting at the end of it. The liaison officer certainly seemed quite blasé about it all. Here Tez was about to be strung up on bogus drug-trafficking charges, and he treated it like a poker game, played with wild cards! Who were these men? It was these very same bastards Tez and I would now have to face in court. Japanese or Javanese, no difference whatsoever.

Yes, a trial was inevitable. I resigned myself to the fact. Everything up to now had just been skirmishes. First-round eliminations. Now the real battle began.

I met with Attorney Gatir. We had to hire him now, I guess, so we needed to talk money. Inagaki had said he was highly competent and well connected and influential, but all that came at a price. Well, whatever the expense, I couldn't just stand by and do nothing. For the time being at least, money was one factor that could be dealt with.

The attorney estimated the total expenses for the trial would come to one and a half times Tez's annual income. That included his own fees, plus incidentals and running costs. (Just what these running costs were, I didn't ask.) He couldn't promise the outcome, of course, but he would make every effort to steer clear of a death sentence. Attack weak points in the prosecution's case. And ensure that the fake testimony got thrown out of court. He'd also try to work various angles behind the scenes. What choice did I have but to believe him?

Now to come up with the money. So far I'd been operating out of Tez's bankbook. Sufficient for a no-trial perhaps, but no year-and-a-half of Tez's earnings. The balance had dwindled considerably, and on top of the court costs, I needed money to keep chasing around here in Indonesia. So I flew back to Bali and met with Tez. I told him the embassy wouldn't do anything and that we'd have to go to court.

Tez just sat there, pretty much as I expected. "Have to borrow from someone. It's not so much I couldn't pay it back with two or three years of solid work and no traveling. *If* in how-many-years I get out of here and start painting salable pictures again. *If* I still have it in me."

"Don't say that."

"*If* I can survive this, that, and the other thing," said Tez gloomily.

"Everything'll be fine, you'll see," I answered out of pure reflex.

"I don't know. Big powers are at play here, forces neither you nor I can see. I feel like a mouse who's wandered into an elephant cage," he protested weakly.

"Anyway, we've got to try." Where did I dredge up these platitudes?

"Sure," he smiled sadly. "For the time being let's assume no death sentence. We borrow the money from somewhere and hire that expensive lawyer and stand trial. If all goes well, I get a short sentence and, some years later when I'm free, I earn enough money to pay back the loan. That's assuming my pictures will still sell into the next decade, but trends change."

"Since when did you ever pay attention to trends? People have always come running to you. That's popularity. I wouldn't worry, by that time you'll be a legend, an Old Master. Your signature will be worth hundreds of thousands. You'll have *carte blanche* to the big annual shows, the Cultural Medal of Honor. Think optimistic, or you'll never do anything." Inside I was almost in tears. Looking at Tez, I could feel the weight on my shoulders. There was to be a trial. My brother's life would be debated, his murder contemplated dispassionately in the name of justice. And us trying to tilt the scales of life and death to the side of the living.

"About the money, I'll go back to Japan and talk to Mom and Dad. We'll figure out a way." In all this time, had I even mentioned the folks to Tez? Maybe right at first, to say they were worried. No, this was nothing Mom or Dad would understand. This was our territory. Change countries and all the bases for reasoning change. And the situation here was totally unreasonable, out of bounds to Japanese common sense. Both Tez and I could see that as clear as day. But money was different; *that* we could talk about. Money was common international ground—for just about anything.

I flew back to Japan. There just wasn't much time. Gatir had also told me to gather material to lend credence to Tez's background—the Outstanding Career and Reputation of Tetsuro Nishijima. Not that producing some of his paintings in court would induce the judge to drop the case; the important thing was to give Tez a face, to establish his standing. Articles and reviews of exhibitions, letters from big names, magazines with Tez's artwork, interviews —I had to scrape together whatever written and visual stuff I could find.

While one part of me was listing up these character references, another part was wondering what good it would do. A talented artist should be spared some degree of punishment—was that the idea? Would a judge think like that? Tez is a talented artist, clearly. Someone not half as gifted, like myself for instance, wouldn't have a thing to show. I could just see me standing there before the judge, an empty-handed nonentity. But then again, why should a scrapbook of my brother's work as an illustrator in Japan mean anything at all on this island? What is "reputation" anyway?

Back in Tokyo, I went and told the folks that a trial was unavoidable. "Damn fool," was all Dad would say. Exactly the sort of thing a Japanese father could be expected to say. Though the sad thing was, not only couldn't he fathom Tez's art, he couldn't understand the upcoming trial either. If anything, he felt embarrassed by the whole thing.

"Can't something be done?" Mom implored. "Can't we appeal to some-one with influence?"

"Professor Inagaki is plenty influential, but all *he* could do was find us a good lawyer."

"We'll find the money somehow. We're his parents, we can't just aban-don him."

"But do you have any?"

"Whether we do or don't is not the issue. If we mortgage the house, we can borrow three times the amount. Or sell this place. With both of you flown the nest, I'd been thinking Father and I might as well be living in a smaller place, anyway. A condominium or something."

"Don't be ridiculous, it's not *that* much," said Dad.

"He'd pay you back with interest fair and square," I suggested.

"Do parents charge their own children interest?"

I tuned out. It would have been even worse if Tez had been there to listen in. Championed by his kid sister, bailed out by his parents, and he himself unable to paint one measly picture. All I meant by the idea of paying interest was that it would make things a little less emotional, given that the folks were bound to get worked up.

The next day, I went to Tez's apartment, packed up his artwork and paints and books, and arranged to have them put into storage. The rent wasn't all that much, really, but every little bit helped. Not much in the way of furniture anyway; he'd told me to sell it or toss it.

It was a few days afterwards that my mother rang. "I was just reading in the newspaper. Why don't you try to contact these people for help—Amnesty International? It says right here, 'Helping innocent people everywhere.'"

I knew the organization by name, of course, but hadn't made the connection with Tez. I sort of had the impression they dealt more with political cases.

". . . And Tez *is* innocent," Mom stressed tremulously.

I thought it over, and the next day, when I called Professor Inagaki with a progress report, I asked him about it. He practically blew a fuse: "You haven't got a clue, I swear! That's a bunch of self-righteous Western crusaders who blindly foist their values onto developing countries. Activists dead set on fanning the fires of American media to apply pressure."

"And what's wrong with that?"

"What's wrong with *that*?" he fumed. "Well, just you listen here. There's all sorts of countries in the world. Countries that even imprison and torture and execute their political enemies and opposition groups without warrant or trial. Yes, I know, sometimes outside observers can help improve the situation a little. But the people in that organization don't understand what makes countries tick. Because all countries have their pride. Even in places suffering under a dictator, if you start pointing fingers from the outside it can backfire. It's never black-and-white.

"You see, this Amnesty crew of yours simply can't abide nationalism. But without some kind of unifying gravitational force, no country's going to last. In the final analysis, no matter how reprehensible the system, it's better than no system at all. And the people know it—being reduced to refugees without a home leaves 'em totally exposed and unprotected. That's why they rally around the banner of nationalism. Look at Japan—after the Sino-

Japanese War when we grabbed part of China, then were forced to hand it back, the average citizen didn't give a hoot about international politics, he just went on shouting. That was nationalism. Pride and outrage. It's a messy thing, because there's no accounting for emotions."

"No, I suppose not." I gulped down my ignorance.

"Now, if Amnesty got into the act, the Indonesian media would play it up in a big way. 'Japanese smuggles in drugs, international organization schemes to cover for villain.' Coverage inside the country would blow it all out of proportion, and that police chief in Denpasar would be grinning all the way to Jakarta, am I right?"

"Yes, I see your point."

"Indonesia is a multi-ethnic nation. That alone should tell you why they need nationalism for unity. It's not just the leaders pushing, the people themselves want it that way. If they hear outsiders saying it's a horrible country that arrests innocent foreigners on trumped-up charges, they're going to build up that trial just to prove what a wonderful, law-abiding place it is. They'll boast far and wide how fair and honest they are. In gambling terms, you've just raised the stakes. And with the eyes of a hundred million Indonesians on him, that judge's going to hand down a death sentence whether he wants to or not. Am I right?"

"Yes," I agreed, my voice shrinking.

"Trials are theater. Showmanship. Forget any notions you might have about justice or truth. Big words, that's all they are. No, if I was you, I'd inch things forward as quietly as possible, slowly and surely past the public eye and right out the back door. That's why I was saying, spend however much you've got to spend behind the scenes for a no-trial. Only we were up against the wrong opponent. That promotion-hungry police chief got in the way."

"Yes." I shrank even more.

"Don't make this thing any bigger. Don't call in any more players. There are folks both inside Indonesia and out who'd love a chance to make a name for themselves. The same goes for the Japanese media. They're out for blood, too. Amidst all the commotion, any discussion of what your brother did or didn't do will go up in smoke. Am I right?"

"Ye-es."

"The public's always looking for scapegoats, too. Gets them all excited. Thumbs up or down—it's all the same. A soccer match with a human ball. The public is always bored, ready and waiting. And the media are in business to feed 'em what they want to hear. Some poor fool's bound to toss himself in as the next ball to be kicked around."

"Yes, okay. I see your point." Did I ever! I saw Tez's precarious position only too well.

Three days later, I returned to Bali. Not knowing how long I would be staying this time, I decided I'd slum it at backpacker lodgings in Kuta, instead of my fancy hotel in Sanur. Fall in with those eastbound hippie customers for my bargain fares out of Paris. Only *I* didn't have worlds of time for touring or trekking or anything. I had to economize, conserve energy—those were my priorities at this point.

I considered staying at Pandra Cottages where my brother was arrested —for about half a second. No, I had to lie low, remain inconspicuous. Who did I think I was, a detective? Did I really think I could sniff up evidence after the police made their clean sweep? Inagaki made sense—don't make a scene, get the trial over with, slip Tez out of the country.

The place I found was in an area called Legian. A little one-room cottage. One bed, small desk and chair, mini-kitchen. No air conditioning, just windows with screens and shutters. If I was going to be living here, I needed to stick to a daily budget.

Meanwhile Gatir was hard at work: conferring with Tez every day, doing the rounds to size up the situation. I now had cash in hand, so we all got together with Tez—the four of us, Mr. Kondra included—and signed contracts. And with that, the trial really began for us.

The first time I went to court was the day of the first hearing. Entered through a corridor waiting area, the courtroom was barely twice the size of a kindergarten classroom. Lots of tall windows and a large fan circling slowly on the high ceiling. Extra spectators turned out, so many it made me nervous. Maybe even some newspaper reporters. Why couldn't they restrict this to concerned parties only? I felt exposed. Who were these prying eyes, these stares? Both for Tez and for me, the real agony was yet to come.

The judge entered directly through a door at the back. Everyone rose. The judge was a woman, wearing square-framed glasses that looked like two TVs. *Please*—I addressed her in my heart of hearts—*please look carefully. Listen carefully. Think carefully. Judge Tez correctly.* It was all show, Inagaki had said, but if somehow the truth did get across to this judge, if she just saw things for what they were, she couldn't make such a bad ruling. *Politics might force its way into this courtroom, but please don't knuckle under.*

The righthand door opened and in came Tez. He was in handcuffs. Eyes downcast, he bowed once to the judge, then took his seat and was uncuffed. He didn't so much as look toward the spectators' gallery. From where I sat I could see the side of his face, and Mr. Kondra directly behind him. The judge sat up straight and the whole courtroom went silent. The bailiff then announced the court was in session. It was all in Indonesian so I didn't understand a word; I could only just make out my brother's name and that of the country in the case—The People of Indonesia vs Tetsuro Nishijima.

Tez rose when his name was called. The judge looked over her brief, then formally addressed him: "Is the defendant the Japanese citizen Tetsuro Nishijima?" Mr. Kondra translated this into Tez's ear, and he answered "Yes, that is correct."

The prosecutor, sitting to the left, then rose, walked to the front of the courtroom, and began to read from his papers. I glanced at my notes (Attorney Gatir had given Tez and me a rundown on standard court proceedings); this was the bill of indictment. He was accusing Tez of bringing two hundred grams of foreign heroin into the country from Thailand with intention to sell. The syllables assaulted my ears like accusations. The statement drew to a close.

Now the judge spoke, and my brother was brought forward to plead—guilt or not guilty. "I admit to buying two grams of heroin after arriving in Bali," he said in Japanese, "but I deny all other charges." Kondra translated for the court, then Gatir proceeded to read out a brief statement to the same effect, while Kondra simultaneously interpreted back to Tez.

I grew antsy. I wasn't getting the essential parts. Apart from my brother's Japanese, I hadn't understood a thing that was being said. I could observe the judge and prosecutor and attorney, their expressions. I could hear the buzz from the spectators' gallery. But I couldn't follow a word. For me, the whole court session was a pantomime from start to finish.

8

TETSURO

↑
○

"People always tell you how wonderful life is," Inge said out the window to the rain. "What a blessing it is to emerge from the cold, dead void and breathe warm air for however long, to hear the proteins at play in the body. To fall in love, to lie in the sun—every good experience the cosmos has to offer. Everyone says so."

Her voice sank lower as she gathered herself in. Smaller, but still a large foreign presence. Then, leaning closer to you, she looked you straight in the eye. Her voice so chilling you forgot you were waiting out a tropical storm in Thailand.

"Life, the so-called miracle of existence. Most wondrous work in all Creation. Maybe even *the* reason why the whole universe exists. Everyone sings its praises—but I tell you, it's not like that at all. Life is only a tiny bubble on the surface of a deep, dark sea. Go down three meters, there's not even a ripple. Things underneath are on a far grander scale."

"Okay. The rocks and earth and stars and nebulae may not be protein, but in a way they're living, aren't they? In the long view of things. They're born, they change, they die."

Inge's face lit up, a crystal with an inner light. "Exactly my point. We die, but we don't revert to absolute zero. We don't turn into *non*-phenomena. Only the speed changes. After death the body quickly decomposes, but that's just the life-spring winding down, uncoiling from such impossible compression. After that, we slow to the pace of the rocks and stars. That's the real thing. Life's just in too much of a hurry."

"But that one flash of life *is* beautiful."

"No, wrong again. The glacial, inorganic world, closer to what we call death, is far more beautiful." Spoken like the looking glass to the evil queen's "Mirror, mirror, on the wall." "People are distracted by what moves before their eyes. More important is what lies underneath. Not the waves on the surface, the unmoving depths of the sea. Eternal calm in thousand-year increments. You have to see things at the speed of bones petrifying."

"And what if I happen to like to paint morning flowers that bloom for only a few short hours?"

"Don't get me wrong, I like your paintings. But not because you paint flowers that fade. Behind each blossom you can see an eternity . . . far beyond the life of the flower—that's what makes your flower paintings beautiful. They pretend to exalt the moment when actually they aspire to eternity. Life is short, but it only looks precious backed up by eons of mineral time. I don't have to tell you, you know it already yourself."

"Do I?"

"It's very simple. Contrast. Here's a hundred-year human lifespan alongside rocks that never change in a hundred thousand years. Here's a morning glory that's open for scarcely two hours against the two-billion-year blue of the sky."

"I never think about things like that when I'm painting."

"Not consciously perhaps, but somewhere deep down inside you *know*."

"How can you be so sure?"

"Just look at your pictures."

You couldn't dispute her logic. Who knows?—maybe that's where the critical difference lay between your best paintings and the rest of your output: this dual time frame.

"The reason movies never escape the secular is because they're trapped in realtime. Film is a device for counterfeiting time. Useless. You can't film a rock that's not going to change for thousands of years. That's where painting and carving differ. What's painted already belongs to mineral time. A thousand years from now and the painted rock will still be here. Think of Lascaux—the painting itself is stone."

"So, say I paint in constant awareness of the rocks and stars, would that be better?"

"It's not that simple and you know it." Inge made it sound like she'd known you for decades, through each rise and fall in your career. And what if she were right? "Turn to stone, and discover the happiness of stone. The pleasures of living are all too brief. A stone is far more secure in its happiness, if only because it has no way of changing so quickly. That's what you've got to realize. I'm a Westerner, but I think Westerners are crazy. Always chasing after the fastest, latest, and greatest, forgetting the unchanging firmament that's behind everything. Christians think they have to beat the Last Judgment. Whereas the Eastern ideal, according to my studies, is to make oneself stone-still. To transcend the pulse of life into timelessness, a still point looking on the phenomenal world. Go beyond the pain of *doing* to merely observing. Ultimately to just *being*. A Japanese ink painting of a waterfall may seem like a fleeting image, but really it's about *being* a waterfall— a singular, eternal waterfall. Western artists don't even paint waterfalls."

"What about mandalas?" you asked out of nowhere. Inge was taken aback.

"What do *you* think?" she hedged a second later.

"They represent the truth. Pure principle. On the level of the eternal, not the here-and-now."

"Well, maybe. I wouldn't know . . ." She went silent, staring off into space.

"Basically, if you ask me, painting is technique. There are good painters and bad painters, and that's all there is to it. No need for your difficult philosophy."

"No." She met your eyes head-on again. "As long as you think that way, you'll never go all the way. You'll just be a very skillful, very boring painter."

Touché. You could think of several artists who fitted that description. No, didn't want that fate.

Neither of you said another word. The rain was getting heavier and heavier. Thinking back on it later, would things have gone on to the next level if it hadn't been raining so hard?

After a while, Inge dropped a peculiar comment into the silence. "I come here once a year to get stone-still and enjoy my own death. Then I go home."

Some cryptic reference to sex? Were Thai boys her thing?

"To live as an organism is to respond to the outside world in minute increments. It's so much nicer just to stretch out and do nothing. Unresponding, completely self-sealed. Not moving a finger, existing on sight alone."

"And how do you do that?"

"By experiencing death ahead of time."

"Like I said—*how*?"

"It feels so good. To turn to stone, to stop measuring time in decades and centuries. A living thing is half pleasure, half pain—that's just how life is. But a rock is granted pure pleasure rarified over a very very long time. No pain. Like sleeping, only fully conscious. Not dreaming. Seeing this reality as the dream of a stone."

You became apprehensive. What was this woman talking about?

"You'd see. Paintings embody a different light. Up to now in your work you've been oblivious to the most important thing. You've been going about it the long way around."

"How's that?"

"Do it once, and everything from then on is different. Like a steel blade once it's been tempered. The cutting edge changes."

What was she saying you should do?

"I come here once a year to fossilize, pass millions of years in a few hours, and with the strength that gives me I can just about carry on for another year. I gain a superhuman perspective on all things human—from local neighborhood goings-on to office relations to international politics. Nothing fazes me any more after that. Viewed on an absolute scale, from the viewpoint of a rock, everything is relative. Nothing matters very much. But to ensure that mental state, I have to come here once a year."

"And do what?" She still hadn't said one thing concrete.

"Lie down, not do anything. Not even think. You're a thing that happens to occupy this shape—it's bliss! No mind, no real body either. Just the contour and position of each finger, inside its skin. Volume and displacement, filled up with you. That simple fact converts into pure pleasure. And not by force of logic, no pleasure you get any other way."

By that stage you didn't even bother to ask. You looked past her, backlit in the gloom, lips reflecting a faint glint of light, until her droning voice sounded like distant thunder.

"If I tempted you here and now, what would you say?" Inge's expression relaxed slightly.

"I'd say yes, I'd love to," you heard yourself answer.

Was she waiting for a proposition? Hadn't really considered it, but okay. "I've been well behaved—up to now. Trying not to think about it. Out of courtesy. But talking to you here like this, I can't very well stop these thoughts. I don't ordinarily chase after women, but you radiate such . . . In my mind, I'm already undressing you."

Inge defused you. "No, I've given up on all that. There were times in Germany, an affair that lasted half a year . . . but no, here I don't feel a thing. Stones don't have sex."

You moved over beside her. "Stones aren't this soft or warm." You reached out and took her hand, almost grazing the swell of her breast.

"You're very nice and flattering. But like I said, it's no good." She withdrew her hand.

You weren't really serious, so no harm done. Only a casual foray that fizzled. So you got up and returned to your place on the bed.

"There's a TV camera mounted at the busiest intersection in Frankfurt," Inge began again, all serious. "Shoots all day in time-lapse. At first light there are only a few people about, cars speeding through each green signal. But lengthen the intervals and even those flickering ghost-images vanish. All you can see are the buildings and streets and a few trees—things that don't move, though the trees do blur a little if there's a breeze. When I saw that, I said to myself, that's what a stone sees. Living things are just squiggly residues, hardly even visible. Leach out everything that moves in micro-dimensions—an hour, a day, a year—then the real landscape emerges."

The rain seemed to be letting up. Outside it grew a bit lighter, bringing some slight definition to her backlit face, her eyebrows, the tiny golden hairs on her cheeks, even as the shadows deepened in the room by contrast. For a second you considered getting out your drawing pad, but you were captive to her incantation. Immobilized.

"And the same with man-made things. Ever been to Angkor Wat?"

You shook your head. Your face in the window light must have been visible to Inge, your intrigued expression. No, never been to Angkor. Wanted to, but wasn't Cambodia still in a civil war?

"Fifteen years ago, I went. It's incredibly beautiful, truly a marvel. One whole day I spent walking around it, examining the sculptures one by one. Overwhelming, the sheer scale, the human labor to create it. There was just one thing I couldn't understand. Something that made it seem greater-than-man-made, something in the combination of stone and light. An unidentifiable element, though at the time I had no idea what."

You had no idea where this story was leading either. So just sat still and listened.

"Ten years ago, I came here and found the means of decelerating body and mind. And what I discovered, what I hadn't understood at Angkor Wat, was the time factor. The initial construction must have taken a matter of decades. But then the millennia began seeping in, wholly transforming it. And *that* is what I saw. An immensity of time stored up in the thing itself. An otherness to rival the mountains and the seas."

You listened, just listened.

"Discarding all that's ephemeral, wiping away the telltale hand, the chisel marks, leaving only the unwavering inertial mass. Time goes to work all by itself. The most breathtaking thing at Angkor Wat is that gallery of mythological carvings, the *Mahabharata* there in solid form. And what makes it so beautiful is, all those Hindu myths have weathered such eons. Myths aren't made of stone, yet over the ages myth becomes as durable as stone—myth made manifest in those carvings."

The sun had shifted, illuminating the left side of Inge's face. A glow from behind her ear.

"Through that secret something, I experienced myself as one of the gods in that myth, carved there forever in solid joy. I understood what it is to be divine. Immortal. Pleasure beyond the phenomenal, pleasure that is existence itself. That's why I come here every year. I see everything, I see through death, nothing frightens me."

She fell silent, having apparently said all there was to say. You too said nothing, but your next words were already swelling inside. *What is this something that justifies coming here year after year?* So near your fingertips, yet still out of reach. No, don't ask.

"What is it?" The words escaped.

"I can't tell."

"Can't tell what?"

"I can't tell if you're up to it. Here I've led you on this far . . . I just don't know if it's the right thing. Maybe not everyone is meant for myth."

"No way of knowing unless we try."

"I suppose. Yesterday, I saw your picture and I gave you my thoughts on it. One meter to the side and it would have been completely different. That one meter is the difference between living organism and rock. This may be overstepping my powers of judgment, but when I saw that painting I thought, he's still caught in the temporal scale, the minor workings of clock time."

You let your silence coax more out of her.

"To be honest, you're one of the most powerful painters I've ever run across. Last night, thinking about your picture, I couldn't sleep. A very powerful image. I remembered what you said looking down over the temple. I couldn't help thinking, what if he were to experience that same liberation as I've known? What if he were able to escape biological time, move his vantage point just one more meter to the side."

"So, let me ask you one last time, what is this secret thing of yours?"

Vietnam is a gentle place. Remember when you rode the train for thirty hours from Ho Chi Minh to Hue, and spent the next few days there sketching around the quiet old capital? The palace and girls in their white *aodai* tunics. Then another short train ride north to Quang Tri, and a couple of days there before taking a bus over the Annam Mountains to Khe Sanh. Instead of staying at this site of some of the worst fighting in the Vietnam

War, you boarded another bus. Two hours south over mountain roads, you got off in a small village—just a place where a clutch of locals unload their masses of bags and boxes and baskets. One of them even dangles three chickens tied together by their feet. Your only luggage is a smallish backpack with an aluminum frame that doubles as a campstool and a drawing board.

After a short walk along the main road, surfaced but rolling with rises and falls, you're way up in the hills. People walk past half-looking at you, curious but too polite to stare. You need water, but where to get it? No watercolors then. You set down your pack by the side of the road, and start a pastel tableau of the village houses and the mountains beyond. All soft and misty, but not the natural province of pastels. Paper's too slick, no tooth to it. Still, your roadside artist pose has the desired effect: kids gather around, looking over your shoulder, pushing each other aside. Saying whatever they're saying.

Once you've finished your first sheet, you look up at the kids. Shy smiles and naughty squeals, trying to hide behind one another, pointing fingers in judgment of your picture—they can scarcely contain themselves. You pick the smartest-looking one of the bunch and gesture for him to step out in front. The other kids all jostle to push him forward. As soon as he crouches down, you pull out a new sheet of paper and begin to draw his face, now suddenly all serious. A hush falls over the kids. They watch spellbound— your hand in motion, roughing in the outlines, deftly adding the features, touching up shaded details, finally shifting his head-on gaze slightly to put a far-off look in his eyes.

You can now relax, turn the board around, and show the boy your handiwork. What does he make of his own face? Does he even have a mirror at home? Not that this is a mirror image. But not a bad likeness, hmm? After a few seconds, he breaks into a shy, happy smile.

Now to move on to the real task at hand and begin negotiations. Out with the canvas pail. You pantomime drinking, you want water. He understands in a flash and flies off with the pail while the others give chase. Meanwhile you file away the boy's portrait in your travel portfolio. Five minutes later the water arrives. You start looking around for a nice bit of scenery. The kids trail after you as expected. A short climb brings you to a small shrine where the surrounding greenery makes an attractive composition. Now to paint in earnest. The kids huddle behind you to look on, surprisingly well-behaved. This time, however, it's slow going. Over an hour to get all the elements—form and color, light and shadow—down on paper with your brush. Slowly, patiently . . . it's looking good.

Half the kids have deserted you. The rest are fooling around, only occasionally checking back on your progress, dipping fingers into the brush water to see if it stains. Only the boy who posed for you is standing guard like a watchdog. He seems to be the oldest, the most interested in art. Maybe you should leave him some paper and crayons?

At last the picture is finished. You put away the drawing board as soon as it's dry. The sun's already starting to go down, time to find a place to stay tonight. You stand up and bundle up your equipment, toss the leftover water, and look over at the boy. You gesture bowl-and-chopstick, arm-and-pillow, counting-money, then trace a house shape in the air and motion in the direction of the village. Right away the boy nods and tugs you by the hand.

The boy leads you to his own home. A small thatched house on the far edge of the village, backing onto a mountain forest away from the rice fields. No, this is too small, they won't be able to put you up. Usually they lead you to the biggest house in the village, where the extra burden won't be felt, but this boy's just so happy to have met a foreign artist, he never considered what his parents would say. Don't want to disappoint him, but they'll probably raise a fuss and you'll have to go elsewhere. Okay, wait and see.

Soon a young woman comes out, the boy's mother. While the son beams with pleasure over his catch, she looks more than a little upset—but lovely to look at. Hard to gauge Vietnamese ages, they all seem so young, maybe early thirties? Cinnamon skin like her son, dark eyes, broad nose.

"English? You speak?" she surprises you by asking. Not fluent, but plenty understandable. "Tahn, my son, he bring you. You are looking for place to stay?"

"Yes."

"This house very small. But Tanh say he really want you stay. So I no have husband, so you cannot stay here in house. Village will talk."

"Fine. Thank you. I'll look for somewhere else."

"No no, Tanh not want that. You eat with us. I will make bed, maybe there." She points out back. What's out there? You detect a slight hesitation in her voice. She turns away, a mere half-twist that brings her slender figure into silhouette, breasts pressing against her gingham blouse. Then a rhythmic stride as she heads inside again, her back swaying under a fall of hair down past her thin shoulders. If only you had paper and charcoal; you just missed a beautiful opportunity. Artist's eye coinciding with male leer. The boy Tanh stays beside you, buzzing with delight.

You stay outside keeping Tanh company, drawing cartoons until it gets dark, while his mother prepares dinner. Simmered *cá muối* catfish and stir-fried *rao muống* water mimosa with a hefty helping of rice. The fish is seasoned just right with salt and coriander; likewise the garlic and *nguoc mam* of the stir-fry. Simple but satisfying. Only two people, mother and son, in this household—is it a temporary thing? Where is the husband? Is he merely off traveling somewhere? But then, an only child, in this country?

While you're eating, Tanh asks all sorts of questions via his mother. You came from Japan? Why come to Vietnam? Why this village? Do you always draw pictures? Is that your work? How can he learn to draw like you? How long will you be staying in the village? The boy seems starved for intellectual stimulation. Seems you're the hero of the hour. Maybe even a father/big brother figure.

His mother merely translates, interjecting no questions of her own, smiling enigmatically when you ask where she learned her English. Now and again, she pauses as if to rephrase her son's words, compensating for his directness.

"Are you going to stay here a long time?" Tanh asks.

"I don't know. Depends whether I can paint good pictures here."

"No problem. There's lots of things to paint."

After dinner, you bring out the drawing you did of Tanh and give it to his mother as a thank-you gift, on top of the meal money you plan to give her anyway. She pores over the picture in the yellow glow of the kerosene lamp, saying nothing in reaction, but obviously recognizing her son in the lines. She accepts you at face value, an adult who draws for a living. Her profile, half-lit in chiaroscuro, asks to be painted. All the more vivid for long hours of work and sun, a face alive with joy and sorrow.

There's a small shed out behind the house, which mother and son proceed to empty of its farm implements. They swing several sacks of rice off to one side in the dark, then retire to the main house while you stretch out in your thin sleeping bag. It's not really cold enough for any covering, but there's always mosquitoes. The shed smells of rice and burlap, dirt and chicken shit. As you doze off, you swear you can hear the soft breathing of your hostess and her young son.

The following morning you walk around the village with Tanh, painting pictures. He's showing you off, amazed how your fingers can turn what's before his eyes into something completely new. Other kids come take a look, but eventually bug off, bored. Tahn, however, sticks with you the entire day. You give him paper and crayons, and urge him to draw. He's no born talent, still his lines are free and vigorous, like vines, his use of color simple, bold. Mustn't praise too much, but the potential is there if he keeps at it.

That evening, after Tanh gives a full-color account of the day's activities, his mother asks, "What you paint today, I can see?"

You show her a few pictures. She knows the buildings and places depicted, so she can judge your skill for likeness. She takes particular interest in a couple of them, looking at length and smiling. Today there's a nod for your work.

You discreetly offer money for food and lodging, a little over what you estimate to be a fair per diem, but she pushes it back into your hands. Visitors are to be shown courtesy, she wouldn't hear of it! On the other hand, isn't it customary for the visitor to thank the host in kind? If she won't take the money, then tomorrow you'll have to look for somewhere else to stay. Kindness is kindness and money is money. There are two standards in this world. When that's made clear, she accepts. Are you really not an imposition?

Or is she merely an indulgent mother putting her son's wants first?

First thing next day, Tanh makes signs he's going to take you somewhere. He packs a basket of leftovers from breakfast and a canteen, stuffing them into a rough cotton shoulder bag, and you're off. Tanh presses ahead with confidence, brushing the other kids aside. You carry only your own art supplies, respecting his arrangements. Wherever it is, it's far. Almost an hour back down the Khe Sanh bus road, you turn off into a valley. Why didn't you think to ask his mother to translate what it was he wanted to show you? Or didn't he tell her? Maybe this was a secret between men.

Before long the path narrows and the jungle closes in overhead. No sunlight penetrates, but the heat and humidity are tremendous, completely soaking you in sweat. A decade ago, foot soldiers from both sides would have tramped these hills like this. You can almost see a Vietcong unit cutting across the marshes up ahead.

Where the valley bottoms out, you ford a small stream and the path begins to ascend. Tahn shows no sign of tiring, but halfway up the ridge you beg for a short breather. Here at least there's a breeze. In under a thick green drapery of creepers, the fresh air feels good, a flowery fragrance sifting through the underbrush.

All too soon Tahn is on his feet again. His mind is set on his destination, no time for dillydallying. You follow, soon out of breath again. On the very last bit, you have to scramble down a steep incline holding onto gnarled roots. How the hell did Tahn ever manage to find this place? How can he keep ahead on this path that hasn't been a path in ten years?

At long last, the boy stops. The slope levels off into a glade of low grasses and saplings where an open patch lets in sunlight. Tahn walks out into the middle of it and grins, pointing at something. Something really big, a heavy shape half-swallowed into the hillside beyond. A man-made object, metal no less, with a curved, factory-forged surface covered in a tangle of time and gray-green moss. An airplane, probably a downed American fighter, totally out of proportion with the surroundings. Big dead bird.

You straddle fallen tree trunks to get closer to the behemoth. The tail end bares its twin anuses, the jet exhaust ports. The vertical stabilizer still points upright, but the horizontals slouch to either side in a circumflex. They don't seem to be broken. Maybe that's just the design?

Tanh leaps across the wild topography toward the fighter hulk with the surefootedness of repeated visits. He grabs a hank of vines to scale up the side and onto a wing. You follow his route and climb up beside him. The head of the plane is angled down into a gulley. You couldn't tell from the ground just how long the thing was, but it's the length of a train. The wings are clipped short, the right span mostly sheared away. Fat fuselage, narrowing where it merges into the tail fin. Ballooning underbelly—an extra swell to house the jet engines?—looking grotesque and obscene.

Tahn works his way down the nose-dived plane hand over hand by vine. You follow, hoping he's not leading you to a dead body. Cautiously, yet enjoying the slippery thrill of the descent, you slide seat down on the duralumin plating all the way to just behind the cockpit. There you latch onto Tanh who's secured by a single sinewy tendril that snakes down from above. Look inside, the cockpit's empty. A twin-seater apparently, windscreen gone, even the seats are missing. What's left is literally a pit of composting leaves and plant debris. The dials and switches are buried thick and unreadable. No bones, no mummified remains, no pilot at all. Bailed out probably. The plane died instead, burying itself in the undergrowth, never to fly again. Tanh lords it over the spoils as if he downed the thing himself. A gigantic war trophy. Who knows? Maybe he really did find it himself and kept it a secret until now. How long ago did the war end?

Give the duralumin hull a kick—the metal echoes with a hollow thud. This proud issue of America's factories flew halfway around the world to unload a payload of bombs—and for what? It's scrap now. Or worse, totally unsalvageable. Not even rusting, a heap of non-returnable, non-refundable parts. A massive *thing* lodged in the forest, an affront to nature, though the plants and dirt do their best to hide it. Above the wreck, the sky is the same brilliant blue as always in this part of the world. Bright tropical birds wing past. You brought your paints, but this doesn't inspire you. And no way to compose a picture on such a steep incline. So you play along with Tanh and go inspect the crashed-in nose, run fingers over the ganglia of plasticized cables severed at the wing stump, wipe dirt from the hull to read the urgent stencils. IN CASE OF EMERGENCY, OPEN WINDSCREEN HERE TO SAVE CREW. DO NOT STAND HERE. DANGER! LIVE EXPLOSIVES INSIDE. The emergency, the urgency, pilot and copilot all long gone.

No, you've changed your mind, you *will* draw the thing. But where to get a view of the whole fuselage? You struggle down the slope to the left, but find so many trees in the way the precarious, tilted shape through the branches is barely an airplane. A quick pencil sketch will have to do. The collision of opposites—metal, vegetation—a study in contrasting textures. Poor dead plane. Tanh watches from a few steps back.

The way back seems twice as long, and when you reach the village by late afternoon you go soak in the river with Tanh. The boy's naked body is beautiful, sun glistening off his skin. To draw that, or better yet to sculpt it. Not sexual, but not really paintable either. Warmth sensible only to the touch. No, say that and you might as well give up painting. You know you can paint skin so the body heat translates, your art is *that* physical.

When you were a boy, you always hated how they included "fleshtone" as one of the twenty-four oil-pastel colors. The rest of the box was so logically organized according to color theory, and then they went and shoved in "fleshtone." A concession to the faces and hands kids always draw but never color right, they'd pre-mixed a standard shade. Homogenized fascism of a thousand different complexions reduced to one muddy blend, living color into dead chemical. You used it often enough, though it never looked like your classmates' faces. Try as you might to correct it, that pasty peach-pink stubbornly resisted.

Once when you went to America, you thought to check the supermarket shelves, but in the school kid's twelve-stick set there was no such color. Kids were supposed to mix their own colors—if that was the idea, then great. Afterwards you went to a drugstore and asked if they had band-aids in different minority colors. The clerk gave you a dirty look. Band-aids were made for white skin; all other races—Hispanic or Asian or Black—had to highlight their scrapes. Yet another skin color policy.

Tanh would never need band-aids. If he cut himself, his own antibodies would do the healing. The same way his country never needed American fighter planes. The living can't be sealed over with dead bodies; the land heals its own scars, however slowly.

Tanh doesn't tell his mother where you two have been all day. That evening at dinner, there's no talk of any secret jet fighter. Instead, he steers the conversation toward Japan—a fairy-tale country of big cities where everyone's rich. You struggle to correct his simplistic view, but Tanh goes on dreaming aloud. As if the more he talks and keeps his mother translating, the less she'll suspect. She, however, doesn't even ask; she seems mysteriously anxious, her eyes flashing secrets of their own.

That night, pleasantly exhausted from the day's outing, images from some invisible script reel you into a deep sleep. Then suddenly Tahn's mother is there, kneeling beside your sleeping bag. No telling how long she's been waiting for you to wake. Despite the darkness you know right away it's her. Not unexpected, not after your eyes met across the dinner tray. How much was the desire to paint her confused with plain desire?

You couldn't go to her in the house, she had to come to you in the shed. Your hand reaches out, drawing her in close. Wrapping her in your arms and rubbing up together. There's no hiding any more, only wanting. Desire pours from your bodies, both of you aware of what's happening, both helpless to do anything else. Clothes peel off. She snuggles her hips up closer, kneading hungrily. Your open palm smoothes her back, travels down behind to trawl in the fullness below. Her breasts hover before you, moist and breathing—roundness and warmth and weight, resistance and contour. Two handfuls of flesh, two bodies sleek with sweat, panting ragged involuntary mouthings. Legs tremble open to the thrust. Still more, a little more, yes, hold on, there. Working each other, like drenched clay. The feeling mounts and mounts, until finally the intensity boils over and evaporates . . . though you rub together this way and that, milking the least last leftover of pleasure as you fall away, breathing heavily. Pleasure made all the keener by the knowledge of shared transgression . . .

"What's your name?"

". . . Mmm?"

"Your name, I never asked." You tickle a whisper in her ear.

"Tanh's mother."

"No, here with me."

". . . An."

"An?"

"An. Ngyuen Ti An. And you?

"Tez."

"Tez, Tez." She tries out the name, the pronunciation somewhere between English and Vietnamese. Sounds cute. How did you both stay nameless until now?

The whispered words go on into the night. Words inviting lips to ears, lips to lips, tongue to tongue. Licking the line of her neck, fingers exploring, fondling each other, thighs and hips swaying. An's round behind brimming in your cupped hands.

At some point you ask: "Where did you learn your English?"

"In city, now many years gone."

"Saigon?"

"Yes, big noisy city. This my grandfather grandmother village. My family leave to Saigon. When American War end, I hate city so I come back here. Better to farm in mountain field. Here I meet my husband, here Tanh born. We very happy. But my husband he must leave to war and he never come back."

"Another war after the other one ended?"

"Cambodia."

You picture fighting down in the flatlands. Machine-gun cross fire and grenades and howitzers, landmines and explosives. A foot soldier setting off from the village, leaving her warm body for active duty. You feel for him, linked through this woman you've shared. *Did you forget her in the heat of battle? Does sleeping with your wife like this make an enemy of you? Or a fellow partisan? Does this slender waist, this smooth skin, connect with you? What about it, comrade? If you're still there, come back and fight, in arm-to-arm combat. That's what life is all about. But if you're dead, well, just eat your heart out. Ghosts are meant to envy the living, right?*

These imaginings only heighten your enjoyment, which communicates itself to her. And so you ride out the dawn on Tanh's secret plane. Poor broken bird, wants so badly to hide away in the trees, to be covered completely. Too late, we already found you.

You turn An over and lie on top of her. Slide yourself in, slip both arms around her sides, lock onto her shoulders and extend. Pumping from behind, chest to back lubricated with sweat, sobbing sounds coming from your mouth. Our airplane, riding higher and higher, never to come down. Until you find yourself back on the ground, nuzzling softly at her ear.

"I want to paint you."

"Me?"

"I like this just fine"—you squeeze a breast and she lets out a soft nasal moan—"but I want to paint your picture. Your back. From your neck on down."

"Nowhere to do. Everyone see."

"Not even up in the hills?"

"No. People talking even more. They thinking we doing this." She rubs your chest. "No good. Even you stay here make big problems. You know I am widow, outsider to village."

"Yes."

"Village men interesting me, right? I say no, they thinking me too proud. I say yes, now village women all talking. Big problem."

"And me?"

"People already talking, but okay. First time Tanh bring you here, I thinking, this man he can stay."

"Did you think we would be like *this?*"

"Never!" She looked so startled, you had to laugh. "My dead husband mother, she very nice to me. She headwoman very powerful house here in village, everyone look up to her. She always look after me. Sometime she send helper for work in field. She know about you. I see her yesterday and she already know you and Tanh go together where you go. Tahn only grandson, so he happy she happy too. So okay you staying here."

"But not okay to paint your picture."

144

"No, never. That too much."

The following day you begin doing portraits of the villagers. Two drawings each, one for you and one for your subjects, beginning with the mother-in-law matriarch. Tanh proudly leads the way. She's big and fat, a wonderful face. Thanks to her, you're accepted in the village. After that everyone comes to you to be drawn in turn, regular as an X-ray clinic.

These ties linking you with everyone—not just with Tanh and An, but the whole village—are unusual for you. Ties you'll have to break sooner or later when the traveler returns to Japan. In the course of your nightly pleasures, you talk it over with An. Eventually you must leave, both of you know that. But not yet, not tonight. Tonight you're still here with her. No way to see a life together, you the foreigner and she a villager. *You'll be back, she'll wait. But will she now? Will you return? Will she wait?* The only answer is now, what feels so right, so happy. Bodies like this, here doing this, see? Yes, it's so good.

In the end, you do draw An. One day, after sending Tanh to the next village on some errand, the two of you go up by different paths to meet in the hills. There in the filtered forest sunlight you draw her back. Facing away, clothes let down halfway, lovely and graceful. Then you have her face this way to draw her breasts firm between her arms, her shoulders and face. Three drawings, five drawings, until you're out of paper. Heartfelt works all.

And so, after several weeks, you leave the village. You've drawn everyone there is to draw. Run out of supplies. Can't put off your work in Japan any longer or they'll lose all trace of you. Leaving Tanh so sad, An hollow in body and heart, rumors flying. Days of drudgery ahead to pay for the pleasures had. The wrongs and debts you leave behind. Punishment for coming to a strange land and making ties, though it's not you who pays most for it. Smiling your back-in-a-month smile, knowing it's a lie, you board the bus, look out at An and Tahn, and wait for the engine to start.

Living is a long ride, through turbulent patches of free-fall skies. It's not the destination, it's not even the route. Things a dead airplane wouldn't understand.

9

KAORU

After the first session, I got a rundown on the day's proceedings from Kondra. As expected, Tez was charged with smuggling in 200g of heroin from
Thailand. The prosecution was completely serious about this make-believe,
and of course the name Agus never once came up. Nor was there any mention of Tez signing an altered "duplicate" confession. I couldn't believe
so-called officers of the law would stoop so low. Gatir, however, took an
altogether cut-and-dried view: he would simply object to the transcript,
obliging the judge either to reject it as evidence or overrule the objection
on some other grounds.

Thus the question became, how to attack the prosecution's story? We
needed to anticipate and discredit whatever pieces of evidence they might
submit, meanwhile establishing that Tez had indeed been framed. A tall
order, was the typical Gatir understatement. We had next to no evidence
on our side, only those character references from Japan to prove Tez wasn't
a deadbeat hippie but a renowned artist. I myself could testify to that. Fair
enough, but the real point of contention was his actions, not his reputation.
By the same token, though, they had no hard proof either; they hadn't
caught him at the airport in the act of smuggling. It was all of ten days later
they arrested him. Not much of a case, really.

"Couldn't we find this Agus character?"

"Not very likely. It's probably an assumed name, and we've got nothing to go on but your brother's recollections. Not one photo. The police could be hiding him; he might not even be in Bali any more. And even if we did find him, they'd never let him testify in our favor. He's theirs."

"We could get someone from Padra Cottages to say they saw a man come visit that day. It would at least establish there was someone else."

"Panda Cottages is a lax sort of place, with large grounds. Anyone could go in and out without attracting the attention of the front desk."

"And if the judge accepts the prosecution's story?"

"Very bad news for us."

That evening I went walking in town. Tez might be in jail, but why stay locked up myself? I had a lot on my mind, but I thought I might as well see what I could of the island. At that point I still imagined I had the luxury.

The first time, when I stayed in Sanur, I saw nothing but fancy hotels, self-contained resorts filled with busloads of tourists. At night the streets were practically deserted, so I never felt like going out for a walk. But here in the Kuta-Legian area, things were much livelier. Narrow streets lined with souvenir shops and restaurants, taxis and three-wheeler *bemo*s putt-putting around everywhere, lane after lane of cheap lodgings like the place I was staying now. The *quartier* was jumping with hippies and surfers, young people low on funds but high on exuberance. Around them jostled Balinese and Javanese, peddlers and would-be guides and people just trying to be friendly.

Out on the town, I was nobody special—which was great! I felt free and easy, no longer the Kaoru Nishijima who was in court today, conferring on legal strategies. I was tired of all that. Tonight I was just another tourist, completely anonymous.

I turned a corner, and a few doors up a busy sidestreet was a café—*warung* they called them. A low-key "hangout," the sort of place I'd frequent if this were Paris, not Bali. But here on *Bari* not *Pari* I had yet to savor the *ambience*. All the streetfront terrace seats were taken, so I had a quick look inside: two tables of loud conversations—regulars, obviously—a few couples, but otherwise only a few singles like myself. A lone woman can be read as an open invitation for male propositioning, but I can generally hold my own in that department. I didn't feel like eating, not just yet, so I ordered a *café au lait*. With the day's work done, the farcical formalities of the first session over, I guess I was entitled to a nice hot cup.

Five minutes later, returning from the toilet, I found on my table not the coffee I'd happily anticipated but a large plate of rice heaped with vegetables. It looked pretty good, but it wasn't what I ordered. "There's been a mistake," I called to the waitress. "I ordered *café au lait*."

"That's mine," came a voice. I looked around to see a thirtyish European man in a green shirt and chinos sitting nearby. "The *nasi champur* is mine."

When the waitress came to pick up the plate, the man turned and said, "That's all right, I'll move. The plate doesn't have legs, but I do. Okay by you?" I guess he was talking to me.

Before I could answer he came over and sat himself down at my table. Talk about pushy. "As you like. Be my guest," I said, trying to tack on a note of sarcasm. I just hoped he wasn't totally obnoxious.

"Were you waiting for someone? I'll go away if I'm bothering you."

Fine time to be asking, I thought, but I shook my head. "What's that called again?"

"Like I said, *nasi champur*. Care to try some?"

"No thanks, not today."

Finally my coffee arrived, which spared us from speaking while I drank and he ate. And did he ever eat!

"Sorry. I'm disturbing you, I know." He suddenly looked up, as if only just then noticing that he was making a pig of himself.

"That's okay. Seeing how you're putting it away, it must be awfully good."

"Yesterday I slept the whole day, so I'm famished."

"You don't look sick. Or couldn't you be bothered to eat?"

"No, I nearly died the day before, so yesterday I just collapsed from exhaustion."

"Oh, sorry to hear that, but aren't you kind of overstating things? People don't usually 'nearly die' so easily. So how did you almost do yourself in?"

"It was in a sea kayak."

"Those little boats that you paddle?"

"Right. To the east of here is a small island called Nusa Penida. It's about ten kilometers off the coast of Bali, about an hour and a half paddling. Not too far. In fact the day before I'd paddled across to the island from Chandidasa."

I gave him the benefit of a listen. He was dark, not too tall, and spoke with a slight roll of the *R* in English. My guess was he was from somewhere in southern Europe.

"So, well, I thought I'd take another route back, just for a change. Go halfway around Nusa Penida, to the opposite side of the island, before heading back to Bali. Which ought to have taken two hours at most . . ."

"Only . . ."

". . . only the current on the south side of the island was much, much stronger than anything I expected. I do a lot of kayaking and I know most of the tides and currents around Bali, but this was totally out of the blue. My little boat was swept away just like that."

"Aren't they dangerous, kayaks?"

"No, not at all. It's a safe, fun sport—usually. But to make things worse, a wind blew in from the south. I was paddling like crazy, but I wasn't heading anywhere near Chandidasa. The current was sweeping me east and the wind was driving me north, and this combined northeast direction would put me right out in the middle of the strait between Bali and Lombok. If I kept going like that, I'd wind up in the open sea with no land until Sulawesi, a thousand kilometers away. My kayak could stand a little water, but I had nothing with me to eat."

"So you really could have died."

"No joke. I wasn't just saying things to get your attention. What's your name, by the way?"

"Eh?" I was taken aback by this sudden gear-shift. "Kaoru."

"I'm Manolo. So anyway, there I was being washed further and further away. My arms and shoulders were sore. I mean, I was paddling for dear life. I knew I'd only make myself more tired fighting the current head-on, so instead I paddled at an angle across it. It meant getting pushed way off course, but eventually I'd be clear of the current."

"Like being on an expressway and missing your exit by not being able to change lanes."

"Exactly. And missing it by a long shot. I could tell from the profile of the island. Mt. Agung was hiding in the shadow of Mt. Seraya, which meant I was already north of Bali."

"And . . . ?"

"And still all I could do was paddle. Bali was so far away by now, I thought I was dead for sure. I'd reached my limit. My muscles hurt, my lungs hurt, my heart hurt. Yet somehow I kept going, cutting westward, westward, until finally I wound up near the beach at Amed. By then there wasn't any current and the wind was blocked by Mt. Seraya. The very last stretch, I was using as little energy as I could, letting myself drift slowly closer to the beach."

"And you survived."

"I survived."

"Good for you. You should eat some more."

"No, really, one helping's enough, even for me. That was the *nasi champur deluxe*, twice the regular portion. It's time for coffee." He called the waitress and ordered a *kopi Bali*.

"When you were really scared, did you pray?" The words just came out. I'd had nothing to do with religion for ages, so what made me think about praying? Why then?

"No," was the answer. "It was all I could do just to keep paddling. I knew I couldn't depend on any external powers, only my own muscles. I'm pretty much an agnostic, don't generally pray at all."

"Same here."

I wanted to talk more, but the reality of Tez's situation called. It had been a nice interlude, but Tez and I were out at sea ourselves, and if we didn't flex muscle we'd really be in scary straits. Yet how were we even supposed to paddle? My interest in the kayak adventure evaporated, suddenly I just couldn't stay.

"Thanks. Great story. See you around," I said, leaving him there with his mouth hanging open.

That night, thinking back over the events of the day, I began to worry all over again where everything was heading. Yes, the trial *was* a sporting event, a face-off, nothing to do with truth or justice. The words let fly in court bounced back and forth, probing for the opponent's weak points. Both offense and defense had to hustle. The only difference in this game was neither side knew the score midway. A general hunch as to who was ahead or behind maybe, but no actual tally until the match was over. And Tez was not the ball; Tez was the trophy, to be handed over to the victor. Which reminded me of Professor Inagaki's Amnesty lecture: how an incident like this could fan the fires of nationalism like at a soccer match. And while no one would be so dumb as to dive in voluntarily to be kicked around, it was Tez's bad luck to happen along at the wrong time.

We'd try our hardest, but things didn't look good. Tez might get life imprisonment—or worse—and all so some horrible police chief could make a name for himself. Could there be anything so insane? I'd felt powerless hundreds of times before in my life, but how could I live with myself afterwards if my fumbling effors let the worst come to pass? The room was so oppressively hot I could hardly sleep the whole night.

The next morning, on my way to breakfast, the front desk boy waved me over.

"What is it?"

"About you, in paper." He held up an Indonesian newspaper. There on the front page was a big photo of me sitting in the courtroom. I nearly keeled over from the shock.

"What's it say?"

"Eh, it say, catch Japan drug man, make big trial. Today first time." Lousy translation, but enough to tell me that Tez was front-page news here. "Criminal bring much drug to Bali, sister from Japan come in court. Dark dress, white skin, look so sad. No speaking *Bahasa*. Pretty lady (see photo)." The boy looked up at me and smiled. Just what was so funny?

"I'll take that paper," I said and, grabbing it out of his hands, beat a fast retreat to my room.

I sat down on the bed and took another look at the newspaper. The photo showed me in the front row, taken from the side. I hadn't realized, but obviously I was a news item myself. Was my skin really that white? Maybe by Balinese standards, but I'd never been called a "pretty lady" before in my life. Certainly not in Japan. I felt like an exhibit. Was this going to happen every session? Everyone would remember my face and say, "There's the drug smuggler's sister." I couldn't possibly fend off this sort of flak, not at least in their impossible language. Yes, that's how the rumor would spread.

None of the article meant a thing to me except the letters of my name. But who had informed the newspaper? The hotel? The police? No qualms about giving out a person's name; no reservations about swallowing the prosecution's allegations either. Now I understood how the average Balinese would view Tez's case. So far my contacts had been pretty much limited to the Japanese consul and Professor Inagaki, Gatir, and Tez himself. In court I'd been face to face with the judge and prosecutor, each with a special agenda. And there was that awful police chief with his own devious angles. But most of the island people, they just read this paper and saw this photograph of "the drug smuggler's sister."

Tez and I were a set, him the main item and me an extra bonus. An object of public curiosity, a bit of journalistic titillation fallen right in their laps. I'd been on the other side of the camera myself as a media coordinator, so why was I so surprised? Because this wasn't Japan or France. But now even Indonesia had entered the tabloid age, and I was fair game for any hack reporter with a camera.

From now on, I had to be on guard out there on the street. No way would you catch me going to places like last night any more, even if it meant eating every meal here at the hotel. I was committed to staying on the island for the length of the trial, but how was I supposed to pass the time? What face was I supposed to wear? Everyone would be watching, pointing at me. The tourists wouldn't be haggling with shopkeepers over the price of a T-shirt, they'd be discussing our trial. The *bemo* drivers waiting at the corner for rides would be making bets on the sentence—already a guilty verdict as far as they were concerned. The café hippies would take a drug interest in Tez's case, and sooner or later the talk would turn to the poor joker's sister. That kayak guy had probably seen my picture by now.

I bought some sunglasses, big ones. Three pairs. I went to a beauty salon in a big hotel and had my hair cut. A naff bob, but at least it made me look like a different person. I wanted to borrow a mask, I wanted to be the invisible woman. If I must stay on this island, then let me be someone else. I even thought about handing everything over to Gatir and Kondra and just hightailing it back to Japan, but that would be like defecting, turning my back on Tez. Now that the trial was on, I couldn't *not* be there. He absolutely needed me.

Waiting around the hotel between sessions would be no fun. And knowing it was a lot worse for Tez didn't make it any easier. I hated that grinning boy at the front desk. I hated going to the dining room and dealing with the people there. I didn't have any appetite anyway. I never liked eating alone, and now I couldn't even taste half of what I put in my mouth. I'd point to the menu at random, wait for the stuff—whatever—to appear, eat a few bites, and then feel their eyes on me all the way back to my room. Once safe inside, I'd lock the door and plop down on the bed, a long, sweaty night ahead. My whole system was out of whack, my heart beat out of rhythm. If—heaven forbid—we got an unfavorable verdict and we appealed, the case would move to Jakarta for how-many-more years like this? My stomach lining would wear to a frazzle. Well, let it. I wasn't giving in.

The next session began with the prosecutor, quite the little orator, arguing his case. I couldn't understand a word, but obviously he was asserting that this evil foreigner had schemed to lure innocent Indonesian youth into drugs for his own selfish profit. The judge listened expressionlessly. How much weight did this case carry? How separate were law and politics in this country? According to Inagaki's intelligence from Jakarta, Tez's trial might tie into an American anti-drug campaign. Maybe this lady judge had even heard that pumping our case up into a big affair would boost her career. I gazed up at the bored look on her face behind the glasses and begged her, *Please don't give in to those pressures.*

Next came the presentation of evidence. The prosecution's number one piece of evidence was the transcript of the interrogation—Tez's "confession." The prosecutor read it out at great length, pausing after each paragraph for Kondra to translate for Tez. Too far away for me to hear, but I could see Tez shaking his head now and again.

"The transcript isn't at all what I said at the interrogation," Tez told the court. "Those are not my words."

The judge summoned him before her and showed him where he'd signed the transcript.

"Yes, that definitely is my signature. But the statement is wrong."

The judge scowled, probably saying, "Weren't you read the transcript before you signed?"

"Yes, they read me the transcript, I listened to the translation, then I signed. But what was translated to me then was completely different. They read it out sentence by sentence, translating each time, so I know there shouldn't be any difference. But I also know I *never* said anything about smuggling two hundred grams of heroin from Thailand. Why would I admit to something I didn't do? So I do find it very strange to see my signature here on this paper. Only, now as I recall, I was made to sign two copies. The second one was a duplicate, I was told. I didn't check, I couldn't check. Nor was there time. Please ask the prosecutor where that second transcript I signed went." He was playing it very cool.

The prosecutor, of course, flatly denied Tez's claims (it was obvious from his tone of voice). "He is insulting the dignity of this court! Why would a member of the legal profession resort to patent lies and trickery?"

Gatir quickly rose and pressed for a motion (as I learned later). "Since there is some question of duplicity and hence a reasonable doubt as to whether this transcript constitutes a fair and accurate representation of the defendant's words, it should be dismissed as evidence."

To which the prosecutor countered, "This ex post facto denial of the accused's own verified testimony can only be construed as a highly irregular maneuver to buy himself time" (again later).

The accusations flew back and forth. Finally the prosecutor moved on, bringing out Tez's belongings as further evidence. A table was set up in the middle of the courtroom for his backpack and portfolio, art supplies, clothes, and other personal items. The prosecutor pointed to each in turn, asking Tez to identify it as his. He opened the portfolio and showed its contents —just blank sheets of paper. Whereupon the judge said something to Kondra.

"I was arrested before I had time to draw anything in Bali," Tez replied to what must have been a query about why there was no artwork. "Though at the time of the interrogation, I know I definitely drew a portrait of the interrogating officer. Maybe he has that drawing?"

The prosecutor heard out Kondra's translation, and the judge pressed the query.

"*Dadit*," came the one word reply. The inescapable Indonesian negative —"No have."

"Okay, I'll do another. Give me five minutes please." Tez waited for a nod from the bailiff, then grabbed a sheet of paper and a pencil from the evidence table. He took up a position to the left of the prosecutor and began to draw the man's portrait. The prosecutor looked pretty uncomfortable, the judge waited and watched without comment, and meanwhile I was on the edge of my seat—but smiling inside. *Tez, you're really something!*

Five minutes later Tez placed the drawing before the judge and returned to his seat. For one brief moment, the judge let down her guard; she called over the prosecutor to let him take a look. A complex mix of emotions came over his face: to allow that the drawing had any merit was to pride himself on his looks, which he badly wanted to do, but doing that would also boost the defendant's character and undermine his own arguments. The internal tug-of-war was almost comic.

Gatir asked to see the portrait, then held it up to show the court. It was a good likeness, the very image of an able lawman, if a tad pandering to the man's ego. A buzz went through the room. People were smiling, reacting more favorably toward Tez on the whole. The prosecutor frowned, only then realizing how badly he'd lost out. Tez's standing as a talented professional artist had been established in court.

There was little the prosecutor could do but bring out the next pieces of evidence, laying them on the table, each in an individual plastic pouch: one ordinary red-and-white twenty-cigarette pack of Marlboros with the seal broken; one ten-pack Marlboro carton with nine packs inside, seals intact; two tiny pouches of white powder, one with about half the amount of the other and held shut with a clip; one used hypodermic with cap and two more syringes still in their factory packaging; a small bottle of mineral water, teaspoon, and cigarette lighter. The prosecutor named each item in turn for the court.

"Are these yours?" asked the judge. "Please look them over carefully."

Tez went over and carefully divided the things into two groups, left and right. The pouches of white powder, the used and brand-new syringes, the mineral water and teaspoon and lighter he pushed to one side of the table. "These I bought for $200 in my rented room at Pandra Cottages from a dealer who went by the name of Agus."

The remaining pack and carton of Marlboros he pointed to and said, "These I didn't buy. Agus used the pack of cigarettes to conceal the heroin, then tossed it into a corner of the room. Or at least that's what I thought. That carton I never saw before in my life."

The prosecutor rose and began to speak. From what Kondra told me later, he explained that the little plastic pouches contained respectively 1g and about 0.8g of very high-grade heroin, and that the Marlboro pack bore the defendant's fingerprints. The Marlboro carton originally held ten packs of 20g of heroin each, in readily salable 1g pouches, all stuffed in together with cotton wads for padding, making a total of 200g of heroin. And for reference's sake, an ordinary pack of twenty cigarettes also weighed about 20g, so that the overall cellophane-sealed appearance and weight were virtually identical to any real pack of Marlboros. Here was a special "heroin kit" painstakingly prepared by someone planning to smuggle it across international borders. In other words, the willful intent was self-evident—thus ran the prosecutor's argument.

Tez stood up. "I can explain the fingerprints. After the arrest, at the interrogation, they asked me about the pack of cigarettes, just like now. I said I remembered Agus bringing it in. But then when they showed me a lot more heroin and I knew I'd been framed, I got so upset I threw it across the interrogation room. That's where the fingerprints came from."

The prosecutor said nothing. Gatir then launched into an impassioned speech, which set off a chain reaction of fervent retaliatory debate for the next few minutes. As I later found out, Gatir first asked whether there were also fingerprints on the carton, to which the prosecutor responded "No." Gatir then asked how was it possible to remove one pack of cigarettes without touching the carton? Wasn't the absence of fingerprints unnatural? Not necessarily, said the prosecutor: the defendant may have been careless enough to touch the pack during the interrogation, but otherwise his "criminal instinct" would have been to wipe off any telltale fingerprints. "Nonsense," insisted Gatir, the defendant's own explanation was far more logical, whereupon he formally requested that the judge strike those items not recognized by the defendant from admissible evidence.

And with that the session came to close. Both Tez and Gatir had made heroic efforts, but now it was up to the judge to decide. Not exactly reassuring.

The following morning, after a shallow sleep, I was heading for breakfast when the front desk boy waved at me again. I had an ominous feeling, but I couldn't very well ignore him. I went over—another newspaper, I just knew it. I switched my mental guard to full and took a look: there front and center was another big photo of me, this time getting out of Wayang's car at the courthouse curb. Taken front-on and lengthwise to show me walking, the photographer must have been lying in wait with a telephoto lens.

This time the shock wasn't as strong as before. I could pretend to be calm. I thanked him, took the newspaper, and walked at a normal pace to the dining room. Inside I was a wreck, but I had my pride. The pressure of others watching me actually made me contain myself. I put the newspaper to one side and ate a good-sized breakfast. Then with the newspaper under one arm, I walked—chest out, chin in—leisurely back to my room and spread the front page out on the bed.

They couldn't photograph Tez in court—ever here there were limits—

so they kept running the same grainy arrest mugshot. But me they'd blown up along the right side of the front page, white blouse and longish navy skirt, handbag in hand as I made to cut across the lawn, looking down behind sunglasses. Not even seated in court, but full-length, outdoors. Which meant that I could be photographed anywhere at any time. I could feel the air around me buzzing with it all. I sat there on the bed, head in my hands. I didn't want to go anywhere, didn't want to leave the room, didn't want to be on this island one second longer.

There was no session scheduled for that day, so I just stayed in. Really I ought to have gone to see Tez to talk over recent developments, but I simply didn't have it in me. It was all I could do to phone Wayang and ask him to visit Tez and have him write down anything he needed. By now the police knew Wayang and would let him meet alone with Tez even without papers from the Japanese consulate.

I didn't eat lunch. I paced back and forth in my room all afternoon. By evening I was going stir-crazy, I just couldn't stay cooped up any longer. For the last few days, the hotel had been fumigated every evening, and I knew I'd get a pounding headache from the insecticide smell—the *whoosh* of the sprayer reminded me. Reluctantly I grabbed my handbag and stepped out. Luckily the hotel was near the sea, so I headed for the beach and sat myself down where the wild grass met the sand. There were few people out walking at that hour, so there was nothing much to see but bored waves sluicing toward shore and the flat, faceless expanse of the sea beyond. Gaze on and on as I might, the sea suggested nothing at all. I'd never been so low in all my twenty-odd years.

Why was I so depressed, so wrapped up in myself? Traveling had always been part of my job. Go to strange places, stay a while, look around, eat the food, befriend the people. See the good things, make good impressions. Mind warnings and steer clear of bad places. I'd done it before, why couldn't I see the good side of Bali? I had to be missing something (though another part of me was saying the whole of Asia was rotten to the core). A trumped-up trial like this—there hadn't been anything so phony in France since Dreyfus. Even Arab countries weren't this backward. At least they had their charm. But here—what was the attraction? This was supposed to be a tourist area, but what's there to it? No striking scenery, nothing like the *muezzin*'s morning call to prayer from the minarets. What did these people think or feel or believe?

Several days of mulling things over at the hotel conspired to make me feel generally miserable and insecure. In the end, Gatir had to practically pry me out of my room to go meet with Tez to discuss our defense strategy.

"If they deny that Agus exists, who does the prosecution say tipped them off to arrest me? Why single me out of all the other tourists to come busting in with guns?" Tez had obviously been considering different angles on his own.

"That's simple enough. Word from the hotel, report from the doctor, strange behavior out on the street—they could make up anything."

"The police chief said an 'honest private citizen' informed on you," I added.

"Can't we find some hole in their argument?"

"Their weakest point is the ten-day gap between your arrival and the time of arrest. Even supposing that heroin were yours, they can't prove you didn't obtain it *after* coming here to Bali. Not unless they caught you red-handed in Customs."

"So does that work in our favor?" I asked, jumping to conclusions. Typical me.

"Not necessarily. We can't disprove anything either. All our claims about Agus, about two grams being increased to two hundred—there's no real proof. The judge is just faced with two conflicting stories: the smuggling scenario and the police conspiracy scenario."

"And to the judge, the foreigner's story carries that much less weight."

"Not only that, this has become a highly politicized trial. Just this morning the word was that the next session will be pushed back. No specific reason, but my guess is that it has something to do with the U.S. president's upcoming visit."

"How's that?"

"One of the lead topics on the table for the upcoming Yogyakarta Summit is drug control. It seems drug problems in America have gotten out of hand since their last administration, so they've launched a worldwide anti-drug campaign. Which of course in itself is admirable; we'd all be better off without drugs. However, before any substantial changes can be made, officials everywhere—regardless of the country—will want to make a show of their vigilance. Thanks to this summit, pressure will be put on the judge to deliver an anti-drug verdict."

"Can she be trusted, this judge?"

"That I do not know. She has a good reputation, and for the moment she seems to be honest and conscientious, but whether her final ruling will be fair . . ."

"Political ambitions?"

"Some perhaps. They're our real nightmare."

The following evening, in a corner of the dining room pretending to eat, I looked up to see a young but rather large Western woman standing there. I'd seen her now and again around the hotel.

"Excuse me, do you speak English?"

"Ye-s," I answered warily.

"Are you Ms. Kaoru? From the newspaper?"

That did it. I went on the defensive. Good thing she was white; if it had been an Indonesian I'd have walked out on the spot.

"No need to be alarmed, I'm not a journalist or anything. My name is Margaret, from Australia. I'm in the same boat as you, really. You see, my boyfriend's on trial here for drugs."

Strange to think that her troubles could put me at ease, but they did. "Have a seat," I said, motioning her to a chair.

"It's just that I saw you sitting here all alone, looking so stressed out, and I've been pretty stressed too . . ."

Margaret had her dinner brought over to my table and I ordered an extra salad to share. A small gesture. We talked for the better part of an hour. Mostly we bitched about this rotten country, its pathetic legal system and its awful people. She fidgeting constantly, eyes darting around, even more paranoid than me, probably because she was ten times more informed about the courts here than me. And that was because there were other Westerners in similar straits, and word traveled fast among their friends and relatives. There were so many others charged with drug smuggling like Tez and her boyfriend that she joked sadly about a "Foreign Druggies' Fan Club." She knew of one Brit who got a bad verdict the first trial, so he shelled out a lot of money for a supposedly top-class attorney only to be saddled with an even worse verdict than before. And a Canadian who refused to trust any lawyers, so he boned up on Indonesian law to act as his own attorney— and failed miserably. And a woman—where was she from?—who'd been asked to put out for the prosecutor in exchange for a no-trial—anyway she refused.

"If I got propositioned like that, I'd really have to think," said Margaret almost in a whisper. "If it meant reducing Barney's sentence by two years, I just might do it."

"Though the idea itself is outrageous."

"Of course. It's a cheap shot at someone in a weaker position. But after the anger, what else can you do? What choice do we really have? Think about it."

"Would you discuss it with Barney?"

"Absolutely not. Never a word, not as long as I lived. That'd be the end, even if it were for his sake. It wouldn't be right, but still I just might do it. Maybe the sacrifice would poison my feelings towards him, or maybe our just being back together would settle everything, so I'd forget and we'd live happily ever. Who's to say?"

I might do it for my own sake, to save my own neck—but for Tez? Brother or lover, I just don't think I'd put out like that for someone else. I don't know why, even hypothetically it seemed a heavy issue to me, a painful decision either way. If it meant the difference between death and a few years for Tez, I might. But not with that evil police chief, anything but that. The more I thought about it, the angrier I became at this country— without any real grounds for it!

"Americans have it so much better."

"How's that?"

"If they get arrested, their embassy pulls weight and gets them deported, under a smokescreen of 'extended diplomatic immunity.' Their country takes a different view of things."

So what the Japanese consul told me about no diplomat ever interfering in the legal affairs of his host country, it was all just lies. Some countries *did* bail out their citizens, if not exactly exonerate them. Japan or Australia, however, were just weaker diplomatically.

After dinner, over coffee, I told her how Tez had walked right into a police trap. Buying and possession he admitted to, but the smuggling part was pure police fabrication. The whole thing must have been a set-up right from the sale on down.

"I wouldn't put it past these cops."

"You said it."

"Though when it comes right down to it, there are bad cops everywhere."

I didn't respond to that one. Whose side was she on? She seemed nothing but a source of depressing information, a catalog of failures. I was grateful for the various tips, but really, she said too many things I didn't want to hear.

She lowered her voice a notch: "These past few days, I've been so scared."

"Why?"

"I think I'm being followed."

"Who by? The police?"

"I don't know. A man in a yellow batik shirt and black trousers. I turn round and he's always there, pretending to look the other way. I steer clear of deserted streets, let me tell you."

"It's just nerves, got to be."

"That's what I kept telling myself. I'm under stress, so all Indonesian men start to look alike. But I've just seen him too often by now. I remember his face. It *is* the same man. It's as if he were *trying* to let me see him following me. Whatever, it can't be good."

Glad as I was to have company, Margaret put me in a bad mood. We parted on a rather empty "Let's not give up hope." The terrible thing was, the next few days I began to check behind me, too. The police chief's threats came back with a vengeance. I stayed up at night thinking, what would I do if he demanded sex in exchange for Tez's freedom? The days were dragging me deeper into quicksand. I hated this horrible country, this horrible island.

Delayed or not by the U.S. president's visit, the next court session began a few days late. The prosecution called its witnesses to the stand: staff from Pandra Cottages, the doctor who treated Tez, and a forensic chemist who verified that the content of the Marlboro packs was unadulterated high-grade heroin. During cross-examination, Gatir asked the chemist whether the defendant had been administered a naline test upon incarceration.

"Naline?"

"To test whether there was heroin in his system. Isn't such a test required if the charges include using heroin, not just possessing?"

"No, we didn't test." How could they conduct a procedure they didn't even know existed?

Next came the defense's witnesses, though we had none to call. Instead, Gatir read off Tez's résumé with his various awards and commendations, as well as letters of character reference and support from publishers and associates in Japan. Kondra had translated them all into Indonesian, but it still took a good two hours.

After that it was my turn on the stand. I told the court how close I was to my brother (a bit of an exaggeration, admittedly), yet the last time we met in Japan he'd never said a word about heroin. Which made me believe what he said now—that he strayed into addiction this last trip overseas. No, my brother was not short of money; he made quite a good living as a painter. Why would he even consider smuggling or selling heroin? (On Gatir's advice, I stopped short of revealing Tez's actual bank figures. The difference in income levels between Japan and Indonesia would only invite envy and bad feelings.) There was no cross-examination from the prosecution. It couldn't have taken more than fifteen minutes, but when I stepped down I felt as if I'd been up there for hours.

That evening, I hadn't the slightest sense of having made myself useful to my brother. No satisfaction, only wasted effort. What difference did it make? The trial was rigged anyway, wasn't it? They were going to do what they wanted regardless. Tez and I were mere pawns, showpieces set up in plain view on this island. Did I really expect otherwise?

Better I became a total recluse. Staying put, for fear of finding my sunglasses staring out of the front page. But they'd *still* reprint my picture. I felt exposed, naked, an object of hostile fascination. Pacing around indoors all day long like a bear at the zoo, I knew just how Tez felt in that cage where I first saw him. This bear was miserable.

By the evening fumigation hour, I'd worn a path on the floor. I could hear the *whoosh* of the sprayers, smell the chemical fumes drifting into the room. My head began to pound, my sinuses swelled. No way could anything so toxic to bugs be good for me. I slipped out again to the beach and sat watching the birds; an equatorial blizzard of white flecks, and me with my wings folded around me. I waited—for the poison dust to settle on the hotel lawn, for me to get hungry enough to brave the dining room, for the day when I'd leave this island for good and Tez would be free to paint again. If only I could dig a hole and crawl inside. Let some kind soul come shovel sand over me, make me invisible. Sweet oblivion.

Even so, I didn't pray. I thought how wonderful it would be if all this were over. I wanted that day to come so badly, I said it to myself a hundred times a day. But still that wasn't praying. A pep talk maybe, a plea to myself. I was paddling desperately. Getting swept away, with no one to call to for help. I was caught unprepared—which was how I got into this mess—and there was nothing to do but paddle. I had to fight. Not for Tez—I'd only end up resenting him as a burden—for myself, for the real me.

Or was I already praying? These last few days when I felt at my wits' end, was it only my pride that refused to admit it? Had my mind shaped a prayer, to whatever God or gods were out there? Was that strange Paris baptism still with me somehow?

10

TETSURO

"Heroin," said Inge.

You go wide-eyed. "You can't mean . . . ?"

"And why not?" she taunted.

"Even if it does do all you say it does, it's just too dangerous."

"Oh, really."

Silence. Only the rain outside. Falling on and on till the end of the world.

"And you can live with that?"

"As I said, I come here once a year. And for a month I do heroin, a little at a time. I enjoy being a sentient stone. The sensation is very special, I admit. My first time I didn't even vomit, which they say is rare. And in ten years I've never varied the amount at all. When my month is up, I get on a plane, fly home to Germany, and for eleven months I forget all about it. My accountant self couldn't be further from heroin than a devout Muslim from pork. I've done all right so far and I'll keep doing it. Everyone says it's so dangerous, but that has not been my experience."

"Maybe you're not normal."

"What can I say?—it works for me. I get through a year on the strength of my one month here. There I lead an exemplary German life. I'm respected professionally; I do volunteer community work and even have something of a name in contemporary art criticism. I'm not misleading anybody, I just never tell any of my German friends. Nor will I ever. The dealers here know me as 'that once-a-year German woman'—which is all they need to know."

"Do you know anyone else like that?"

"Only one other, the person who first brought me here. He'd trained his body little by little over time, and he taught me. He's dead, though—from cancer, not from heroin. The pain got so bad by the end he was swimming in morphine, which is basically the same as heroin. Ironic, isn't it? Well, I have the same constitution. If I get cancer, I know I'll go the same route," Inge laughed. Not cynical or self-mocking, a bright, happy laugh.

"And you're happy you were born with that kind of body."

"I guess. At this point I can't imagine life without heroin. We're like an old married couple. You can't just say, 'Yes, but what if you were married to someone else?' Not apropos of old couples or anything, the person who taught me about heroin was my elder brother. Wounded in the war and weaned off morphine, so twenty years later when he got hooked on heroin, he knew how to tame his habit. Since his body could take it, he thought his sister could too."

"But I'm not your brother."

"No, but I sense some kinship in your paintings. If I saw them at an exhibition in Germany, I'd have heaped praises on them. And here you are, so I get to know the artist."

"Is it true what they say, you know, about drugs and creativity?"

"Depends. American jazz musicians take coke and speed because jazz depends on fast improvisation. The more you put into one short phrase—the more variations you come up with in one set—the better the playing. Music is all a matter of timing, of compressing time. The faster your head and ears and fingers do their tricks, the better you are—at least that's my impression. That's why they go for cocaine and uppers."

"Are heroin and cocaine so very different?"

"Complete opposites. Taking heroin won't make you a better artist, nothing like that. But it may change how you see a picture. Not while you're painting, but when you're imagining what to paint next. If I painted, I think I'd experiment with heroin."

"I'll go it my own way. What I could do in five years on heroin, I'll do in thirty years without. The end result is the same."

"Figured that way, what you could do in thirty years on heroin would take you 180 years without. You haven't got that much time."

"It's a tempting argument."

"But the decision is entirely yours. I'm merely offering the benefit of my experience."

The next three nights you ate dinner with Inge. The talk was all art; neither of you said a word about heroin. You showed her the pictures you painted each day and she came back with very incisive criticisms. Topics ranged from the Old Masters to the Americans. Warhol was a whore, but Johns maybe had something. Could you see a Southeast Asian Fauvist movement?—after all, the French Fauves were tropical in sensibility. Judging from his excellent *China Diary*, David Hockney did the best work of any European in Asia in recent years. (You made a note to order the book when you got back to Japan.)

The whole while, Inge showed no sign of any change. Was she on heroin or not? Could it really be so low-key? No mention was made, but heroin was on your mind. A dangerous gamble, but maybe it could push you further, to a different level of art. And if it didn't work out, well, you'd deal with that when the time came. Just wash your hands of it. Or would you become addicted? The thoughts came and went, spiraled and vaporized, but the embers remained, just waiting to flare up again. Yes, she was a strange lady, this one.

Was heroin intensified morphine? Well, both came from opium. Remember that story about the old opium addict? You heard it from a girl who chatted you up while you were painting in Singapore. Got kind of friendly, but that was it (somewhere you had her name written down in a sketchbook—Huang Suyin—the Chinese characters came instantly to mind, the brilliance of having a shared written heritage). Over dinner, she started talking about her grandfather, who'd lived half his life on opium. He'd been a skilled shipyard worker, with lots of children. Earned a good salary, so ordinarily the family would've been quite well off. Except for the fact that half his earnings went up in opium smoke. He put in a good day's work, ate supper, then holed up in the attic and smoked. She'd seen the old man up there when she was small. As far as she could tell, he was always good-tempered, though on the quiet side; she remembered how, passing in the hall at night, he'd move out of the way of his grandchildren.

Sometimes, though, he couldn't get any opium. Like when there wasn't any money on hand in the house. He would be flat on his back, mouth and nose gummy with saliva and snot. Coughing the whole time. Withdrawal symptoms. But then didn't she say he was off to work at the shipyard the very next morning? Didn't he lead a normal life until he could get enough money to buy the stuff again? At least their family life didn't seem to have fallen apart.

Even so, if it hadn't been for her grandfather's habit, all the children would have had high-school educations. That's what her father, the old man's number-two son said. The whole family would have been one step up the social ladder. She was in college now studying art, but that was her father's doing. Grandfather's habit didn't ruin the family, but it delayed progress toward a modern life by a whole generation (as if "a modern life" was so worth having).

You understood the bit about opium walking off with a good half of a workman's wages. At the time, you thought it was simply an old man's weakness, but now what struck you was how he kept his two lives squared away, his drugs apart from his daily livelihood. So it *was* possible. The nightly opium binges couldn't have helped his day job at the shipyard, but at least they didn't get in the way. And from what the granddaughter said, the old man seemed quite contented, otherwise she wouldn't have reminisced so warmly about him.

Opium isn't heroin. Still, the story did draw you one little step closer to the idea of a separate life with heroin, of heroin changing your art. Not that you'd hit a dead end, but you rose to any mention of new directions, new visions. The difference it was going to make in your creativity, beckoning you to an undiscovered world of light, of timeless color and form. The evening sun slanting across Angkor Wat, millennia encased in stone. Yourself a block of cool weight sleeping happily cheek to the earth.

It was tantilizing, but only an idea, until one evening, after a day of sketching stones in the temple grounds, you find yourself knocking on Inge's door, testing the words, "Once, just once, I'd like to try it."

"Sure," is all she says. She studies your face at length, as if appraising its worth, though in fact not a trace of her inner thoughts show.

"But I'm a little scared of trying it alone. I'd like to try it with you there, under your supervision. Just a little. And if it doesn't go well, I'll quit then and there."

"It's not so easy. Usually the first time you don't come on at all, it just makes you sick. It takes two or three times before you get it."

"If it's not for me, I'll stop. I'll go back to Japan and that'll be the end of it. Just like with you and Germany and your accountant job, I've got my art. In the end, that's what matters."

"So it will be entirely at your own risk."

Was that the German in her speaking? Individual free will and actions duly conscribed within the limits of dignity. And the other person merely looking on. Inge opens her luggage and takes out a small glass vial, some pharmaceutical glassine, and miniature balance scales. "The amount is critical. This is what I use. Let's put you at 5mg for your first time."

She places a leaf of glassine on either dish of the scales, then sets the smallest brass weight on one side, a thin metal postage stamp with upturned corners for tweezer handling and an embossed number "10." Into the opposite dish she taps a pinch of white powder from the vial, then a little more. The scales awaken into motion, the needle swaying left and right of the center mark on the graduate arc. "That's ten mils. Now half that."

Inge deftly moves the paper to the desktop, then divides the white powder into two piles using a needle tool. Out comes a pack of Rothmans. She withdraws one cigarette, snips off the filter and carefully funnels in half the powder, taps the concoction several times on the desk to tamp it down, then hands it to you. The whole procedure has a solemn air of ritual about it.

"Here. Smoke this. Don't puff, just inhale deeply. The powder's all within one centimeter of the tip, so you don't need to smoke any more than that."

The first thing you experience is discomfort. A horrible gagging sensation.

Something awful racing around in your body. Probably like the first time you tasted beer, says a passing thought—you still can't take beer, can't take any alcohol. You don't smoke either, for that matter. But this isn't the harshness of tobacco, not the irritation of the smoke. Before you can think it through, nausea hits. All you did was inhale some smoke and now you're sick to your stomach, as if some foreign object had lodged in your gut and your body's trying to shove it back out. You rush straight to the toilet, but there's nothing to spit up. Only your stomach seized with spasms, pretending to vomit. Then after a while it settles down.

Inge watches you in silence. Not judging, only observing—*on course, exactly as expected.* The nausea has subsided, but now you break out in a cold sweat. The discomfort remains constant. You sit around vaguely waiting for something to happen. It does. More nausea. You kneel there groaning on the cold tiles.

After a few more bouts, what's this? Do you detect a pale ghost of pleasant sensation? Lethargy, a lazy holiday tide. Nothing that asks to be done, no need to resist the tidal drift. Take it easy, sit in a chair, physical mass supported by seat and backrest. Or no, now your body weight evaporates as well. A vaporous nowhere sensation. Is this it? Impossible to get a grasp on. Don't think.

Ages later you get up and say "Thanks," then return to your room. The feeling still rides on. Lying on the bed, you lazily entertain ideas for painting. Like this, wouldn't that work? Can't get up the strength to paint just now, but you'll do it soon enough. Just like that. Simple. A good strong image. Anyway, feels great. An echo of that contented old Chinese grandfather in Singapore. You go to sleep that evening without eating.

The following morning, you're famished. You head out in search of sustenance, and there's Inge alone in the breakfast nook with her toast and butter and honey and coffee.

"Morning," you call out.

"Morning. I've something to tell you. Later." Her tone is cold, dismissive. That's okay. You tuck into your own breakfast, then head back to your room to collect your paints and brushes.

What Inge tells you as you walk together through the village is this: the next step is up to you. There are people who destroy themselves with heroin. There's no denying that. On the other hand, one person right here —herself—knows how to coexist with it. So take care. She's catching a plane back to Germany today and can't offer you any more heroin. From here on it's up to you to decide, though to be honest, it's a bit worrying how far you went your first time. You may not be the right body type. Still, not everyone who drinks becomes an alcoholic, and the same goes for heroin. Don't say she didn't warn you.

"There *is* one school of thought that says users out working real jobs in society rarely succumb. It's those whose lives center on heroin who get in over their heads. They pour in all their money, then can't pay for the next round. Those with confidence and solid social lives are relatively resistant to addiction. Still, it only takes one slip and down you go."

"These past few days, you didn't do any?" you ask her.

"I was in the weaning-off stage. I was hardly using it by the time I met you up there painting. Otherwise I wouldn't have had any interest in anyone else. I was trying to resurface into the external world, trying to get back quickly to my German persona, which is why I even spoke to you."

"I couldn't tell, one way or the other."

"When I'm totally on heroin, I never leave my room."

"Is that how it goes?"

"I can tell you now, you were *this* close. When you took my hand, I nearly came on to you. If you'd been just a little more determined, if you'd been more forceful like a European man, I might well have given in." Inge gives you a teasing look.

"I'll keep it in mind." Your joking response chases up a residual wash of last night's happy lethargy. The pleasure is still in you, it hasn't left. Your brain responds in kind, simply can't resist. Like getting a kinky turn-on from being tied up, only softer, more subtle, seemingly inexhaustible. Are you imagining things, or replaying, or waiting for the next round?

"And how was it for you, last night?" Inge asks.

"It was good. Don't know if it will make a difference in my art, though.

I'm still trying to decide whether or not to try a second time."

"Your decision. But if it's any help, should I leave you the scales? I can always buy another set in Germany. It's very important that you do not increase the amount."

You think it over. Just how much did you really want to do it again? How about spending a few more days here to repeat the experience, then take off like Inge? Couldn't be much harm in that. "Okay, I'll take you up on it."

"Actually, there's a little left, so I'll throw that in too. But I want a painting in exchange."

"Fair trade. Which one will it be?"

"The temple. The one you were painting when we met." And so Inge returned to Germany with one favorite watercolor of yours under her arm.

That afternoon, you measure out precisely the same amount as the day before, mix it in with cigarette tobacco, and light up. This time you only vomit twice before that slow diffusing otherness kicks in, total pleasure filling out every recess in your viscera, taking you far, far away from all the excitement and commotion to what you can only describe as some great unmoving sense of affirmation. You know you're here to paint and the scenery is right there, but you just don't feel like going out. It's not that it's too much trouble or you're too listless; the endeavor itself seems wholly unnecessary. The world is beautiful enough—why try to put it down in pigments on paper? Yes, it's all perfectly beautiful as it is.

After coming down, an aura of the pleasure still lingers. No particular aftereffects, only a lack of appetite. You eat only a light supper, then go out walking. That night you sleep soundly—not so bad, eh? Maybe it's like drinking, a quieter version of alcohol.

Next day you decide to paint. Pack a single-dose cigarette together with your paints and some lunch, then head out. Find a spot on the hillside and begin to sketch the vista below. Your body doesn't really want to. The doing seems somehow beside the point, a leftover of yesterday's complacency. Okay, don't force it. You hardly touch the lunch you brought with you. Instead your hand reaches for the cigarette, the lightest brand you could find, as Inge instructed. Light up and take deep drags. You know you're not going anywhere once it kicks in, so you find yourself an isolated patch of shade where no one will bother you, then lean back against a tree. This time it comes on straight away with no vomiting. You stay until dusk, returning to the inn after it wears off. Slightly nauseous, but nothing serious.

And so it goes for several days. Hovering at a fixed plateau of pleasure, never increasing the amount. Outside is better than in your room. No shortage of places, no prospects of rain—that's what so nice about tropical countries like this. (Spoken like an expert.)

In another two days you'll run out of the stuff. A good place to stop. Make this village your regular thing, perhaps, and come back next year to meet Inge, a happy users' reunion. Packing it in doesn't sound so difficult. But just in case, what about buying some to take back to Japan where it's next to impossible to find? No, wonderful as the stuff is, it's nothing to get stuck on. Even if it were legal, maybe you'd only take some on weekends. You're okay, not causing problems for anyone else, what's to go wrong? Just a little risky fun.

The next day you find a spot by a stream. Don't bring any lunch because you're not going to eat anyway. Drink a little water, then light up. The same fixed amount. The same feeling, slowing time down to eons. Not quite a stone yet—a tree maybe, trunk pushing upward, branches spreading, leaves sprouting, drinking in the sun. One minute equal to a day in this other body time.

The stream is about thirty meters away, the width of a two-lane road. Muddy, but a fairly strong current. Banked in dirt and grass, with a bridge a little further upstream. You spend the entire afternoon just watching it flow. The water rushes by, but its course remains the same, unchanging; for some reason that seems incredibly important.

Children come, a whole gang of them playing on the bank. In your mind's eye you can see Tanh and his cohorts, maybe ten at the oldest, three at the bottom end. They're rafting leaves and twigs downstream for their friends to catch. Yes, and some rafts get whisked away into the middle of the current out of reach. The kids cheer at each exaggerated lunge. No one notices you sitting up there. So this is how kids play here, you smile to yourself.

Looks like fun. Everything positive, everything natural.

They start to scatter. No, there's one left, the very youngest, squatting there in the grasses on the bank. Good, you like their little games. He tries to throw something in the water. Tears off a blade of grass and drops it in, just like the older kids did. Over and over again he repeats the gesture. That's right, repetition's the thing. Always the same, that's what counts. That's what keeps the cosmos on course. Yes.

The child leans out over the water, wobbles, then falls right in without a sound. The stream swiftly bears him away. *Oh, he fell*, you think. *Sank in the water. Gone.* Sometimes the cosmos reclaims lives before they mature. All carried away on the water's flow. So be it.

The shock of recognition hits—a minute later? Ten minutes? Like a gust of wind sweeping away the fog. Why did you just sit there watching? You just saw a child to his death. All you had to do was run down there and dive in after him. You're an excellent swimmer, and the stream doesn't look all that deep, not over adult height. You sit there paralyzed.

Stand up, scan the stream; there's no sign of him. Of course not, he's long gone by now. Maybe someone saw him and saved him further down? Maybe he's still caught in the current? No, you saw a child lose his life, just stood by looking on. An infant playing alone by the water's edge and you hadn't the least premonition of impending danger. And by now, what can you do? Nothing. Still you go down to the stream and look. You strain your eyes far downstream—in vain. Start to walk along the bank, break into a trot, then a headlong dash. No child anywhere. Utterly exhausted, you collapse.

Some time later you drag yourself back to the inn, not a whiff of all-affirming heroin left in your system. You're less than human. The infant slowly turns and falls, turns and falls, over and over again in your mind. Mustn't tell a soul what happened, can't look anyone in the face. You head straight for your room and fall flat out on the bed, plunged into remorse for your crime—*You just killed a child.*

You lie there shivering late into the night, but sleep doesn't come. For all your wonderful heroin high, your glorious cosmic affirmation, you couldn't save that kid's life. He's bobbing face-down somewhere. Or else someone downstream recovered him, and a grieving mother is now cradling the cold little body in her arms. Just think how An would grieve if it were her son Tanh, sole keepsake of her dead husband!

Dawn approaches. You've got to do *something*. To put yourself out of your misery, you smoke your last dose, a messy half-measure mixed with tobacco. As it comes on, softening and soothing—*forget it, it couldn't be helped*—the voice condemning you retreats into the distance. The all-knowing cosmos gathers in young life again and beckons you to insensate sleep.

Next day you decide to pack your things and leave. Gone is the numbing calm, as is the heroin itself. All that remains by daylight is a bleak despair. Villagers are gathered out in the road, whispering in somber tones.

"Did something happen?" you ask the innkeeper as you settle your bill.

"Yesterday, child missing."

"Oh." You quickly pay your money, grab your things, and start walking in the direction of Chiang Mai. There's an afternoon bus, but you can't wait, not for anything. What if those villagers found out? Scared shitless, you walk at a furious clip. A villain fleeing the scene of the crime. Got to get out to the main road and flag a ride, fight the urge to rest.

Hours later in Chiang Mai, you wearily unload your baggage at a hostel. A room to hide in, any room will do. Curl up on the makeshift bed with your head in your hands. You've come this far, you're safe, everything's all right. Yet the child bobbing face-down in the water won't go away. You can see the villagers coming after you, the bleary-eyed mother leading the mob. *You killed him! Molested the child, strangled it, floated the body downstream!*

No, it wasn't like that. *Just watched, didn't do anything at all, that's what's so horrible. But it couldn't be helped.* You try in vain to conjure up that heroin haze of reassurance.

Got to silence this pain. You suppress your fatigue and stagger out into the busy tourist street. There's a shifty-looking man standing on a corner eyeing all the *farang*.

"Any heroin?" you wonder out loud, acting as unobtrusively as your state will allow.

"What—H?"

The man doesn't have any, but he knows someone who does. Down a dusty backstreet you find an ordinary-looking house, and in a dirty back room you ask for the very smallest amount you can buy. Was it really this easy to purchase? More expensive than you'd imagined, but luckily that's no concern. Anything to relieve the anguish.

Back at the hostel, you weigh it on the scales. Pick some of the tobacco out of a cigarette with a straightened paper clip, stir in the white powder and tamp it down, light up and breathe deep. After a while it starts to work, but for some reason it's not like before. You mix up a chaser, the same amount again. And finally a soothing calm visits you with assurances that, no, it couldn't be helped.

Only this time when it runs out, it hits hard. Naked, icy pain. Your gut doesn't lie—it *was* your fault and knowing it is torture. Misery eats into your cells, ravages your tissues with sub-zero fury. There's no defense, not against the helplessness of an infant so innocent, so tragic. No denying or dismissing, no adult evasiveness or pretense of forgetting. The child's avenging angel flies straight at you with a sword, sharp as the sorrow of the lost life. Hunts you down, drives you into a corner. And you take flight.

And so the amounts increase. In three days you've used up all you bought, which should have seen you through a week. You go back to buy more. Five times your last packet.

"You not want needle?"

"Mm? How do you use it?"

"You not know? Strange customer. I teach you, needle more faster." He shows you how it's done.

And further down you slide. Each time, the lingering calm is wonderful —while it lasts. Inge recedes into the distance, but then the Sad Child Angel looms ever closer, driving you to increasing doses, a good customer for any pusher.

"Turning to stone" just about describes the inertial mass of your thoughts. If all you have to do is exist, stay motionless as a rock, why wear yourself out doing anything? . . . Or no, not a rock. You're stratosphering. High in the sky where the angels fly. Suspended blissfully above it all, animate and inanimate alike. Nothing but light, aerial blue far and wide. Viewed from this arc of infinite time, the death of a single child is nothing, the fate of any individual nothing. To the transcendent eye what matters is the big philosophical picture.

Brave words for chasing off an angel. But the pose crumbles as soon as the heroin wears off. You're the world's most pathetic loser, not a thought for art or anything else in your head.

One time only, you painted under the influence. By some fluke, the heroin acted as an upper, jolting awake the painter in you. The angel taunted and accused as you charged your brush with paint and drew—a shape. Or no, why bother with shape at all? The lines that came from your brush were utterly meaningless. Better no shapes, no form. Matter is strangled in form, that's why ordinary things suffer. Go further, beyond. Let the rock slip from its delineating skin and blend into the air. Liquify and escape, free from all bonds of superficial form. *That* would be something to bring off.

You try this and that, quickly tossing each sheet and starting another. How to express the essence of things? How to render the absolute in paint? The solution eludes, never quite *there*. You're so tired, but this is work, *your* work. It takes effort to make a breakthrough. If you just sweat this through you'll have a masterpiece, transcending every human effort in paint so far. A portrait of god done right under the angel's nose. The colors are still too dark; make it lighter. Air is hydrogen and helium. Weightless. Pale and ineffable, an airborne cosmos. Space floating in space. Eternal stone time. Isn't that right, Inge?

You painted nonstop. Until the drug did. Your body drooped, like an astronaut returning to ground level G-force. A game of tag, as it turned out —keeping one step ahead of gravity, moving the brush held firmly in your hand, to finish this masterpiece to end all masterpieces. Then, finally satisfied that you outmaneuvered the angel, you tumbled into bed for a short nap, all blissed out from the opiate still streaming though your system. A smile of satisfaction drifted over your lips at your accomplishment.

Three hours later you woke to the dreg discomfort of it all and confronted your ultimate artwork. There was nothing on the paper. No shape, no color—nothing. What on earth had you been up to? Wash upon wash, lighter ever lighter, back to hydrogen and helium, thinning the pigments that tainted eternity. Which meant you were painting with water alone. The sheet had been wiped clean, the rippled surface the only sign of ever having seen a brush. Your great masterpiece, a picture painted in water alone. The reason no artist ever produced the ultimate picture was paint itself. Some great cosmic revelation.

You began to cry. This was much more pathetic than that watercolor washed off by the rain.

After that, all hell descended. When the heroin ran out, your trauma at the stream became a fear of water. All water. You couldn't even bare to look at what little it took to dilute your paints. Couldn't drink a sip. The glass at your lips summoned the Sad Child Angel, knowing the kid swallowed much more than that. Another fix to drown out the voice of the drowned.

Withdrawal comes fierce. The angel does not forgive. The dosage claws higher and higher. For four months it lasts, until some last-ditch instinct for self-preservation pushes you to throw away the scales, crush the syringe, and run for that temple outside Bangkok.

Looking back now, when did you actually make the biggest breakthrough in your art? It was twelve years ago, in your mid-teens. After a childhood spent with crayons and pencils and watercolors you begged your parents for a set of oil paints. Your element was already shape and color, the way light hit things and created shadows, the way objects and light made colors and textures. That was your world, and you were adept at capturing it all in drawings and sketches. Want to be popular with your classmates? Draw a kitten or a child; it's recognizable shapes that have most impact on us.

Flowers—real, unidealized flowers—are more difficult. The same with sunsets. Artists have painted sunsets for centuries, but no matter who paints them they're a cliché. There ought to be a way to see them with new eyes —but how? From Leonardo to Lichtenstein, you could mimic anyone's hand. You could be an expert forger, as if that held any attraction. Art history doesn't need two Michelangelos. "Genius copyist" is a contradiction in terms.

There are times when you just grab some big, fat brushes and slap oils down on canvas, forget detail and act on impulse. It was like that when you painted your kid sister. Not that you ever thought to ask her to model. Late one spring morning (it had to be a Sunday, because you were both at home), returning from the corner store, you ran into Kaoru moving a pot of flowers—bougainvilleas, they were—out of the shade. Pressed into carrying that big, heavy pot, she was being careful not to break it, the stress visible in her face, brought out by a shaft of spring sun. A fantastic image.

"Hey, hold it right there!" you called out, then raced into the house to grab paper and pencil. Ever-obedient Kaoru stayed glued in place.

"This weighs a ton, and Mom wants it over by the front door."

"Yeah, I hear you. This'll only take a sec." You sketched the basic forms and it looked great.

"C'mon, this is killing me. I'm tired already."

"Kaoru, whatever you want, just name it."

"A jumbo jet."

"A plastic model?"

"The real thing. Eight hundred billion yen. Make me an airline and I'll be a stewardess."

"You can test for stewardess without buying a plane," you said, keeping your hand in motion.

"No way. It's got to be my own uniform design."

"All right, all right. I'll buy you one, just hold that pose."

"It's heavy!"

You kept the pencil racing. Something special here, you could feel it. You had the overall composition down, with little notations about the light. This was an oil, for sure.

"If you let me put down the flowers, you could draw me as long as you want. Be loads easier on my arms, too."

"You can't pretend weight. The body shape looks completely different. When you carry something heavy, your shoulders and elbows tighten up, your waist drops. There's a nice tension to the whole posture."

"C'mon, I've never seen any painting posed like this."

"That's why I wanted to do it. To paint something no one's ever done before. The flowers are pretty, the light is just right, the tension looks good."

"And my face?"

"Your face, too. I've got it in the picture."

"That's not what I meant and you know it! My face is pretty, too, isn't it?"

"It's not for your own brother to say."

"What's *that* supposed to mean!"

The payback for the joke came much later, but meanwhile the sketch was brilliant. You transferred it to canvas and dabbed in some color from memory, then a few days later at approximately the same hour you set up your easel in the garden to recreate the scene. When Kaoru came home from school—your middle school got out early—you had her stand wearing the same outfit. "This time without the flowerpot?" Then the following Sunday, in the calm light of late morning, you painted her face in detail. Still a child's, it was nonetheless full of character. Not exactly everyone's idea of beauty, but yes, even beautiful—though you'd never tell her that.

The picture was getting interesting. Now to really paint it. No fine brushes, only flats and palette knife. Lay it on thick, practically molding the face; overpainting *impasto*, scraping away occasionally; building up the surface in dense layers. The result, when you finally stood back, was a far cry from a portrait. Kaoru saw the finished piece but didn't say much. Maybe she was glad she'd made herself useful to her brother, but she would never admit it. Not to him.

And the thing about it was, the painting did prove a major turning point. The confidence that you'd painted something original changed you. Thinking back later, it was around this time you began to get concrete ideas about making a living by art.

Exactly what changed? Hard to say for yourself; easier to see in others. When Gauguin painted *Jacob Wrestling with the Angel* he probably didn't see it as a turning point, but for you at the time it was a revelation. His angel with the yellow wings had you transfixed. Jacob is fighting him with all the strength he can muster. Everyone has to wrestle his angel sooner or later— that hard truth is right there in the painting. Or at least you thought so as a teenager. Maybe it was more the literary theme than the work itself, but pictorially the sheer daring of it swept it way out of reach of mere mortals like yourself; the extreme conception of it, pushing the two main fighting figures all the way to the back and bringing that woman in prayer forward so big. As if to say, when elemental forces go at each other, life-and-death, those looking on can only pray. That gap, that distance.

Not unlike how your sister looked carrying those heavy flowers. She could have been carrying anything, of course: a puppy, a hot pan off the stove, it would have made no difference. The important part of handling things is in the focus, the solemn attention you give them, as if your life depended on it. And sometimes maybe it does. The resolve is the same, the care and caution in each step. That was the way your little sister stood there with that unwieldy flowerpot—those bougainvilleas were her sparring partner, her angel of the hour.

Of course, all this occurred to you in retrospect, a paltry rationale. Back then, it was forget the words, just paint. You placed a tall tree and sky in the background behind Kaoru—or rather, beneath her and the flowers— and there was the finished image. Not a doubt in the world.

And as it turned out, your *Burden of Flowers* was a critical success. It took Gold Prize for Painting at the All-Japan High School Festival of the Arts. One art magazine even hailed it as an "emergence of genius." Whatever, the award went a long way toward convincing the folks you could make it as an artist. That's the nuts and bolts of how you decided to turn professional. In those days all you ever heard in school was study-hard-go-to-university-get-a-job. Painting wasn't even an option. But the session with your sister in the garden changed all that, made you abandon the beaten path and find a life of your own.

And for what? You came all this way only to paint a pointless picture in plain water! The artist in you is dead.

11

KAORU

Sinking and sinking, never to float up. Deeper and deeper the more I kick and thrash. Lungs taking in water, impossible to breathe, I'm dead for sure. If only I could touch bottom to push up. Just hope my breath holds out. Hope there *is* a bottom.

The trial was excruciating, hotel life was excruciating. Everything was so uncertain. What if Gatir's best ended in the worst? I lay there in the dark, trying to think of something else: favorite restaurants in Tokyo, wonderful meals—all unreal and without taste.

I was sick at heart, said Kondra. He suggested I go out somewhere for a change of pace.

"I'm in no mood for a 'change of pace.'"

"That's exactly why you should go. If you can't be more *genki*, Tetsuro won't perk up either, and he won't look good in court."

I didn't have it in me to even argue. I was in his hands. "Where to?"

"I suggest Uluwatu. The air will do you good. I'll tell Wayang to take you."

Uluwatu—what or wherever that was. I had a guidebook, but I'd been too preoccupied to even look at it. All I knew as I got into the car was that the name had a vaguely magical ring to it. We drove past the airport, veered due north, then headed up into the hills. Out of the cluttered town into something more like real landscape. Beautifully lush vegetation, I remember thinking. What season was it here? Habitations grew fewer and still we climbed. After twenty minutes of woodland, we pulled into a big parking lot.

"Here is temple of Uluwatu," Wayang announced.

A temple? Hmm. I got out of the car.

"Please borrow sarong," he advised.

"Should I have worn a skirt?"

"No problem, but no trouser at temple."

At least I wasn't wearing hot pants like some dumb American tourist, but even full-length cotton slacks were no good apparently. I did as told and borrowed a plain green cloth wrap at the entrance counter. If only to put me in a more respectful mood.

"Take off earring, too," added Wayang. "Monkey steal for fun."

"Monkeys?"

"Yes. Maybe jump on head, pull earring."

What kind of place was this? Anyway, I obliged.

Wayang said he would wait for me here at the bottom, so I climbed the steps by myself. The sun blazed down. How could any place be this hot? My legs dripped with sweat, soaking my slacks under the sarong, making it hard to bend my knees and climb.

At the top, I headed through a stone gate and was suddenly hit by a blast of sea wind. What I'd taken for a mountain was a promontory jutting out into the sea. High above the surf, water spreading far and wide to either side, the temple building ahead blocked what I imagined was also sea. Kondra's "air" was so strong any sweat from the climb was soon a memory.

In the forecourt sat rows of people, all of them Balinese, all praying. A priest or head celebrant—he wore no special costume—handed out flowers and rice to each worshiper, then sprinkled them with water. Each raised the flowers gratefully with the fingertips of both hands, and daubed the wet grains of rice on their forehead.

How long I watched this I don't know. How beautifully they prayed! Why couldn't I pray? The desire was there, but not knowing the rituals or even who my own god might be, I couldn't see myself, a foreigner, sitting among them.

There were monkeys, like Wayang said, furry gray figures clambering over the stone walls and railings, climbing the bushes. Moving in droves, with sharp eyes and nimble little hands, babies clinging to their mothers' bellies. Fun to watch, but so far from anything I was used to, my emotions wouldn't reach. I shouldn't have come. These people, these animals, the sun and wind and sea—what were they to me? I was from another world, hermetically sealed in glass. Bring the jar here and nothing changes. I'd told Kondra I wasn't in the mood for a change, and this certainly wasn't the place for it.

I turned to go, back through the gate and down the steps. My mind was a blank. To the left was the parking lot; to the right, a path skirting the edge of the cliff. Shame to come all this way just to turn around, I thought, why not have a quick look in that direction? The path was dusty, with a stone retaining wall. I leaned over to discover a sheer drop to the watery blue below. I could see tiny white swirls of surf, the whole sea surging slowly, relentlessly. Huge waves rolled in from far offshore, their breaking crests spreading sideways as they neared. Curling into themselves to gain mass before they hit the shore, the blue went pure white, covering the whole surface with a froth that seethed up the rocks, then hesitated a thinning moment before withdrawing, white vanishing back out into the blue.

I fell into the rhythm, the slow, steady cycle of the sea feeding on itself. The waves came surging to me, a strong tang in the air each time they turned tail. I could make out each measured rumble of the undertow, the hiss of the spray, though in fact I was too far away to hear anything. The wind up on the cliff teased at my hair as though trying to pick a fight. I stood there, mesmerized.

As the sea swayed its ancient dance, I could feel myself growing more serene. My heartbeat slowed, my breathing became deeper. Salt air forced its way inside me, penetrating the knots in my head. And gradually my mind, too, began to move in phase with the sea, tangled nerves unfraying in the breeze.

I stepped back from the wall and sat down on the grass. The light from the great blue sky had changed in only the time I'd been here. I could think about Tez without agonizing. All this time, I'd been a mental case—that I knew. I'd been running in the wrong gear, overheating, corroding myself and everyone around me. "What's eating you?" people usually say, but with me it was definitely the reverse. It made no sense, but the strangest notion kept playing hide-and-seek across my mind: if I made a change *in here*, it might just change everything *out there*, altering the way things actually were. The idea came into sudden focus, like the view opening up atop the cliff.

Look around. Stand on this ground, this spot. *Here.* The events all happened here on this island, the trial was being held here. Sea and sky, *this* sea and sky. Everyone here lives and moves to the rhythm of this sea. Since coming here to Bali, when did I even look at the shape of the clouds, the swaying palm fronds, the bowing stalks of rice? (Just how often did they harvest here? Every field I passed always seemed heavy with grain.) The way people walked, their smiling faces, I'd ignored them all, never seeing the simplest significance in them, when it was staring right at me, so obvious, so natural.

But now another me was looking down on the person who sat looking at the sea and sky. Even from that high angle, this little me was anchored firmly in place, calmly scanning the horizon. Not cut off from her surroundings, but truly *in place*. In communion, sea and self. I sat there for about an hour, I suppose. Then finally I got up and went back to the car. As I got in, I remembered to put on my earrings. I could feel my fingers touching my ears, fully aware of what usually was an unconscious action.

The scenery out the window on the return trip was like water to a parched throat. I was spellbound. I was on this island. In this landscape. Between the patchwork houses, I saw so many dry, almost leafless trees, bursting with fluffy white pods.

"Wayang, what are those?"

"Kapok. Make soft inside pillow."

We drove past a field where a farmwoman looked up from her work and actually waved at me. To her it was nothing, a casual gesture, but it filled me with joy. I was happy as a child. She whizzed past out of sight, but her image stayed with me. I waved back at the absent figure in the car window. Tears came to my eyes. Like a thin trickle of tap water into a paper cup, the tears brimmed up and overflowed. What came over me? The tears just wouldn't stop. I gave in to my emotions. I pounded the cushions, pulled at my own hair. I couldn't tell if I was happy or sad. I was a baby curled up in the back seat, helpless to do anything but cry while Wayang kept on driving.

"Wayang, take me to a beach," I said. Not seen from above, somewhere I could reach out and touch the sea with my own hands.

"Where?"

"Anywhere, just a beach. With not too many people."

"We go Jinbaran."

We turned off the main road through a tightly clustered village to the shore. Children were running around playing, but otherwise the beach was deserted. The sea was calm.

"I'll be right back, just wait here."

I kicked my shoes off in the car and stepped onto the sand. I walked out to the water's edge and rolled up my cuffs to get my feet wet, then crouched down to dip my hands in. I splashed some water on my face, cool and sparkling. A tiny wave rode in, soaking the cuffs I thought I'd rolled up. I couldn't hold back, I had to walk out into the sea. It got deeper sooner than I thought, ten steps and I was up to my thighs. I wanted to plunge right in. Another two steps and slowly I lowered myself. The cold penetrated my clothes before I felt my skin get wet. The water enfolded me. I gave in to the sensation and ducked my head under. I could feel the seawater between each strand of hair, the salt washing over my whole body. I lifted my face. I was a different person from the one I'd been that morning.

After a while I went back up the beach, water gushing out of my clothes. My white blouse was plastered to my skin, plainly revealing the outlines of my bra—how embarrassing! Arms clutched across my chest, I hurried back to Wayang's car.

I found Wayang asleep in the driver's seat with the doors flung wide open. Not wanting to get the seat wet, I squeezed down onto the floor behind him with my knees tucked in, and that's how I rode back to the hotel. My Uluwatu high had mellowed into a lingering sense of physical well-being. Yet something in me still wanted to come out. It was only when I got out of the car that Wayang saw I was sopping wet, clothes and all. His eyes popped.

"I went for a little dip in the sea, thank you," was all I could say. I rushed into the hotel, picked up my key from a similarly wide-eyed front desk boy, dripped a fast trail to my room, and went straight to the bathroom, where I stripped off my things and took a nice hot shower.

Once that was done, I wrapped up in a bath towel with both arms clutched around myself and sat down on the edge of the bed. I rubbed my shoulders like a mother trying to calm an overexcited child. My hands were not my own; it was someone else soothing me. I got under the covers, closed my eyes, and began to rub myself all over. Easy now, calm down. Something welled up from deep inside. All right, you want to be touched, do you? How long has it been since you felt like this? I gently massaged my tummy, my skin still moist. Now I knew what I'd been missing. My body was mine again. This is *me*, this is the feeling. Touch, rub—yes. Making me sleepy, then wide awake again.

The feeling got stronger, coming on for real. A hot cloud gathering in my stomach, hot and juicy. I held my breasts with both hands and rolled the nipples with my fingertips. The delight built slowly, slowly. Like *this*. The body of a beautiful young god came bearing down on me. I heard the sound of my blood in my veins as that hand reached down below. The great waves of Uluwatu came surging in to meet me, drowning me in the world.

A funny thing happened at the next trial session. Witnesses for the prosecution were to take the stand: the policemen from the arrest, now called on to swear the planted carton of Marlboros had been there all along. We'd prepared our best counterarguments. It was sure to be the most crucial point in the proceedings.

Only, when the court convened and the judge told the prosecutor to call his witnesses, the prosecutor barely answered. The judge asked one more time, and again the prosecutor repeated the same thing. An expression of puzzled dismay came over the judge's face and a murmur rippled through the courtroom. Kondra leaned within whispering distance of Tez's ear.

Something strange was going on. The witnesses had failed to show, apparently. Sick or injured—or threatened into hiding, which was very possible in this country? But wait a minute, if anyone tried to prevent them from turning up it should have been us, the defense. And how could we have threatened the police? Tez had said there were half a dozen of them. All these cops couldn't take ill at the same time. Food poisoning? Hardly likely.

Gatir and the prosecutor conferred with the judge. The day's session was over in ten minutes.

Once we were in the car, Gatir confirmed that the witnesses had suddenly become "indisposed." But when the judge asked why, the prosecutor gave no answer.

"For so many cops not to show at once, it can't be for personal reasons."

"No, almost certainly not . . ." Gatir preferred not to speculate, saying we should wait and see what happened at the next session. The judge might hold the witnesses liable for contempt of court if they still didn't show.

"What's this all about?"

"I don't know. But whatever, it does us no harm. If these witnesses default on their testimony, the prosecution's argument falls to pieces."

I felt lighthearted. Things were beginning to turn. Ever since Uluwatu, the sun was shining on me. The rays even reached Tez. I was still wary, of course—I didn't want to be tricked by any false signs—but as I looked out the car window I just knew this was no hoax, things really had taken a turn for the better.

Later that afternoon, at fumigation hour, I decided to go out. Not to the beach, this time I braved the town. People's eyes were no longer menacing, I no longer had to slink about. Not a soul remembered me from the papers or even gave me a second look. They were too busy with their own lives and having a good time, and by the time they folded the newspaper they'd forgotten about some brother and sister on trial. My face meant nothing.

I went back to that *warung* where I'd heard the kayaking story. This time I took a terrace table by the street. I was wearing sunglasses, but I could see all the passersby. And for a fact, no one—man or woman, local or tourist— paid any attention to me. I blended right in, just another tourist. It felt good.

I ordered a coffee. The waitress brought it out, and I drank slowly, thinking things over. Yes, I thought about Tez. Was the change in the trial real? Could I trust a little sign like that? Only time would tell. I pictured myself at Uluwatu, seen from above. My sky-eye saw me sitting on the grass gazing out to sea. Why couldn't I see the whole panorama of time like that? Why couldn't I see Tez next year, a tiny figure roaming through an Asian landscape, painting away happily?

The far half of the table caught the sun, this half was shaded. An ant on the tabletop was walking in the shadow, getting close to the sunny side, but it still didn't know. The minute it reached the light, its body temperature would rise. Probably feel full of energy. It was the same with people. Tez just happened to stray into the shadow and I followed along after. We were both wandering around in the dark, though anyone looking down from above could tell we were almost out into the light. Was there any point in praying to whoever could see these things? "Whoever"—God or Buddha— would just look on, never lift a finger to move the ant into the light. The ant had to walk for itself. So of course I never prayed.

The ant made it into the sun. And the next thing I knew it was gone, run off somewhere, probably down the table leg and across the blazing ground. I suddenly felt very hungry. I asked for a menu and studied it carefully, then ordered a *nasi champur, soto ayam*, and beer.

The *nasi champur* came, a heap of rice in the center of a big plate, surrounded by meat and fish and vegetables. The *soto ayam* chicken stock was nice and thick. And the beer—Indonesian Bintang, what else? I was ravenous, I could practically feel the nutrients recharging my body. I was back in the world.

The following day, I got a call from Gatir. "I've learned a few things. It seems the police chief is on his way out."

"That evil creep?"

"Yes." I could almost see Gatir's sardonic smile at the other end of the line. "The word is that his wrongdoings came to light. He may even be indicted."

"That's great! Makes me feel wonderful. And the trial?"

"The prosecutor is probably due for substitution, too. He was rather too close to the police chief. Very likely the whole case will have to be restructured."

"Which is good news for Tez, isn't it?"

"Well, I should imagine so."

Gatir was still guarded, but I was jumping for joy. I felt so sure in my own mind, I decided then and there to go visit Tez. I'd been seeing him regularly together with Kondra and Gatir for consultations about the trial, but when was the last time we met just the two of us? I'd given up going when I got so paranoid, and Tez hadn't insisted. The-worst-that-could-happen still sat square in the center of both our thoughts. Even discussing the most commonplace things, his food or laundry, one false word would make us clam up. It seemed easier on both of us to sit things out apart until some decision was reached. He didn't have to tell me, I knew. But now the waiting was over.

My brother didn't seem so very changed, but he was obviously surprised to see me on my own.

"Did you hear about what's happening?"

"You mean about the police chief getting the boot? Yeah, I heard."

"This changes everything."

"You think so? Well, maybe. Still too early to tell." He remained as cautious as our attorney. Okay, I could understand that he didn't want to fall prey to false hopes. But more than the news of the police chief's downfall, I believed in the change in myself, or—at the risk of exaggerating—the change in my fate. What changed at Uluwatu was me.

"Don't worry, I've got a feeling things'll work out."

"I'd like to believe that. But considering how things tend to 'work out' in this country, I don't feel so secure about a magically disappearing police chief."

Okay, Tez, let's change the subject. "A few days ago, I went to Uluwatu."

"It's a temple, right? Out on a sea cliff, isn't it?"

"You know about it?"

"Just what I've heard."

"It's a wonderful place. You look out from the top of a cliff and there's the wide open sea, big waves rolling in. Makes you dizzy just looking at it. Gets you high."

"I'll be sure to go see it, once I get out of here."

I sensed an irritated edge to his voice. It was just like old times—Sis screwing up again. I was such a slow, clumsy child and Tez would get after me for every little thing. Only this time *I* was right. Everything really was going to get better. Not that I could take Tez to Uluwatu the day after tomorrow, but still lots better. That's when it struck me: whatever I told Tez wouldn't make any difference. He'd just think I was dancing in my dreams. It was kind of frightening, I had no guarantee to back up my optimism. Better just shut up.

Actions, not words. Maybe not now, but in a few days' time, the simple fact of my coming to the jail alone and talking a happy streak about that temple might give him a lift. Strange I could suddenly be so confident. There was so little to pin it on, yet I was completely convinced the course of my life had changed. Miraculous Uluwatu! Strange place, Bali. I left Tez still looking glum, but I'd done my bit.

That evening, I went back to the *warung* and had a nice cup of coffee, then an early dinner. It was becoming a daily routine. Off with the armor and I was just one more face in the place. I'd go the same time every day and meet the same regular customers. At first I'd simply nod, *Oh, you again*, but soon it was "Hey!" and "How goes it?" and "Where you staying?" When it got around that this Japanese girl could speak passable English and French, there were lots of people to talk to. A repeat performance of Paris. Most were fellow-travelers of hippiedom and I knew a lot about traveling—if not always firsthand—so there was no shortage of talk. Hippies had become something of an endangered species, but what few remained claimed Bali as their paradise. Listening to them, I could practically plot the route of their pilgrimage.

Agnès and Jean were a French couple I befriended. Which is to say we only talked inconsequential travel tales, nothing deeper than that. Neither knew about Tez. Or if they did, they didn't let on.

"*Il y a un spectacle de danse ce soir, on t'amène? Tout le monde y va,*" said Agnès, inviting me along.

"Quelle espèce de danse?"

"Des maîtres de la danse Legong."

Some sort of Balinese dance? I had no idea where they were going, but I was in my Keep Active mode, so why not? I quickly polished off my meal, then fifteen of us crammed into two taxis, and we headed out of town. I felt like a student again; my first group activity in ages, like putting the clock back ten years. I sat on the floor of the car, someone's knee in my face, my elbow poking someone else in the behind. Everyone was talking up an Esperanto storm. All I knew was that somewhere at the end of this trip something was supposed to happen.

After a while the taxi pulled to a stop, and we untangled our limbs and got out. The place was an outdoor amphitheater surrounded by dark trees. A large crowd was already gathered. We filtered into any spare patches of ground we could find, us few foreigners diluted unnoticed into the mass of Balinese. I for one was glad we didn't stay clumped together in a group, and the locals around me didn't seem to mind us either.

There was a slight breeze, but still it was hot and humid. The sun was on the wane. I sat there amidst a drama of different smells—the damp earth, leafy trees, people sweating, food being eaten, flowers and perfume—all alive with expectation. The ground felt nice and cool. Everyone crowded in around an open square spread with plaited grass mats. Otherwise there was no real stage. Musicians were seated toward the back, behind a row of strange percussion instruments. Unnoticed, they were already playing. Gently, patiently, never insisting, all but drowned out, a fine stream of music filtered through the noise.

Gradually the audience quieted down. And when it was almost dark, a little girl who had been sitting in front of the musicians got up, walked out to the middle of the mats, and just stood there. She had on a showy costume and flowers in her hair, but I only took her for a warm-up act. Suddenly the music changed. They were performing for real. At a clash of gongs the girl sprang into action: treading the ground with lithe legs, arms outswept, fingers fanned, her whole body snapping sharply into position with each pounding beat. This was no child's dance, this was the art of a professional, polished to a taut precision after constant repetition. She looked like a kid, but maybe she was just very small. No, with those proportions, she could only be a child.

Her body shook from bottom to top in minute pulsations. Tiny volcanic tremors vibrated from the dancer's body down into the earth and up into the sky . . . only to snap to a halt, her arms and legs each snaking now to rhythms completely independent of the rest of her. Several times she leaped across the space, then struck a pose with each gong beat, stillness and motion, stillness and motion. It was wonderful.

The dancer picked up two fans from the mats and, while she slowly strutted about, two more girls stood up from their places in front of the musicians and joined in the dance, both wearing far more ornate costumes than the first girl. Crowns piled high with plumeria blossoms, bodices intricately worked with gold brocade—or were those gold-leafed ornaments? They too were maybe ten or twelve years old. As it turned out, these were the main dancers of the evening. The first girl handed a fan to each of them, and so began a long, elegant, intense dialogue in dance.

The moon rose. A full moon, so the dance floor needed no artificial light. Poses barely discernible in the dying afterglow of sunset were floodlit under the night sky. Halfway into the performance I realized the dance was telling some kind of story, which everyone in the audience apparently knew. I couldn't tell the characters by their gestures or expressions, yet I was drawn in, too. I forgot I was sitting among hundreds of others watching a dance. I couldn't be bothered to breathe—I often hold my breath when I'm watching something amazing. I had no idea there were things like this on the island.

Who *were* these island folk? Where had these children learned to dance like this? Here I'd been shunting back and forth between the hotel and the courthouse, oblivious to all of this. I'd practically turned my back on the island. How much more culture lay behind this dance? If the children were so good at it, what did the adults do to compete?

The two dancers' counterpoint grew more and more technically demanding. Moving at incredible speed, their steps were always perfectly synchronized—so perfectly, in fact, that the second they stopped, their silhouettes were absolutely identical. The splayed arcs of their fingers, the tilt forward from the arched soles to the knees, the bend of their backs from waist to ribs, the tucked-in chins—everything matched immaculately. Even the curves of music molded smoothly to each posture, moving them on and on. When they darted their eyes sideways, the whites glinted in the moonlight. The palms of their dark-skinned hands shone white as they turned to face the moon.

When finally the long dance ended, the moon was high in the heavens. The surrounding trees etched shadows on the ground. I'd been so breathlessly involved in the sheer intensity of the performance—part of me just wishing the excitement would let up, another part wanting it to go on forever—I'd lost all track of time. But then everyone got up to go. Exhausted, glad of the night air, I followed the flow of people.

"*C'était quoi, tout ça?*" I asked Agnès, once I'd searched her out in the crowd.

"*Mais, la danse Legong.*"

"Yes, but what *is* the Legong dance?" I pressed, switching to English in frustration.

"Is what you see. *Les Balinais* all love it. They do it so often. We invite you again soon."

"*Merci bien.* But those children dancing, who were they? What were they supposed to be?"

"I do not know. But the one, she is very famous." Which one? She didn't explain.

"And the story? *L'histoire?*"

"*Hélas, qui sait?*"

"You should ask Manuel," Jean suggested from the side.

"Who is . . . ?"

"*Très expert. Il connaît tous ces trucs balinais.*"

"Is he here now?"

"*Non. Pas ce soir.* But go to the *Warung Made*, you will meet him sooner or later."

The next day was another court session, but it ended almost as soon as it began. A new prosecutor appeared due to "unspecified circumstances," and he asked that the court be adjourned until such time as they had reviewed their case. The judge grudgingly agreed. "Until they had reviewed their case" had to mean they'd dropped their former charges which hung on a thread of false testimony and friendly witnesses. Very good news indeed. I felt so relieved, and even Gatir looked pleased once the session closed.

The following afternoon we all went to the jail and told Tez the news.

"What do you think's going to happen?" I asked Gatir point-blank.

"Well, they'll certainly drop the 200g charge. However, Tez has more or less admitted to buying from Agus, so there is little hope of a total acquittal. Which means, if we can't get a waiver, we have to try for a lighter sentence."

"Does this rule out the possibility of a death penalty?" asked Tez. It was the first time I'd heard him ask anything so directly or realistically about his own future. I was overjoyed.

"Unless Jakarta takes a hard line. And as far as I've heard, the new prosecutor has no special political motives," said Gatir, serious as ever, though the message itself was encouraging.

"He's a relative of an acquaintance of mine," Kondra put in. "Born in Bali, stayed in Bali since university, so I don't imagine he has any strong connections to Jakarta."

"Then I guess we can relax a little and just wait for the next session," said Tez.

Hearing my brother say the word "relax" made me loosen up as well. Up to now, the very idea of relaxing, of trying to cool down, had been next to inconceivable. No lifeline of hope, no flimsy tightrope to security was worth the risk—if only to keep some semblance of sanity. Both Tez and I had been on guard against all species of hope, trying not to think about the future. Trying to stall, unplug our thoughts, all the way through till now. But now that was gone, the freeze-out against hope had melted.

The death sentence itself kills; the judged man is already dead. Even before the verdict, through each stage of the trial, the growing possibility of a death sentence tightens around his neck. Now Tez was spared the stranglehold. Even if deportation were out of the question, he could survive a few years' imprisonment. And I'd probably be back here often, fly in to give him my support. We could begin to picture a life ahead.

But would this change in attitude in my brother and me win us the fight? One thing I'd learned in Paris was to argue. The idea of debating is fundamental to Europeans. They've refined it to an art, which is why they rely so much on words as a people. It's sort of like dueling, but in most cases it stops this side of real violence. With them, thought is an instrument of will, the bottom line being that only through asserting one's point of view versus someone else's can one put it to use. A showdown of words better or worse. Words are the chosen weapons, not fists or foils, but the win-or-lose stance is the same.

But in Asia, different principles seem to hold. I remembered Margaret and her scare stories. How a Westerner put on trial for similar reasons said he couldn't trust the lawyers here and studied the local laws to be able to hold his own in court, only to land himself even deeper in the hole. Or how another paid through the nose for a fancy lawyer, only to end up with an unfair ruling anyway. Gripes and grumbles. Bitching about how much money and time and energy they'd wasted. Complaints from the penalized and their countries of origin about how "backward" Asia is. About the trials not proceeding logically. How nothing is transparent, how everything is rigged behind the scenes. How low the level of social justice is. Etcetera, etcetera.

But you know, I couldn't help thinking maybe it's the Western way of looking at things that's out of place. On this side of the world, people don't set out straight off to debate something. Before lining up their arguments, they read the flow of things, not fighting their way against the current or talking others down, but assuming an almost *laissez-faire* attitude so as to merge into things. Just what it is I couldn't say, but the basic stance of Asians and Europeans does seem to be different. The way they hold themselves, the way they act.

It's not giving up and it's not giving in. Not passive resignation, but then neither is it being at loggerheads. Like in the kayaking story: when you're swept out to sea, paddling against the current only wears you out and gets you nowhere. So the thing to do is to paddle sideways, at an angle. There's only so much force to the current, a limit to its scope, and eventually you'll find yourself out of its path. After that, it's up to you to make for shore under your own power.

That visit to Uluwatu broke me clear of the current. Jibed me onto a different course, a parallel drift with a different end in sight, one where my brother gets saved. Or no, maybe my luck just shifted direction. Maybe it'll change again. Mustn't be too optimistic.

Before Uluwatu, at my lowest point, was I praying? Or was that just casting wishes to the wind? Prayer is a contradiction. The moment it comes true you're locked into a deal with god. A transaction, like having something you ordered by phone delivered to your home. Up until delivery it's prayer pure and simple. So how about this sense of relief we all felt now? Was this the answer to my prayers? Certainly the goods had arrived, but I couldn't remember having ordered them. Maybe it was just a lucky chance delivery.

Or was I just too self-important? In this corner of the world, it almost seems as if no one specifically orders anything, they all just sit around waiting for a chance delivery. And maybe there's something to be said for living like that.

A personal pact with god called "prayer"?—no, I doubt it. In these parts, in Asia, it's the undistracted, singleminded act of asking that summons the gods; that's what counts as prayer here. Bali has so many gods, ask hard enough and one of them is bound to look in your direction. In all of Islamic Indonesia, only Hindu Bali has a surplus of gods to listen to a young foreign woman like me. No going after them with self-determined belief, no bartering faith for fortune, only your plight will turn them your way.

Which must mean I actually was praying. And the visit to Uluwatu was a pilgrimage. At least that's what I told myself.

12

TETSURO

You were still in third grade.

One fine day in early summer, you file out with your classmates to a public square fifteen minutes away on foot: a special life-drawing outing for two hundred kids during Fire Prevention Week. They've lined up five big, bright fire engines there.

You go to the biggest truck. All red and shiny, blue sky and white clouds reflecting in all that chrome. Matte black tires, dull cloth hose—those'll be easy. You draw a heavy outline in pencil, big enough to fill the page, then start filling it in with watercolor. Lightly at first, let it dry, then a bit darker. And there—real fire engine red! Highlights where you see sparkles on the bumper, a few touches of white paint on top as you've learned to do. Brings out the color.

Friends come over to look mid-exercise. Just fooling around, they've given up on their own pictures. "Wow-o! Get a load of Nishijima's picture! It's like the real thing!"

Ignore them, try to concentrate. You know you're the best in the class, they've given you a special ranking—"gifted." When the teacher comes over, you don't even look around. "Yes, that's it." She pats you on the shoulder, then goes elsewhere, nothing more to add.

That's when it starts to go funny on you. The colors are off. See where the sky blue breaks into the vermilion red? You try for it, blending a little

198

orange on the tip of your brush, diluted just right, but the minute you put it down on paper it all starts looking odd. That's not the color. And you can't get it back to where it was before.

Wash it out with a wet brush, maybe? You spend the better part of the outing toying with the picture, but it only gets worse. Let the color dry for a while and go back to the shape. You want more power in the fire engine, make it jump off the page. The pencil lines are still strong and solid, nothing wrong there. How about painting beyond the outline? Try seeing shape and color separately. Hard, but worth a try.

Only that doesn't go well either. A dirty scum spreads from the pencil marks, a smudge is all it is. Nothing seems to work.

Okay, back to the color? The paint must be dry by now. But the whole thing's muddy, not a bit like the gleaming red machine in front of you. And it's all bloated out of shape.

Have to fix it, but how? The more you fiddle with it, the worse it gets. You begin to hurry. You want to catch the way things look—white clouds and green trees bending around the fender—and make them brighter, better than the real thing, too. So why does everything just go murky on the page?

You're panicking now. Where's that sparkle it used to have? It's getting impossible. Maybe you should move on to another sheet? No, too embarrassing. And time's up already, you hear the teacher's whistle.

You pout. Can't hand in the picture like this for the teacher and all the other kids to see. Want to throw it away, start over with a clean sheet and not mess up this time. Slowly you gather up your paints and pencils and trudge away. If only you weren't so "gifted" in art. Wish you were good at sports instead. Everyone would like you then. With sports you'd never mess up like this. Never going to paint again, ever.

You're two years old and someone gives you a piece of chalk.

Little white stump in your hand, shove it up against something, move it across—it leaves a white mark. What fun! Move your hand, make a line. Swing your whole arm and there's one great big happy arc. Now a long straight line, nice and strong, up and down. Twirl your hand all the way around—a chalk ring. You just made a circle! Divided the world inside from out. And the inside's all yours.

Now bigger? Or how about something in the circle? A smaller ring, off center. Two rings, different sizes . . . looks familiar. Must mean something. Almost seems to speak.

Another little ring. Right next to the other—and surprise! Somebody's looking back at you.

Who is it? But it isn't anyone's face, it's everyone's. From somewhere deeper than deep, far beneath the ground, the face calls—*Look at me, look at me, love me.* Drawing draws up love from nowhere. A flick of the fingers forms a familiar face—someone you knew before you were born.

Another circle inside the big one, below the other two small eye circles. A mouth. Even more of a face now. A mouth saying, *Love me, look at me.* And you say—*Of course I love you, that's why I drew you. I brought you to life. Stay as long as you like. Here, I'll give you a nose. Noses are important. Grow you lots of hair. See? You look great!*

You move your hand some more, but hey—what's left to do?—the face is finished. *Brought you out into the light of day, from nowhere into here and now, gave you such a nice face, you should be happy. It was dark back in there, but here you're out in the warm sun. Listen to the birds, look at the flowers over there, the dog next door is barking, and we've now got you as well!*

You waddle two steps back, find a spot on the ground for another circle. Another face. Mouth and nose and shooting streaks of hair—and presto! *So who are you, stranger?*

One face after the next. Draw one, then back up two paces and draw another. And another and another. The faces multiply, each a little further away from the last. Hours and hours of faces. Behind you suddenly there's a sharp *scre-e-e-ch*, then a deep engine-throb. Something big. Whatever it is, it can't be as interesting as this. What your own little hand produces is so much more fun. This face you're doing is kind of scary, though. A real fright, this one. Is it the eyes? The mouth?

You're drawing up a storm when abruptly you're swept off the ground, far from the scary face. You drop your precious chalk, let out a wail, rage and kick, trying to free your arms. Someone's picked you up. Stinking of cigarettes, he carries you to the door in a tight grip.

"Missus? Ma'am? Anybody home?" the big man yells at the front door, until your mother comes out in her apron. "You can't let the tyke out like that. It's dangerous. Out in the middle of the road like that! I nearly ran him over with my rig. Scared the life outta me, it did. If he's gotta play, keep 'im inside, dammit!"

Your mother apologizes and bundles you inside, then hurries back out in her sandals to the big green truck stopped out in the street. From the front door all the way to the pavement right below the bumper—a thousand chalk circle faces! A daisy chain of all the faces that ever existed, from long before time began. All of them pleased as can be.

13

KAORU

♀
†

That evening I went to my usual *warung*. I sat at a table turning the experience of Uluwatu over in my head, still not understanding how it had changed me quite so much.

"*Kaworu? Genki?*" It was Agnès and smiling Jean. I'd taught them a few words of Japanese.

"*Oui, très genki.* Many good things have happened, *beaucoup de bonnes choses.*" I didn't feel like telling them about Tez; these café acquaintances were much too casual. I certainly regretted telling that Australian, Margaret. Her boyfriend's trial must have ended by now, she'd disappeared from the hotel. No, better not say anything. "Any good dances coming up?"

"Maybe, I don't know . . . *Oh, attends—voilà Manuel. Tu sais, l'homme qui connaît tout sur Bali. Holà, Manuel! Viens ici!*" Agnès made such a fuss about it.

Someone waved from the back of the *warung*, then stood up and started this way. Skinny and dark-haired, olive complexion, Latin-looking.

"*Ah, Manuel. Ça va?*"

"*Salut, Agnès. Salut, Jean.*"

This was their expert? That kayak guy who ate like a horse. But his name wasn't Manuel, was it?

"This is Kaoru. From Japan," Agnès introduced me. "And this is Manuel, from Madrid."

"We met before. You'd almost died and I was sitting at that table over there, remember?"

"Ah yes, I told you my story. After that I didn't see you around, so I thought you left Bali."

"So you know each other?" Agnès said, sounding disappointed.

"Just a little."

"Well anyway, Manuel, our Kaworu wants to know about *la danse Legong*. And because you know all on Bali, we think maybe we catch you and ask. So now we catch you."

"First of all, I'm Kaoru, not Kaworu."

"Ah yes, that's right. And I'm Manolo."

"And Manuel . . . ?"

". . . is for regular friends like Agnès. But you're special, so you can call me Manolo."

"I'm honored . . . So then, Manolo, about the Legong dance. Are you really an expert?"

Agnès sat off to the side looking a little put out, but we just ignored her.

"Did you see it?"

"Yes, it was amazing."

"It's not the Legong dance that's amazing, it's Bali itself."

"Okay, but why? Explain. What makes Bali so amazing?" I asked, the excitement of the night coming back to me. "Assume I don't know anything."

"When did you get here?"

"Let's see, two months ago."

"And you hadn't seen a Legong dance before?"

"There were a few complications. So you might say I only really arrived last week."

"Never mind. The amazing thing about Bali is, well, everything. It would take me three days to explain. And if I took you around and showed you some of the temples and things, it would take a month. Then if you wanted to see all the ceremonies and festivals, it would take a year."

"It's okay, I've got time."

"*Bueno.* I'll tell you about the Legong dance and you can buy me a coffee." A fair enough deal.

The story went like this: long, long ago there lived a Queen Langsari, who was courted by a King Rasem. He was an arrogant ruler and a generally unpleasant character, so the queen spurned him. This enraged Rasem, and he abducted her, to force her to marry him. Even then, she refused. King Rasem threatened, saying he would wage war on her father, but still she wouldn't say yes. The king then proceeded to attack her father, but in the midst of battle a black bird flew across his path. Still he persisted in fighting despite the omen, and so was slain. Peace was restored and everyone lived happily ever after."

"Okay, then who were those three dancers?"

"The first one was a Chondon, a supporting role. The other two were Legong, the main dancers. They change roles constantly throughout. The audience can tell who's who just by their gestures."

"How old were those girls?"

"They retire at fourteen. They only dance at that time in their lives. But don't get the idea this is children's entertainment, it's high art."

"I could *see* that."

"A really talented child may dance for only three years, but her reputation will last the rest of her life. People will say, 'You should have seen her Legong.' There are children who make a lifelong mark, whether they live to be seventy or ninety, by the way they dance at age twelve. There have been star performers whose fame lived on more than a century."

Manolo got so wrapped up in his subject, he forgot to drink his coffee. And I forgot to be more critical and actually began to take a liking to him.

"Only, the ending of the dance with King Rasem dying isn't very Bali-like."

"Meaning?"

"Meaning good and evil are too clear-cut. Here in Bali good and evil mix and change places all the time. Good can be evil and evil good. It's all very ambiguous or dualistic or—I don't know, anything but simple."

"Why's that?"

"To explain *why* isn't simple either. Like I said, it would take three days. But to cut to the conclusion, the place is layered thick in meanings, one piled on top of the other. The whole island is caught in a net of myths, and there's at least two sides to everything—sacred and profane, pure and defiled,

good and evil, life and death. It all swims around and around, in interchange-
able pairs. They offer good things to the gods on high trays, but the lesser
demons still get offerings, too, even if it's crummy things they'd have to eat
off the ground."

"Ho," said I.

"So the Legong is, well, too simple. Really you should see the Barong
dance."

"What's that like?"

"A fight between the monster Barong and the sorceress Rangda. Now this
is truly weird and complicated. The original story is from the *Mahabharata*,
though."

Who was it told me about the *Mahabharata*? Oh, that's right, it was Kondra, with that story about the gambling king who almost lost his wife. Part
of an epic tale, he said. So this was another part? I looked at Manolo and
waited for him to continue. Agnès, meanwhile, was chatting away with
someone at the next table.

"Okay, first there was a princess named Kunti. And she had to sacrifice
her own son Prince Saduwa to Durgha, the Goddess of Death."

"Why?"

"Just wait and listen. It's only one part of a long story. At the beginning
of the dance, the Barong and the monkeys fight with the farmers, but that's
sort of a lead-in. Then comes a bit of Legong dance."

"Legong too?"

"Uh-huh. And then the real story starts. Two of Prince Saduwa's retainers
appear, bemoaning their master's imminent death. First he is to be sent to
the sorceress Rangda to be killed, then offered to the Goddess of Death."

"But why?"

"Just listen. This isn't a modern realist novel, you have to swallow the plot
even if it doesn't make sense."

"Is that so?"

"Yes, that's just how it is. So anyway, while the two retainers are moan-
ing away, Rangda's demon underling enters to give them both a good fright.
The two then go to one of the prince's faithful ministers for help."

I decided to stop interrupting Manolo. It was fun to tease him, but now the story was starting to get interesting. Even just watching him was fun.

"So now the minister appears, together with Princess Kunti and Prince Saduwa himself. The princess is wailing about her son's fate, when along comes that same demon underling of Rangda's and puts a spell on her, which makes her lose her own will and order the minister to take the prince away to be killed."

"And?"

"*¿Te interesa?*"

"*Sí, sí,* go on."

"All this merely sets the stage for the fight between the Barong and Rangda. You really have to see it to appreciate it."

"I'll see it, I'll see it—just point me in the right direction." Maybe it really wouldn't be so bad to have him for a guide around Bali.

"Well, the minister balks at the order, and the demon puts a spell on him too. The prince is led to Rangda's forest lair and tied to a tree. Just as he is preparing to die, though, the supreme deity Shiva appears and takes pity on him and makes him immortal."

"I hate to spoil your story, but that's plain ridiculous."

"Of course, but that only shows you're still too Cartesian in your thinking, too tied up in Western rationalism or its Japanese equivalent."

"Am I so rational?"

"Sure, but listen anyway. *Cállate y escuche.*"

"Yessir. I promise you won't hear another word out of me."

"Okay, so the prince becomes immortal. Then the sorceress Rangda appears and tries to kill him, but you can't kill an immortal."

"Is Rangda beautiful?"

"Beautiful and sexy and . . . well, you get the picture."

"Spellbinding—the way they're meant to be."

"*Bravo.* Well, in the end she realizes she can't kill him, so she gives up and asks the prince to kill her instead. That way the wicked witch can go to heaven."

"*O*-kay."

"The prince kills her as requested. Which summons up Rangda's younger sister Kalika, who begs the prince to kill her too so she can go to heaven as well, but the prince refuses."

"He should've just whacked her."

"Maybe, because the two of them start fighting. Kalika is in human form at first, but then she transforms herself into a wild pig and then a bird. And still she loses."

"That doesn't figure at all," Miss Common Sense had to interject. "I mean, to start fighting because someone refuses to kill you like you asked, only to get killed when you lose. That's just what she was asking for to begin with."

"No, even when he wins, the prince doesn't kill Kalika. So Kalika transforms herself into her sister Rangda and draws on Rangda's magic powers to do battle. Outmaneuvered, Prince Saduwa counters by turning into a monstrous Barong, but neither ever gets the upper hand. The Barong and Rangda, you see, are diametric opposites."

"Like spear and shield."

"*¿Cómo?*"

"It's an old Chinese example of a contradiction. Long ago, a man was selling an invincible spear and an impenetrable shield. Along came a customer who asked, what happens if you pierce the shield with the spear? And of course the seller was at a loss to answer."

"Funny story. Got to hand it to the Chinese. It almost seems more of a satire on advertising campaigns than a logical problem. Ads are always making inflated claims—'Ten Times Better,' 'Thirty Percent More'—and if you don't pay attention, things easily exceed the hundred percent mark. The great thing about that Chinese story of yours, though, is it shows they had these contradictions, these spear-and-shield *dialéctica*, since ancient times."

Hey, this boy had a head on his shoulders. "I guess Ancient China must've really been something, because for over a thousand years Japan was happy enough just to be its satellite. Until China's star sank in the nineteenth century, and we went off the deep end. Now we're a satellite of America."

"Well, that does help make 'Inscrutable Japan' a bit more scrutable."

"You see, we're always half-unsure of ourselves. But enough of Japan, back to Bali."

"Ah yes, right. Well, Rangda and the Barong are equally matched, equally strong. Soon followers of the Barong arrive, all wielding swords, but they end up skewering themselves with their own daggers. Their hands won't move at will, they move by themselves. It's the sorceress Rangda's magic."

"And so—"

"And so the fight goes on and on. It continues for so long, in fact, that finally a priest comes out of a temple and sprinkles them with holy water, saving them from this endless feud. And that's how the dance ends."

"But isn't that a fight of good and evil?"

"Well, yes and no. Good here isn't so super good and bad's not completely irredeemable either. Good and evil, beauty and ugliness, excess and scarcity, they all come in twos. And this two-sided thinking permeates Bali. Here a person can't just stick to good things, it'll never work in the end."

"Mmm." I withheld judgment. Still too abstract, too esoteric for me.

"Consider, for instance, a dance with no Barong, only Rangda," Manolo said, trying a different tack. "Such a dance does exist, they do it occasionally. But it's dangerous. There's no Barong, so sometimes Rangda gets out of control."

"But it's just play-acting, isn't it?"

"The dividing line is very vague here. Dancers playing Rangda have been known to dash out of the circle, wander through the village, and disappear into the hills. Even without going that far, they might go crazy and attack people, and never come back to their senses. The spirit of Rangda possesses them."

"Then there's no borderline between the real and the spiritual?"

"As I said at the beginning, there's just so many undercurrents here. Behind the façade are other sights, layer upon layer through which the villagers see to things you and I can't even begin to imagine. Which is why as many years as I've been coming here I'm never bored."

"And how many years *is* that?"

"About ten. Staying two or three months each trip."

"And the rest of the time?"

"In Kathmandu or Europe. Goa, too."

"My brother's been to Goa." It was the first time I'd ever mentioned him to an outsider. What if he asked what kind of a person he was? It was too early to go into all that, though surely someday we could talk, if I got to know Manolo better. It would probably make me feel better, too, let off some pressure. But he asked about something else.

"And you?"

"Me? I go back and forth between Europe and Japan. I also go to the Middle East and North Africa for work." No one in this café ever seemed to work at all, or if they did they concealed the fact incredibly well. I felt like a heel to even say the word.

"Work?"

"I'm a coordinator-translator for television. And you?" I parried.

"I'm happy to say that Manuel Sanchez-Delgado is a total hippie. And not a poor bum of a hippie, but the lowest of the low: *un hippie desgraciado* who lives off capital interest."

"But that's super!"

"Yeah, thanks, you can see it that way, too. I used to work, ages ago. Terrible what I did."

"Which was?"

"You won't believe this. I was a full officer in the secret police under Franco. *Un agente legítimo de la Guardia Civil de la Falange Española.*"

"Amazing. Top of the most hated list."

"You said it. Everyone despised me, and you know who hated me most? *I* did, that's who."

"I guess I shouldn't laugh, but that's absurd! How did you ever get into that line of work?"

"I come from a good family. In France, we'd be among *les trois cents familles*, and I was the third son. Honestly, I was raised to believe I needn't do a thing. Raised to do nothing. My elder brothers would take care of all money matters, which left me completely without any ambition—not for living expenses, personal resources, power, or status. Instead the family found me a totally secure position that guaranteed strict nonidentity status —secret police work."

"Lovely."

"You said it. I hated every minute of it, saw so many things I'd never wanted to. I quit after two years and became a journalist for *El País*."

"Good for you!"

"And when I learned the ropes, they sent me to Vietnam. Where I saw even worse things. It was a terrible war, but I believe I was truthful as a correspondent. I took a good, hard look at things nobody wanted to see and I wrote them up in detail. I was fairly well regarded."

"Vietnam, eh? My brother went there, too. Long after the war ended, though."

"This brother of yours, what's he do?"

"I'll tell you all about him some other time. We were talking about you. So then, after that?"

"So, of course I got fed up with journalism and quit that, too. That's me all over. I began to drift around, a not-so-young-any-more hippie. And before long I realized a rootless life was what suited me best. No need for status or position, leave the job title blank. I'm just fine as me. My life's much more meaningful without all that achievement nonsense."

"Understandable," I agreed. I really did. Of course, he had a head start.

"I've managed to pack a lot into a short time. I'm a mean *tabla* player. A fair surfer, too."

"*Tabla*? You mean that Indian bongo drum? Which they always play together with the *sitar*?"

"The very same. I sometimes do recitals in Nepal. Not for money, just for friends."

"You're different, I'll say that."

"Everyone's always trying to be the person others will appreciate. When I turned my back on Vietnam, I decided to go by my own yardstick instead. Of course, it was my good luck to be born into money so I don't have to worry about the next meal. If property is exploitation like the communists say, then I'm living easy on top of a pile of stolen lucre. But you know, I'm not the one who did the stealing; I just inherited the take passed down from previous generations and stretched it as far as it would go, creating my life as I went along, like an ongoing work of art."

"And so Bali it was."

"Yes, Bali's the place for me. Hippiedom is, well, a sort of search for a promised land. At one time, the West Coast in the U.S. was it. In Europe there was nothing, but people thought maybe there was something in the East, so we all headed east."

"I know that whole scene only too well. I sold them travel tickets in Paris."

"Really?"

"Yeah. I sold cheap airfares out of a tiny *agence de voyage* in the Quartier Latin, while attending the Sorbonne. Never graduated, though."

"University isn't something you graduate from," said Manolo with a smile. A wonderful smile. "But back to the pilgrim's progress. Place is the important thing; location, *topos*. Those who consider *where* to be the most deciding factor in *who* they are, they're the real hippies. They split up and scour the globe to 'find themselves,' and Bali *is* It—*the* last word."

"So this is heaven?"

"Sure, but not simply by fulfilling a passive paradise wishlist—beautiful women, good food, nice weather all year round. No, there's a wealth of culture here, plus they're open to strangers from abroad. The richness of creativity here is something amazing. Everyone on the island's a singer, dancer, painter, sculptor, festival celebrant, and, on top of everything, a deeply religious believer—where else on earth do you find that?"

"And that's why you're so infatuated with the place."

"You say I'm infatuated, but it's been ten years now, and I'm not starry-eyed about it. Bali is a dance without an end. Remember I was telling you about the Barong and Rangda being diametrically opposed principles whose struggle is never resolved, well, the folks here basically all believe their dances or plays go on forever. For mundane reasons, a priest may intervene and sprinkle holy water to break it up, but really the dancers want to go on dancing and the audience wants to go on watching for as long as they can."

"So there are dances that go on for a week?"

"I imagine that's how it was originally, in the old days. 'When the world was steady,' as they say. And when I realize that, it makes me want to stand back a bit from Bali and just watch. If the whole island's one endless performance, then there must be countless stages, each locality performing its own different scene. It's all *Negara*—super-theater, meta-theater. When you start to see things in that light, then an old woman emptying the garbage is just one more theatrical role. All day long everyone's surrounded by everyone else looking on."

"But doesn't all that become unbearable?"

"No one here seems to mind. The landscape is all backdrop, the buildings stage sets, neighbors fellow actors—if that's the environment you're born into, you can't conceive of a non-theatrical world. Even so, there are times it gets tiresome. You can't watch any play for eight straight hours with the same concentration, so sometimes you want to take a break."

"In Japan, we have little comic breaks during an eight-hour *Kabuki* play."

"Yes, I've heard of that . . . Anyway, that's why, from time to time, I remember to go home. But compared to here, Europe is so bland . . . That's what's so amazing about Bali."

I was starting to get used to Manolo's quirks. He'd get all fired up about something, then pull back to view it from a distance, in panorama. Made him seem to float in space. Maybe living for yourself to the utmost could be a "higher" way of life. Now there's a thought.

"You really haven't taken a look around?"

"I've been to Uluwatu."

"And how was that?" He seemed to be testing me, looking for some common grounds of communication. I'd passed the first part, about the Legong dance. But did I want to deal with the rest of this test? Say honestly what I'd experienced at Uluwatu? What goodies did I get if I passed? Intensive curriculum, enthusiastic teacher.

"The temple itself didn't make much of an impression. My head was full of other worries at the time, but as I sat on the cliff looking at those big waves, I began to feel something *else*. Like I was being taken out of myself, like I was flying, like making love . . ." How to put the experience into words?

"It's like I told you," said Manolo. "Even nature gets into the act here."

"But you know, it really saved me. I was in a bind, and now I'm much more at ease."

"It's that kind of place." Manolo twinkled a knowing, welcome-to-the-club smile.

Prior to the next court session, the newly appointed prosecutor contacted Gatir to request a meeting. After which, Gatir met with Tez and me and Kondra at the jail to tell us the outcome.

"The upshot is largely as expected," said Gatir.

"You mean they're changing the charge?"

"Exactly. Since the policemen who were sent to make the arrest can't take the witness stand, their claim of finding a large amount of heroin falls apart."

"So does that confirm our side of it?"

"For the most part. The rest is largely a formality, but as it's so much extra work to start again from scratch, they're saying they would rather dismiss the interrogation transcript, annul all related statements, and submit another transcript as evidence."

"Meaning the first transcript, in my own words."

"Yes. Government clerks rarely ever throw documents away. So what they want to do is edit out those bits of evidence that support the fake transcript, leaving a pared-down case with most of the witness testimonies intact."

"Fine. They had yet to bring out any witness who did us any real damage. But all the same, why did the police chief get kicked out so suddenly?"

"You mean you don't know?"

"No. No one's told me a thing."

"Me either," said Tez.

"I hadn't realized. My apologies for a serious oversight. But now is as good an opportunity as any, so why don't we read you this magazine article? It's a firsthand account by someone at the heart of the events, so it presents the story fairly vividly."

Kondra pulled an Indonesian magazine from his bag. "It *is* a bit on the sensational side, which is probably why it's gotten so much attention. Everyone except you two—the key people—seems to have read it! Yes, it's a rip-roaring adventure full of swashbuckling action." At times our Mr. Kondra's command of Japanese was wonderfully old-fashioned.

He read us the title, "How I Returned from the Dead—A Special Agent's True-Life Story," then looked at us with a grin. This was going to be good.

I, Anjal Ani, am a policeman. More precisely, I am a detective in the Independent Investigations Division directly affiliated with police head-quarters in Jakarta. My organization's purpose is to investigate miscon-duct in regional police departments throughout our island republic, and unfortunately our services are still very much required.

It all began two months ago, when I was assigned to Bali. We had been hearing disturbing rumors about the chief of police there for some months, and it was my mission to look into them. Specifically, we received an "inside tip" from someone on the force, saying that while this senior officer, Anudan, made a show of being tough on drugs, he was also involved with local criminal elements selling them. Not only did drugs confiscated during clean-up operations somehow find their way back onto the street again, there was talk of him making enormous profits from smuggling foreign drug shipments through Bali and expanding his organization. Nor had these corrupt practices started only since he came to Bali; even in his Jakarta days, the word on the street was that Anudan had used money amassed through shady con-nections to buy off his superiors and climb the ladder.

It was my job to find out whether these "inside" allegations were true or not, but of course I couldn't just walk in the front door. I was sent from the capital in the guise of a police auxiliary cadet assigned to train with the regional police. And while appearing to be investigating the usual run of everyday crimes, in secret I was searching for evidence of Anudan's criminal activities. It would have been helpful if the source of that "inside tip" had realized what my true mission was and had come forward, but whoever it was must have been scared or unaware of my assignment. That's usually the case. Also, it's always safer to work alone.

After two months of undercover investigative work alongside my normal duties, a number of incriminating pieces of evidence had come into my hands. Apparently the "inside tip" was based on reality, though I still had nothing definite to show. I often saw crime syndicate types visiting the chief's office (they did their business right on the premises!), though I couldn't get close enough to catch any of the talk. Whenever these not-so-secret meetings took place, Anudan always bolted his door tight.

I tried recording their conversations. When I was sent from Jakarta I was provided with a miniature Japanese tape recorder that could record ten hours on one mini-cassette. Choosing a time when no one would be around to see, I strapped the recorder loaded with new batteries and tape under the chief's desk. I set it running around four in the morning.

The gods were on my side. The next day at one-thirty, a suspicious-looking pair showed up and went into the chief's office. If they said anything incriminating during their visit, I'd have hard evidence down on tape. I volunteered for night duty, saying I had personal business to see to the following day, and snuck in to the chief's office to recover the recorder.

Unfortunately, when I listened to it, all I could hear was the chief chatting casually with two other men. The tape ran out before they got around to anything of real importance. Only once did Anudan let slip, in among all the jokes, something about a drug case involving a foreigner: "That went well. Well worth two hundred grams to put me on the road back to Jakarta." The specific reference was lost on me.

I tried again several more times. Twice I got blank tapes. But the time after that, I hit pay dirt. The afternoon after my night duty when I arrived at the station, the chief's door was shut. Ten minutes later the same pair as before emerged, with plenty of time still on the tape. I got the whole conversation.

The following night I collected the tape, and in it Anudan was giving very precise instructions about a drug deal—"The goods are in Jinbaran. I told Agus to go pick them up."

Something was in Jinbaran, but nothing would stand up in court unless I had actual incriminating evidence found somewhere the chief had specifically indicated. Not that I intended to go in alone with a warrant, but if I knew the place then I could call in reinforcements from the capital. Word around the station was that while Anudan's home was in Denpasar, he kept a separate house for a "little wife" in Jinbaran. That was probably where he hid his take of drugs confiscated during raids. I learned its general whereabouts from the boys on the job, and my next day off I went exploring in plainclothes and found a house that matched the description. It was difficult to stake out the place with kids playing nearby, but I joked with them whenever they came by, until after about two hours the same pair I'd seen showed up with a third young guy I didn't know. They all went into the house, then came out again ten minutes later. My guess was the young guy was the Agus mentioned by the chief.

I continued my lookout for another thirty minutes and decided that I'd need to call in some backup to go in and search for evidence. But before I could go, the kids reappeared and nagged me into a game of soccer with them (I happen to play forward on the Jakarta Police Department team). We must have played a good two hours. That was my mistake.

This time as I was about to leave and was waving goodbye, suddenly I saw the chief heading this way. I couldn't possibly explain what I was doing there. By the time I thought to look away he'd already seen me. As I turned to run, he shot at me from behind. In broad daylight, with children nearby, he used his pistol. And me in plainclothes, with no weapon whatsoever. I had just rounded the corner thinking I'd got away, when a bullet hit me in the calf and I fell.

Anudan came running up and gave me a whack on the head with the butt of his gun, before grabbing me by the collar and dragging me into his mistress's house. My soccer buddies all watched from a distance, until the chief yelled and waved his pistol at them and they scattered.

"What are you doing here?" he wanted to know, the moment we were inside.

"Me? But what about *you*, sir? And do you always shoot your own men like that without warning?" I said groggily. A young woman was watching from a corner of the room. My leg was bleeding all over the floor. Not a serious wound, no bones shattered, but it really hurt. And the bump on the head hurt even worse.

"No one comes here by accident," he insisted. "What were you snooping around for?"

"I was just walking by when the kids invited me to play soccer," I explained. "Do you have any bandages to stop the bleeding?"

He balked: if I really was there by chance, then he'd fired on his own officer for no reason. But no, where he'd found me was too close to be a coincidence. I had to be onto him. The very fact that I'd been sent from the capital only two months before was suspicious. Either way, now he couldn't let me go alive.

Anudan told his mistress to wash and bandage my wound, but this dolled-up honey was too put off by the sight of blood to be of any real help, so in the end I had to do it all myself. The water in the bucket turned bright red. The chief kept his gun trained at my head the whole time.

Could I use the girl as a shield if I tried to escape? As I wound the bandages, I decided he wouldn't hesitate to shoot a woman he'd only met six months ago. A .38 bullet would rip right though that pretty body of hers. Realistically, I knew there wasn't a chance. Whenever she came between him and his target, the chief yelled at her to move out of the line of fire.

The bullet wound throbbed with each heartbeat. Anudan kept his eyes fixed on me, and the window was too far even if I could run. Another shot and I'd be dead for sure. The wound itself was slight, but having already caught one bullet I wasn't exactly feeling very brave.

Half an hour later a big guy came to the door. He had to stoop to get in. He looked West Javanese. I'd never seen him around the station, so he must have been syndicate. They put me in a car waiting outside, the big guy driving, me in the back seat with the chief and his pistol prodding me in the side. They took me to their "base camp" in the backstreets of Denpasar, a small room where the usual pair and that Agus character were waiting. Then they tied me with wire to a chair and beat me nonstop.

"What were you doing around there?"

"Like I told you," I repeated, "I was just passing by."

"Then why did you try to run when you saw the chief?"

"You've got it backwards, the chief drew a gun and then I ran." I kept repeating my story.

The chief turned to the two hoods and barked, "You two, go search his apartment. I'll go to the station and go through his desk."

That gave me two hours. I tried to trick the muscleman and Agus into loosening my ropes, but they paid no attention when I said I had to go to the toilet. Even when I soiled myself tied there to the chair, they didn't blink. When Anudan and his sidekicks returned, the chief was empty-handed, but the other two had found the undercover agent ID I'd taped under my table just in case I ever needed it in a hurry. Just wave that once at the station and I'd outrank the chief. But it wasn't my allies who'd found it, and this wasn't a police station.

Nothing I could say now would help me. They beat me again, stubbed out cigarettes in my face, grilled me. How much did I know? Who had I contacted? But my lips were sealed. So in the end they gave up and decided they'd better kill me. We got back in the car, this time with the muscleman and Agus in charge. The car eventually stopped somewhere in the hills. The muscleman dragged me out to the edge of a cliff. Agus pulled out a gun and pointed it at me. Still bound hands and feet, I rolled over desperately trying to half-stand and throw myself over the edge, but Agus pulled the trigger. I felt a piercing pain in my chest as I fell, my tied hands clasped in front of my face. I tumbled and bumped a long way down, banging my head against something, then the lights went out.

It seems I spent several hours caught in some branches halfway down. What brought me to my senses was the splash of cool rain on my face. Pain shot through my body when I tried to move. It was already night. The thugs had probably gone by now. Anyway, I was still alive.

I was dazed, probably from shock and loss of blood. I'd bleed less if I didn't move, but if I stayed put no one would find me and I'd surely die. I decided to wait until dawn.

Gradually it became light. The rain had stopped, but everything around was still wet. I slowly began to move, holding in the pain, trying to size up my situation. I was caught in the lower forks of a big tree, and when I craned my neck to look down, the sheer drop seemed to ease out into a slope three meters below. I steeled my nerve, squirmed out on the branch, and let myself fall. The pain of impact was excruciating and I passed out.

When I came to again, the sun was high. I couldn't afford to pass out again. Little by little I tried to move. The twisted ends of the wire binding my arms and legs trailed outwards, so maybe I could wriggle them loose. Any movement was painful, but with each twist the wire began to slacken a bit. It took ages. Time I had, but there were limits to my strength, limits to my blood reserves. Little by little my hands worked free. Next my legs, this time using my hands.

I struggled slowly to my feet and staggered through the woods from tree to tree. Agus had shot me in the right side of the chest. I was still bleeding, but not gushing like before. The bullet had just missed my lung, but I'd broken a couple of ribs, and if I moved too much those could still puncture my lung. That and the chief's bullet wound in my leg, which still hurt like crazy. I was hot and feverish, probably starting to go septic. Whenever I began to see stars and felt too faint to walk, I crouched down on the spot and waited until I recovered.

Eventually I reached some farmland. I felt weak and fell among the knee-high crops (I'm a city boy, I couldn't say which plants they were). I don't know how many times I'd lost consciousness since they shot me up on the cliff, but somehow I was still alive. The next thing I knew someone was peering into my face. No thug this time, it was an ordinary farmer. I wanted to explain, but didn't have the strength to speak. He gave me some water and tried to make me comfortable, telling me to wait.

After a long, long time he returned with a friend, and they carried me back to his house on a stretcher improvised from two bamboo poles and a roll of cloth. When we got there, they laid me on a bed of straw and I passed out again. By the time I came to, he'd treated my wounds as best he could.

"Who shot you?" my rescuer wanted to know.

I didn't dare say.

"Should I call the police?" he asked. "Are you a bad man?"

"No, it's the police who are bad."

That seemed to convince him. Unfortunately in our island republic, the average citizen doesn't always trust the police. But fortunately for me, I was able to make use of that distrust.

"But if I don't take you to hospital you'll die."

"Do you have a car?"

"No, but the village headman does. I could ask."

"North of Denpasar there's an army hospital. Can you take me there?"

The police were no good, but the army would understand. I lost consciousness again while waiting for the car. When I came to, I was lying in a bed in the army hospital getting a transfusion. I relaxed and went to sleep. It was three days before I got back enough strength to talk.

An army medic came to my bedside. "You must be one hell of a strong fellow," he told me. "It's amazing you're still alive with those wounds and all the blood you lost."

"Yes, I thought I was going to die," I admitted.

"The farmer said we weren't to contact the police," said the medic. "What's that all about?"

"I'm an undercover agent," I told him, "with the Jakarta Police Department." I recapped the events for him and had him contact the capital.

A week later I was flown to Jakarta by military transport. And a week after that, Anudan's whole drug network was mopped up in a clean sweep (only Agus who shot me on the cliff disappeared, whereabouts unknown). This case is now history.

Kondra finished his long translation. Everyone was silent for a while.

"Looks like I've been spared, thanks to 'The Man Who Returned from the Dead,'" said my brother finally.

"So Agus really did exist," I said.

"Of course he exists. I met the guy. I said so all along."

"No, I mean the fact that he existed has now been publicly established. Someday, if you ever meet this detective, you ought to thank him."

"Yeah, someday."

Two weeks later, the court reached its verdict. We more or less knew the outcome beforehand. That is to say, it became clear after the police chief's arrest that the principal charge against Tez of smuggling in 200g of heroin had indeed just been a trap with Agus as bait. The new prosecutor was a reasonable man, so after consultion with the judge and Gatir, charges were brought in line with the actual details of Tez's real confession, which they'd now substituted as evidence.

For a brief moment, there was even talk of doing the whole trial again, but it would have meant a lot of wasted time and effort, and the prosecution had lost so much face they were eager to put the case behind them. The sooner the public could forget this whole thing ever happened, the better. From our side as well, we wanted a quick resolution—a quick and fair verdict, that is. Given Tez's admission to buying two grams of heroin from Agus, it seemed like a good idea to just go ahead and stand trial for that.

So the verdict came down to four years' correction plus a five million rupiah fine, neither subject to appeal. In exchange for which, they promised special parole consideration if he served his sentence at the Foreign Penitentiary without any trouble. As fair a ruling as could be expected, I thought. Release in two and a half years on condition of deportation wasn't such a bad prospect. Add the time from the arrest to the end of the trial and that was only three years out of a whole lifetime.

As I listened to the judge in her twin-TV glasses read out the verdict—in Indonesian, which I obviously couldn't understand—I thought about it all and, of course, I cried. I really hadn't been able to do much, which was kind of depressing. There'd been so much negative thinking, and habits are hard to kick—crying included. If that crooked police chief hadn't been exposed, if that undercover agent had died, what would have become of Tez?...

The day after the ruling I went straight back to Japan. First I had to inform everyone of the outcome—Mom and Dad, Professor Inagaki, and the few friends of Tez who lent their support. Inagaki had already read the magazine article that Kondra had translated for us, but he was still delighted with the news. I thanked him—truly and sincerely—then couldn't help asking: "I know I shouldn't ask, especially after all you've done for me and my brother, but what made you decide to help Tez in the first place?"

"Well, you see . . ." The professor went suddenly bashful, an expression I'd never seen on him. "I guess I, uh . . . I must have fallen for you."

"You *what*?"

"No, don't be alarmed. What I meant to say is, I was *moved* by you. Remember, you did do all that boo-hooing here, didn't you? It may be a bit old-fashioned of me to find your devotion to your brother touching, but I *am* an old man, after all."

I listened, completely dumbstruck.

"No other intentions, I assure you. Oh, I admit I like women, always have. And I've known my share in both Japan and Indonesia. But I never wanted to sleep with you or anything. I think my feelings were more along the lines of an old samurai coming to the rescue of his princess, ha ha."

"But at the time you said you didn't like women crying their eyes out."

"That I did, at the time. But it was only skin deep. When a man gets to be my age, and relations with even his oldest friends get to be more like business dealings, it's hard to be generous about anything. It all becomes a bit calculating. And sometimes even friends let you down. But with this case, there was no way I could take any payment; it was just something I had to do, for old times' sake. No, you know, even old Pirungati got quite worked up over this. It did us two fuddy-duddies a world of good to help a lady in distress. Now I can admit it."

"So that's how it was . . ." I lowered my head again, more than a little embarrassed

"But you know, in the end, we made no difference. Had no effect whatsoever."

"That's not true. You really helped. If it hadn't been for you, I'd have cried from beginning to end and been completely useless. If you hadn't introduced that attorney, Gatir, my brother might already have been executed by now."

"No, I doubt it. Just recently I was in Jakarta, and Pirungati and I spent the whole night talking. And both of us had to admit, in the end the person who saved your brother was you yourself. You changed the course of events. You brought good luck."

"I don't see how. I'm not that sort of person."

"Oh, but you did. At that point and *only then* you did. Out of desperation, you somehow found the strength to turn things around. Much stronger than any ninja or this old warrior."

"How can you say that?"

"I can say it because up to the last moment I was thinking I'd have to pull in some major politician from Jakarta. I was prepared to go that far, if it came right down to the succeed-or-fail line. But you came through on your own, made all that unnecessary."

"I was backed into a corner, that's all."

"Well, you pulled some kind of extra power out of that corner, turned the fight around, that's all I got to say."

"If only it were true. Bali's what did it, not me."

"Granted, it's a remarkable place, that island. I don't much go in for hocus-pocus myself, but what do I know? You must have gotten some Balinese spirit or god or power to side with you, the same way you enlisted me."

Three days later, I headed back to Bali with a large sum of money to pay the fine and settle accounts with Gatir and Kondra. This was the last of my trips to fulfill obligations. All told, these arrangements took two weeks. By then I felt it was time to get back to normal and my own work. No more emergencies. But I wasn't ready to go home just yet, so I put it off for a couple more days.

I waited until evening and went to the *warung*, where for some reason I didn't see any of the usual friends. I just sat there with my coffee, looking out at the street, thinking about Tez.

The Foreign Penitentiary he'd been transferred to was fairly easygoing, as jails go. The inmates were allowed to do whatever they wanted all day long; and instead of the usual prison slop, they could cook for themselves, with stuff brought in from outside. One Italian prisoner, a trained chef, collected money from everyone and did the communal cooking. Which was like saying the prison had its own private restaurant. Private rooms—meaning single cells—it didn't have, but there was plenty of individual space, so Tez could go out in the yard and paint if he wanted. When I visited him earlier that afternoon he'd asked if I could send him some art supplies from Japan or Paris.

"So what are you going to paint?"

"Weeds in the prison yard. Sky and clouds. Faces. I'll become a master portraitist."

"There any good faces among your jailmates?"

"Ha! No way. We're all baddies on the inside."

"And that makes the faces bad?"

"Of course not, just distinctive. But any face will do for practice."

"The problem is, they're all men."

"Can't have everything. Màybe I can pay to have a woman come in on visiting days."

"I'll put in a request with Wayang and Kondra."

"Well, eventually maybe."

The move to new surroundings really lightened Tez up. He'd be all right, I thought over my coffee. I'd come to see him several times a year, reassure myself that he was okay, ask what he needed, then go home saying I'd be back.

"Hey there!" came a voice. "*¿Qué tal?*"

I looked around and it was Manolo. "How goes it?" I greeted him.

"I just heard. About your brother and all. Congratulations," he said, pulling up a chair. Seen without a load on my mind, he suddenly seemed sharper than before. And not too bad-looking either.

"You knew?"

"Sure I knew. But I didn't want to say anything until you brought it up. That undercover agent's story made the rounds everywhere, you know. And foreigners here follow these drug scandals pretty closely."

"Yeah, I suppose they would."

"But now all that's behind you, right? You're free just to enjoy the island, no?"

"Not quite, but I'm getting there."

"Shall I show you around? Places where you can see the real Bali?"

"Like, for instance?"

"Like . . . The names Batukau or Besaki mean nothing to you, do they? So many places you've never been, masses of things to explore, an endless show-and-tell. Nowhere else in the world is there a place where people live their daily lives so immersed in myth. *Mágico.* You won't believe how much there is to see!"

He's trying to pick me up, I smiled to myself. That wouldn't be so bad, now, would it? Do me some good to fool around a bit, get over my bad experiences, maybe have a few laughs. A special consolation prize.

"Okay, you're on. Where to first?"

"Around the whole island. On my bike, that's a two-week trip at least. But hey, it might take three months. Ten years. You tell me!"

14

TETSURO

Dear Inge,

Where to begin? Well, first of all, I've been here in Angkor
going on two weeks. I'm a free spirit now, a wanderer again.
Painting what I want to paint, seeing your Angkor Wat, but with
completely different eyes.

By any normal stretch of the imagination, I shouldn't be writing
to you at all. I don't feel a shred of goodwill toward you. You're
the last person in the world I want to see. If I saw your face in a
crowd, I'd turn right around in my tracks. Of course, I can't
prove you had any evil motives, but even to suggest something as
deadly as that amounts to the same thing. Yes, it was my own
doing, plus a few unfortunate coincidences. But you were the one
who invited disaster in the first place, and for that I hate you.

So here I am writing this letter. Not out of niceness or
nostalgia, it's more a matter of pride. I'm telling you, your
temptation didn't work. I came this close to losing myself,
but I pulled through at the last minute. Thanks to my sister and a
determined undercover agent, I escaped a death sentence and got my
act together again. I did my time like a model prisoner.

I'm recovered. Completely better. If I weren't, would I be
writing this?

Today makes ten days since I arrived here. Ten days of painting to my heart's content. No masterpieces, but I'm getting the forms like I see them, that's the main thing. I got my confidence back. I'll do good work again. I'm back to my old artist self, the man you met painting that temple landscape. Though now I make sure not a trace of you remains in my pictures. I've rubbed you out. That's why I'm here.

Ironically, it was in prison I knew I was completely off heroin. Security was lax on the inside, a little money could get you anything. Even heroin was on the shopping list. The guards knew what I was in for, and the very first week one of them brought some stuff around to see if I'd buy, but I just laughed. I wasn't tempted at all. In fact, I threatened to write a letter to the police in Jakarta exposing him—yes, to that resourceful secret agent. That evening, I knew I'd cut all ties with junk. I used to see the guard every day, the whole time I was inside. I never forgot his offer, just didn't take him seriously. A pathetic, second-string pusher was all he was.

Still, my talent, my drive to paint isn't completely what it was. I painted while I was in jail, but with no scenery except walls and sky and a big yard with weeds in it, my main subject was the other inmates. Mostly Westerners, and a handful of Japanese and Koreans. Men only, sorry to say. I could get all the painting supplies I wanted sent in, so I tried different mediums. I did a large oil of the warden in an overblown pose like David's *Napoleon*. Probably still hanging in his office. Crappy pictures the lot. I didn't even think of trying anything new. Creative juices just can't flow shut-in like that. All I cared about was keeping my eye and hand in. Didn't want my touch to go soft.

When we bumped into each other in that village outside Chiang Mai, you talked about Angkor Wat. "You absolutely must see this place," you said. And I thought, I'll show her, I'll lay siege to it with a painter's eye, and make it all my own. At the time, going there was out of the question: entering Pol Pot territory was too risky. I never forgot about it, though. I held on in prison just thinking about this place, how someday I'd come here and paint. After my release, I returned to Japan and spent a year putting my life back on track, preparing myself for this. Now I've got things under control. Hence this letter.

Even now, I'm told, it's not one hundred percent safe. There's a garrison of government troops stationed nearby, but that's not to say the Khmer Rouge couldn't counterstrike at any time. Landmines everywhere, they say. So I don't stray into the bush. Walk only on hard-tramped ground. Never go anywhere alone. So I always have two soldier escorts with me. They keep constant watch. Very young, these soldiers, practically children. The day before yesterday, both guards were girls. Kind of cute, big eyes, full lips. Infatuating in their way. I've drawn their smiles a few times. But make no mistake, their submachine guns shoot real bullets. They can take a person apart. As if I didn't know it.

I get special treatment here at Angkor because of arrangements made in Japan. I didn't want to wander in here like some hippie. An enterprising art dealer friend pulled strings politically, by what channels I don't know, but he got an advertising agency, a travel service, and the Cambodian embassy on board. And one young artist—yours truly—to paint Angkor Wat in an appealing light again for the Japanese public. Predictably, the campaign hinges on the amazing beauty of these ruins and assurances that the Phnom Penh government has the region under control. Another year, they say, and it really will be safe. Which means two years? Three? The only certainty is plenty of tourists will follow us.

Us. No, I'm not alone. There's a cameraman along too, with his assistant and a shitload of equipment. Every day he's off shooting. We meet up each evening and exchange information on the finds of the day. He gripes about the food, can't wait to get back to Japan and head straight for a sushi bar in Ginza. But me, I like the local chicken and vegetables just fine.

The ruins are amazing, the carvings of Apsaras and Devas do

captivate. I can feel myself being drawn into the frieze they call *Churning the Sea of Milk*. But why tell you? An art buff like you knows Angkor inside out, you're a walking coffee-table book. You know how André Malraux got caught trying to steal sculptures from here. Maybe it was even you who tempted him. Not with heroin, but with beauties carved in stone. Or if not you, your grandmother. I'd like to think all evil is your doing or your kin's. A great web of evil.

Malraux's attempted larceny is unforgivable. It presumes no one else is capable of really appreciating beauty. And the presumption is hardly an isolated notion; it's based on that moral superiority the appreciative West foists on the appreciated East. It's the presumption of Lord Elgin hauling away the Parthenon marbles. And yet, seeing the sculptures here up close, the desire to possess isn't so very foreign to me, either. There's so much beauty here right before you, truly wondrous beauty, it makes you feel helpless. That's the first reaction: humbled rapture. And next? There is nothing next. You're spellbound, nailed to the spot. What else can you do but gaze? Sketch it, photograph it—you're only grazing the surface, getting no closer. And when the lonely sense of otherness sinks in, the temptation to own it rears its head. You can't bear the idea of losing it, you want to see it every day, asleep or awake. You must have it for yourself. So you plot and plan to cart it away with you.

Nonetheless, robbing is still wrong. And not because of some tepid morality about beauty belonging to everyone. No, the right thing is to devote yourself to beauty, not beauty to you. To take it in without taking it away, without amputating this beauty from its surroundings. It requires resolve, but it's still much easier than robbery. In other words, all you have to do is live right there, on the spot. Don't go home. Plant yourself down before those beautiful Devas and keep gazing at their smiles. Malraux should have just left Paris for good and settled here. But he was a Westerner, so he couldn't succumb to that.

Now you'd probably say that I, of all people, have other options for relating to beauty: I'm a painter. Instead of camping right in front of it and forsaking everything else, what about painting it? I can just imagine you saying that. But really, Inge, it doesn't work. Faced with a sublime work of beauty from the past, painting can't ever be more than reproduction in miniature. It makes no difference if I can capture those unearthly smiles on the faces of the Apsaras, catch the exact contour of their lips. However hard I work at it, a copy is only a copy.

Every day, then, I indulge in the pleasures of the copyist. I don't for a minute believe this will yield great art. Reference material, maybe. When the light slants across the *Sea of Milk*, it's so impossibly beautiful, I paint in sheer adulation and resignation. I copy it in watercolors on paper, secure in the disheartening knowledge that this most perfect thing was created long before my time. I move my brush to the rhythms wrought by unknown artisans, doing shitty little tracings of the achievements of the ancients.

Nature comes forward and actively intercedes, casting even more gradations of light across the frieze. Encouraging me to work. Nature isn't beauty, but the mother lode of beauty. She teams up with us to mine her beauty-in-the-rough. Luckily, she hasn't yet given up on us, still speaks to us.

Asia is water, at least for me it is. The watery expanse of the Baray. The color of the sky dissolved in it. The air charged with water all the way to the temples in the distance. The diffused outlines of the scenery. It's what I wanted to paint, and what I am painting.

Last night was the new moon. So today is a day of fasting. Finished dinner last night at 9:00, so only water to drink until 9:00 tonight. I've made it a practice ever since then. Not once have I failed to observe my little ritual, which is why I always live with one eye on the lunar calendar. It gives me a certain familiarity with the night. As the darkness deepens, my body prepares for the short abstinence, my mind steels itself to engage the Sad Child Angel in conversation. Though really the angel has nothing to say. No censure, no pardon. It merely listens and nods. Not a word on how the child is getting on in the afterlife.

The other guys inside all soon found out about my fasting days. Everyone in jail lives right in each other's face, no one can keep a secret for long. At first I tried to shrug it off, but soon they were actively prying.

"What's _that_ about? Some kind of Zen thing?"

"Something like that. People fast for all sorts of reasons, physical and spiritual. I could list them all up if you like—got plenty of time here, right?"

"All that means is, you're not going to tell us _your_ reason."

"Guess not. But anyway, today—all day—no food passes my lips."

Ever since that incident, I've carried the burden. I've got the angel sitting on my shoulder, though by now it's second nature to me. The dead child is inside me, and with the angel, that makes three of us living together. If I am to blame for the child's death, then the decades of life he lost I have to bear on my shoulders. That was the resolution I made then.

The child will remain a child forever, seeing the world through my eyes, peering out shyly from the moment his time was cut short. We're one person, with the angel as an enforcer. Every month, the night of the new moon, we extend that contract. I mustn't forget. Never, ever forget.

Once my prison sentence started, Kaoru stayed on in Bali for a while before returning to Japan, then visited several times a year to bring me things and take care of loose ends. Generally looking out for my interests while I was out of circulation. Kondra and Wayang also paid friendly visits. Even old man Inagaki came to see me. Practically broke down, he did, cried his eyes out saying how he'd never seen a sister as devoted to her brother. Typically this devoted sister of mine swung through on her way back from jobs in

Europe. She told me she had a boyfriend in Bali she always met up with, which made me glad she wasn't coming just to look after her worthless brother.

Bali to me was nothing but a trap, a trial, a prison sentence. But Kaoru, she's found the real Bali. At least it sure sounds like it from what she tells me. She's crazy about the place. Travels all over the island with this Spanish boyfriend of hers, seeing festivals and dancing and temples, climbing mountains, buying sea salt on the salt flats, just drinking in the scenery for days at a time.

I may have led her to Bali, but the way it's turned out it almost seems the other way around. She came to my rescue. Just when I hit rock bottom she gave me strength, for which I did nothing in return. I mean, I can hardly boast about being her reason for discovering Bali. The nice thing about family, as I see it now, is that there's no hurry to settle up debts.

When something big blows, it stirs up secondary shocks. My arrest brought Kaoru to Asia, a world she'd never known before. That's what happens: a new destiny opens up and a person chooses to walk that path. Happenstance comes in so many different colors, tangles the strands, cuts them apart only to string them back together. It meshes and twists, sends a shuttle flying across the warps—and before you know it, a life is woven.

The Bali Foreign Penitentiary was hardly a correctional facility, more like a welfare center, it was so relaxed. The inmates were constantly testing the limits of indulgence. You should have heard the requests they put to the warden, just to see how far they could stretch things. One guy asked if he could jog along a set course outside the prison, and it was approved! Which a fellow inmate availed himself of to run away for good! (How clever that was, I don't know. Even supposing he slipped out of Bali and left Indonesia, trying to make it back to his own country without documentation would be another thing altogether.)

Once they gave us a three-day leave, a grace period marking some big celebration they were having in Jakarta. We were allowed out on one condition—<u>return</u>. I negotiated with the warden to have my leave postponed, then wrote to Kaoru and asked her to show me a bit of Bali. Here I'd been on the island for years and all I'd seen was Kuta.

"A three-day leave? Sounds like a pretty stingy company," said Kaoru when she came in during visiting hours.

"Stingy for a company, but incredibly generous for a jail."

"Fair enough. They say Japanese prisons are the worst of any developed country."

"Two months ago there was this Greek guy came in here. According to him, in Greece before the war, they had prisons where you could go home on weekends."

"You're kidding. Then it'd be back on Monday morning, like going to work?"

"Pretty much."

"Anyway, about the next three days Where to? What kind of things do you want to see?"

"Any recommendations? You've been all over the place."

"This last time, I went to Uluwatu on the night of the full moon."

"Uluwatu—isn't that where you had your *satori*?"

"My *satori*, right! Well, maybe. This time I went to see the full moon pilgrims in their white robes. It was wonderful! Since your trial, I seem to be good at praying."

"You mean you're getting your message across?"

"Don't be silly. There's no answer or anything like that. I can't even tell what god I'm talking to. Or if I'm even talking to a god. I just make myself completely empty and then make the least egotistic wish, with all my heart. I erase myself and pray for everyone. Like a very abstract harvest prayer. Drop any thought of worldly gain and everything goes right."

"Deep stuff."

"You're not taking me seriously."

233

"I am too. Thanks to your prayers, Kaoru, I've had a new lease on life."

"Not true. It was your art, your paintings had the power to change things. Subliminally. The gods chose to keep you around so you could go on painting."

"And you honestly believe in these gods?"

"Depends on what you mean by 'honestly.' It's all very abstract, these workings of the mind. How about it, then? To Uluwatu?"

"No. I don't want to go somewhere specially to see something."

That was the honest truth. I knew there was plenty to see on Bali. There were books on Balinese culture in the prison library, all filled with pictures. I remembered with envy the exquisite sketches by Covorrubias. On the outside there'd be no end of places and things to paint. If only I hadn't gotten involved with Agus and that Shunmei Bando in Kuta. If only I'd made straight for the countryside.

Three days was nothing. I didn't really want to paint, not just yet. Didn't want to dabble for three days, then have to spend the rest of my sentence frustrated. Three days' leave, in that sense, is an awkward cookie.

"What about . . .? Is there anything to hear?"

"To hear? Want to go hear some good *gamelan*? I know a village that's really excellent."

"Mm, okay, but how about something more laid back? Something simple and soothing, like wind-chimes, maybe."

"That's a tall order, coming from a jailbird!" She got up, saying she'd be back in the morning.

The following morning at nine, Kaoru came with Wayang. I picked up my special leave papers and got in the car. I couldn't take my eyes off the scenery. I sat in back, but soon moved to the front so I could get an unobstructed view. We stopped now and again and walked, or sat by the side of the road to watch everything that passed. Each Balinese face seemed so radiant, the clothes they wore so beautiful.

In the end, I couldn't <u>not</u> do a drawing. I had the car stop in a village along the way to sketch a tiny temple. I drew the gray stone and red brick gate, its strict symmetry split right down the middle as if by a plumb line. I drew the temple spire wearing its stacked black umbrella-hats. Then Kaoru said we were getting short of time and had to be going. Back on the road, I was drunk on the speed of the car, drunk on the passing scenery, drunk on the freedom.

We headed east. It was a little before nightfall when we reached the village. We got out and walked down a narrow lane into a large compound. The spacious grounds were dotted with various buildings, scampering kids, and chickens. How long had it been since I'd seen children? The owner-headman appeared, apparently an acquaintance of Kaoru's. They exchanged brief and pleasant greetings. Kaoru spoke the local dialect, fumbling and faltering, but enough to communicate. She must have memorized her phrases in advance. It was admirable, though how did she introduce me—"This is my convict brother"?

Before long, they brought out five coarsely woven bamboo cages shaped like overturned bowls, with two pigeons inside each.

"This?"

"Uh-huh," said Kaoru.

"We're going to listen to pigeons?"

"Wait and see."

Presently the headman brought a small basket out of his house. Then, grabbing the pigeons one by one from their cages, he took something out of the basket and hung it around each of their necks. On closer inspection, they proved to be hollow wooden tubes the size of wine corks.

"Whistles," said Kaoru. She demonstrated, blowing in one end, but there was no sound. "Just wait and see."

Once all the pigeons had been necklaced, they were set free. At first they paused under the eaves of the nearest house, then finally one bird took off and all the others followed. High up they regrouped into a broad circle, and now the *hyuee hyuuee-ee*

235

of their whistles reached our ears. The whistles weren't made for mouth-blowing; they only sounded in flight.

"Nice," I told Kaoru.

"There's more."

The pigeons were still flying in their loose ring, linked by their distant *hyu-hru-hru*-ing. Then out of nowhere there were more pigeons. Other flocks of pigeons were flying up to join them from different directions, all with whistles around their necks. These other whistles were pitched slightly differently, producing layer on layer of harmonies from the sky, bending now higher now lower as the birds veered this way and that. The pigeons were quite high up by now, so the sound was growing faint. But the collective volume of so many birds flying in unison lingered on, as if the sky itself were calling from all around us.

"Amazing."

"It's been a pastime in the village for years now. They compete to raise better fliers or carve better whistles, then let them all fly at twilight. They say they can tell their own pigeons apart by the sound. They vary the scales to enjoy the way they overlap."

"A sport for kings and princes."

"Not kings—real people, playing for real. They go to extremes. They're hooked. Others might paint or sculpt or dance—things that might make you money if you're not careful—but for now pigeon-whistling is still safe. No tourists coming here to hear this, not yet."

"Got to hand it to them, thinking of this."

"You said it. Every time I come here, I'm blown away by the Balinese."

Gradually the sky grew dark, turning a beautiful indigo. A slender moon crept out, and around the moon the pigeons circled, still sending the music of the heavens to us below.

That was the most beautiful thing I heard in Bali.

Four days ago, I went with my two soldier escorts to the island temple in the West Baray reservoir, and spent the whole day painting there. I did some good work. Toward evening, I decided to take a dip. I stripped and got in the water. It's just the beginning of the dry season, so the water was still deep from the rains. I had a good long swim, the water nice and cool. Sometimes my legs got tangled in moss. The reservoir is maybe eight kilometers long, if you swam from end to end. Not that I wanted to. Just a little once-around in the immediate shallows. The two guards watched from the shore, obviously worried. I waved to them to come in too, but they looked at me like I was crazy. Probably couldn't even swim. What with the war, they hadn't had anything like a normal childhood or adolescence.

I felt cleansed. Perhaps this is what I came here for, I found myself thinking, so the water could wash me clean. Wash away past failures. Water can be a frightening thing, an ordeal, but if you dive on under, the Devas will be smiling on the other side.

I dived under. I crossed the deep, broad stretch of water. It took fear of death and three years shut in and a year of recuperation to get me here. All that to get out of your clutches, Inge.

With the eyes of the two soldiers on me, I remembered a Vietnamese soldier who died here in Cambodia: An's husband, Tanh's father. What kind of man was he? If An chose him, he must have been a good guy. I wish I could've met him, made friends, even if it meant not getting involved with his wife. There must have been a stretch of water he couldn't cross. To go on living is to keep crossing one and then another channel, sometimes diving under. But then you surface again. Seeing those young Cambodian soldiers with their submachine guns, I tried to imagine him dying in this country. The futility of coming here, never to return to An and Tanh.

Nor can I return to An and Tanh. All through the trial and even more in prison, I kept thinking about An. Those times with her were the best. Good memories can really sustain you through hardships, I know for a fact. An and Tanh were a real strength to me. In jail, lying on that hard pallet through sleepless nights, I relived each day in that Vietnamese village. Tahn's smiling face, An demurely avoiding my eyes. The phantom An who visited me at night, her soothing voice. Thanks to them I could endure imprisonment.

And yet, I couldn't bring myself to write them from jail. I was so ashamed of what I'd done, where I was. I couldn't explain it in a letter. To tell them all that had happened, I had to go see them, spend one whole night talking with them. I'd never open up unless I were holding An's hand. I had all these fantasies about that day when it came.

Then even when I was released I was in no shape to go to Vietnam. I needed to be in better health, normal again, like I was with them. For all my thoughts of them, as much as I wanted to see them, I kept putting off the day I'd climb aboard a plane for Ho Chi Minh. Maybe I'd become so accustomed to my imagined An and Tahn, I was scared to meet them face to face. Maybe An is no longer alone. Maybe Tahn has forgotten me, I haven't written in so long.

I thought again about writing to explain how things were, but stopped myself for the same reason I didn't write from prison. Too painful. My trials weren't over. But whatever it took I had to see them.

And now I think I've finally found what it takes at Angkor, the push I needed. Should I write them a simple "May I come and visit?" Or just go? Talk about the three years of shame when I see her? I can't wait to see Tahn again. Want to hold An so bad it hurts. Just a few more weeks.

Inge, what to do with this letter?

Over these past few years, your presence has gradually faded in me. It's a fact I got hooked on heroin, which means that you, who first tempted me, you must exist—but really, do you? It almost seems more plausible to see you as a witch sent from Europe to lure me away from my path as an artist. Although witches probably don't exist. And it's too flattering to think that Europe would go that far to stop me painting.

But if you really do exist—an accountant in Frankfurt like you said, known as an art critic on the side—you won't be hard to track down. This letter will reach you somehow. Although I'm still of two minds: whether to post it or not even try to re-establish contact. Do I have the nerve? If only you <u>were</u> unreal.

Kaoru once told me a Balinese folktale about a witch called Rangda who gets locked in an endless struggle with the monster Barong. Probably makes a good parallel with us. From now on I'm going to keep painting Asia, until I can show you something to make you change your whole view of art from the bottom up. Give you a taste of your own Malraux malevolence.

I guess I'll be carrying this letter around for a while. Until I paint a picture I'm sure of, then I'll send them along together.

May the fight go on forever.

Tetsuro

（英文版）花を運ぶ妹
A BURDEN OF FLOWERS

2001年10月5日　第 1 刷発行

著　者　池澤夏樹
訳　者　アルフレッド・バーンバウム
発行者　野間佐和子
発行所　講談社インターナショナル株式会社
　　　　〒112-8652　東京都文京区音羽 1-17-14
　　　　電話　03-3944-6493（編集部）
　　　　　　　03-3944-6492（営業部・業務部）
　　　　ホームページ　http://www.kodansha-intl.co.jp
印刷所　共同印刷株式会社
製本所　黒柳製本株式会社